I0618166

THE JOHNSON AMULET

AND OTHER SCOTTISH TERRORS

William B. Meikle

Indy**Publish**

THE JOHNSON AMULET AND OTHER SCOTTISH TERRORS

Copyright © 2001 by William B. Meikle

All rights reserved under International and Pan-American Conventions.

This book may not be reproduced or distributed in whole or in part or electronic form including photocopied or audiotape means and methods without the written permission of the author.

Published in the United States by IndyPublish.com
1487 Chain Bridge Road
Suite 304
McLean, VA 22101

ISBN: 1-58827-050-5 Paperback
ISBN: 1-58827-051-3 Hardback

For family, friends, and Mrs Lang, a teacher who indulged me at the age of twelve and put me on the path to this book.

Contents

The Johnson Amulet — 1
An Early Frost — 22
The Worst Sound — 28
Wee Robbie — 29
Phantom Payment — 39
Overheard in a Cemetery — 46
A Sirens Song — 50
Temper Tantrum — 56
The Elixir Of Life — 59
The Flute and The Glen — 66
The Colour of the Deep — 73
The Strange Case of Dr McIntyre — 82
Animal ,Vegetable or Mineral — 86
It'll Be a Long Hot Summer — 91
In the Coils of The Serpent — 99
The Old Mother — 112
The Last Day Of Summer — 117
Just A Par To Win — 123
Ghost Writer — 128
At The Beach — 135
Can You Hear Them? — 139
The Sweller in the Dress Hold — 144
The Watcher in the Dunes — 151
There's Always a Catch — 160
The World of Illusion — 167
Flower of Scotland — 172
The Dark Island — 180
The Blue Hag — 188

Authors Note — 203
Publication Histories — 204

The Johnson Amulet

The day started like any other. I dressed, I smoked two cigarettes, and I looked at my empty desk and waited for the phone to ring.

At least the view from the window kept me distracted. Students walked along Byres Road, hand in hand, oblivious to the world around them. Old bedraggled men waited for the pubs to open, little old ladies in heavy woollen coats carried bags of shopping that were too heavy for them, and old John from downstairs continued to sing "Just one Cornetto" at the top of his voice every ten minutes. At about ten thirty I opened the desk drawer and took out the whisky bottle and began preparing the long slide down to bedtime.

Just another lonely day in paradise.

An hour later I was eyeing the last of my whisky, wondering how long I would be able to spin it out when the knock came on the door. I almost dropped the bottle getting it back in the drawer and just had time to tighten up my tie before the door opened and all other thoughts were swept away.

She was more than beautiful, she was awesome. She was most definitely the classiest person ever to have walked through the door - I could see that from the cut of her clothes, the way she carried herself, the way her deep black hair was oh-so-carefully tousled. I tried not to stare at her legs as she walked across the office.

"Adams? Mr Derek Adams?" she asked and her voice was just right. The dream of the Bogart case began to take shape. I stood to shake her hand, noticing how cool hers felt, how sweaty mine was.

"That's right. Adams Detective Agency - ADA for short. First name in the book, first when it comes to providing personal service."

I was rambling. I closed my mouth - maybe that way she wouldn't see me dribbling. I motioned her to the threadbare chair in front of my desk and sat down in my own, hoping that, just this once, I could bring off the air of studied nonchalance I had been practising in the mirror.

She smiled at me and I guessed that a dentist had been paid a lot of money for all that sleek whiteness. I sat back in the chair and watched her talk - it wasn't hard work.

"We had a burglary - two nights ago," she started. "My husband doesn't know about it yet - he's out of the country. The thief knew what he was looking for, and only one piece of jewellery was taken - a most valuable piece - he gave it to me as a wedding present and it has great sentimental value. I want you to get it back for me."

Her mouth worked beautifully, but she wasn't telling the whole truth - I had seen it in her eyes as she spoke - but it was a fairly standard request - I had handled such work before.

Besides, she could lie to me all she wanted - I could handle it for a while.

"You realise how little chance we have of recovering a piece of jewellery?" I asked, trying not to notice the expanse of thigh that became visible as she shifted in the seat.

"I don't think you'll have much trouble with this one," she said. "It's a very distinctive piece."

She dug around in her handbag - which on its own would pay my rent for months - and removed a photograph that she passed over the table. I picked up the picture, and almost dropped it straight away. Suddenly I didn't want anything to do with this, I didn't want this woman in my office, and the whisky in the drawer was screaming to be let out.

Then she smiled at me, and I turned the picture over.

It was a pendant, but unlike anything I had seen before. It consisted of a figurine on a heavy gold chain. There was nothing in the picture to indicate size but it looked big. Big and ugly. The figure was of an animal, but not any known to me. The hindquarters were feline and striped, like a Bengal Tiger, but from the waist up it was grotesque, an amorphous blob of some black stone with long suckered tentacles streaming from what would have been the head.

"Nice wedding present." I said as I put the photograph down. "If it was mine I think I would be quite glad to lose it."

I pushed the photograph away from me, turning it face down on the table, and rubbed my fingers on my tie, but I couldn't get rid of a feeling of being dirtied by having touched the thing.

"You wouldn't want to lose it if you knew it was worth half a million pounds," she said, and I sat back hard in my chair. "It is very old - Ancient Arabian I think. Arthur is very fond of it – he'd be very upset if he knew it was gone - that's why I'd like you to find it before he gets back."

I was sure that I wasn't getting the whole truth, but I had the scent of money in my nostrils, and my dream of the big case in my head.

"I cost £250 a day, plus expenses. Two days in advance," I said, then wished I'd asked for more when she agreed instantly.

She put a business card on my desk beside the photograph and my advance cheque. With one last smile she left, taking most, but not all, of her perfume with her. I realised that I didn't know her name.

The card didn't yield any clue either - "A&F Dunlop, Dealers in Antiquities", and a posh address out in the suburbs. I assumed "A" was for Arthur, her husband, but "F", "F" could be for anything. I resolved to ask her the next time.

I resisted the urge to play with the cheque and put it away in my wallet alongside her card and a lonely £10 note. The photograph went into my hip pocket and I went to work for the first time for a month.

My first stop was Glasgow University. I didn't have far to go. Five minutes walk and ten years of my life, that was all. The mock-gothic buildings still loomed ominously over me, just like they did all those years ago, and, for maybe the thousandth time since then, I wondered if I'd made the right decision when I turned my back on it all.

Then, as I made my way down gloomy corridors and stairs to the dark sub-basement where the smartest of my contemporaries worked, I realised, for maybe the thousandth time, why I'd done it.

Doug Lang and I went back a long way. We had been boozing buddies together when we were students and kept in touch, even after I dropped out. He looked much as he had done all those years ago - the unkempt hair, the John Lennon specs and the ill-fitting cardigans, all part of the his eccentric professor persona, but beneath it all was one of the sharpest, most inquisitive minds I knew. And, best of all, he was an archaeologist.

His eyebrows almost raised through his hairline when I showed him the photograph and he got visibly excited.

"The Johnson Amulet," he whispered, and I thought he was going to drool over the picture.

"You know it then?" I asked.

"Oh yes," he said, and lapsed into what I had come to know as his "teaching" voice.

"It was found in Ur, sometime around the turn of the century, and was brought back into the country by James Johnson, a shipping magnate of the time. It's got a long history - something about Devil worship or black magic - hocus pocus anyway - it caused quite a stir in the twenties. There was some sort of scandal, and Johnson died in suspicious circumstances. The amulet wasn't amongst his effects, and hasn't been seen since."

A predatory look came to his eyes. "Where did you get the picture?" he asked.

"From a client. I've been hired to find it."

He laughed. "Better people than you have tried," he said.

"Is it worth much?" I asked, hoping that I might at least expose one of Mrs Dunlop's lies, but I was to be disappointed.

"It's priceless." Doug said, and this time I believe he did drool, "Archaeologists the worlds over would be cutting off parts of their body for just a look at it. I suppose that if it ever came up for auction it would go for, say, a couple of million. But, as I said, it has been lost for more than half a century - probably some rich private hoarder sits and gloats over it during the long winter nights."

"It can't be too far lost," I said, "This picture is a lot more recent than half a century."

I watched the excitement grow in Doug's eyes. I knew it was time to leave - he was getting close to his manic puppy dog phase, and I would have him following me everywhere if I wasn't careful.

"If I find it I'll let you have a fondle before I give it back," I said and left him with my promise of first look at the pendant.

I made my way back to the real world. It was raining again - heavy pelting, driving rain that forced it's way through my coat and my trousers. By the time I'd visited all the pawn shops I knew of and tapped some of my regulars for information I was soaked to the skin and feeling a lot less confident than I had earlier. Nobody knew anything, nobody saw anything, and nobody heard anything - a whole city full of wise monkeys.

I dragged my way home and poured a glass of whisky before settling my damp body into the armchair. Soon it was full dark outside and the whisky bottle was empty. I took myself off to the adjoining bedroom and dreamed of sand and buried treasure.

I don't know what woke me - it could have been the cry of a cat, or the wind, but it brought me out of the dream with a start and the beginnings of a scream that I only just managed to stifle.

Something shifted beyond my bedroom door, a movement in the air so subtle that I almost passed it off as the last remnant of my dream. Almost. I was up and out of the bed quickly, noiselessly, or so I thought. I had just reached for the doorknob, my right hand outstretched, my left foot just off the floor, when there was a loud scratching on the other side of the door.

I stood there, trying not to breathe.

It got cold, then colder, and I could smell a peculiar burning, like incense, only sweeter. Sweeter and yet somehow foul.

And still I didn't move. Not until the door handle rattled in its socket.

I grabbed it, and nearly let go as my palm met intense, icy, cold. I put my shoulder against the door and held it tightly shut.

"I've called the police." I shouted, realising how feeble that sounded, "They're on their way."

The cold left the doorknob, as if a fire had suddenly been lit, and the sour-sweet odour evaporated as quickly as it had come. There was no sound. I must have stood there for another five minutes before I got up the nerve to open the door. Yet, when I did, there was no one there - the doors and windows were all locked and nothing had been moved.

That was it for the rest of the night. I sat up in my armchair and stared at what passes for entertainment on night time television until daylight began to creep through the curtains.

By the time I was dressed I had just about dismissed the incident as a bad dream. Maybe I should have paid more attention. Maybe things might have turned out differently. But how was I to know? This case was about to get seriously weird.

The day went much as the previous one - a lot of legwork and no answers. I was dog tired by the time I walked into the Halt Bar in the West End. The owner, Dave, and I went back to the time when I dropped out of University and he gave me a job behind the bar.

We reminisced about old times for a couple of minutes as I sipped a beer, then I got down to business. I asked Dave if anyone had tried to fence jewellery recently.

"Actually, one of the lads was telling me something this morning," he replied. "There's an east end wide-boy, Brian Marshall, who thinks he's hit the big time. Seemingly he was in his local boasting abut how much money he had coming to him from a strange pendant. Stole it on demand so I'm told."

It sounded as if I was on the right track. I know - it sounds too pat, too simple, but the breaks happen that way sometimes - I like to think that it's all due to the depth of my contact network, but maybe it's just because I spend a lot of time in bars mixing with the wrong type of people.

I sipped on another beer as Dave found out where Marshall's flat was, along with a description of him. It only took him five minutes - he knew a lot of the wrong kind of people as well. As I turned to go he told me not to wait long before my next visit, and offered me a free pint if I came back to tell him what it was all about.

The trip across town reminded me of what I loved about Glasgow. It was just after six o' clock in the evening and the offices were emptying - into the streets, the taxis and the bars. Thrusting young executives mixed with hefty labourers, tiny shop assistants in short dresses rubbed shoulders with old men in overcoats that had seen better days some twenty years before. There was a hint of magic in the air, a sense of possibilities waiting to happen.

The mood stayed with me, all the way through the town centre, but as the crowds got thinner and the buildings got dirtier I began to feel more exposed, as if the magic might not be so benevolent after all.

Marshall's flat was in an old Victorian tenement - four stories high and converted to flats. The communal close smelled, of stale beer and urine, and the graffiti was particularly graphic and colourful. As I climbed the stairs I tried to formulate a plan. Thus far I had been merely following my instincts and I had no idea how to approach him. I stood outside the door, still unsure, and lifted my hand to knock.

Before my hand reached it the door was pulled open and my arm was grabbed tightly. I was pulled inside, hard, and as I tried to regain my balance, I was tripped, falling face first to the floor where the rough carpet scraped across my face.

I was roughly turned over and found myself looking up at the face of a man who I guessed must be Marshall. I heard a sharp click, loud in the confines of the room, and caught a glimmer of silver as a flick knife came up in front of my face. I felt a quick lancing pain as he drew the knife through my left earlobe, then the hot rush of blood against my neck. There was a smile on his face as he did it and I knew then that I wasn't going to be able to reason with him.

He shifted his weight so that he was sitting on my chest and my muscles tightened as I tried to breathe. He brought the knife up again and it headed for my cheek.

I got my left arm in front of it but the blade sliced easily through my coat and the jacket underneath before bringing a burst of red heat as it found my skin then my muscle. There was a scrape as the knife hit bone and a white lancing pain as I pushed, toppling him off my chest.

He got to his feet again before I got off my hands and knees and his foot drew back. I was too late in turning away and the booted foot hit me full in the ribs, sending me rolling away into a corner of the room. I looked up into his eyes as he came for me and saw the wide grin. He was in his element. The knife glistened redly as he brought it up in front of him.

"Got you now you bastard," he said and moved in for the kill, I tried to put my arms up in front of me but my chest muscles screamed in pain and refused to allow any movement.

And then I caught it, the sweet but foul smell that struck in the back of my throat. Marshall must have smelled it as well. He stopped, a puzzled expression on his face, then turned away from me as a rustling in the corner of the room caught his attention.

As if from some unimaginably far distance I heard a sound, rising in pitch, a chanting in a foreign tongue, a tongue that reminded me of the harsh goblin-speak of Mordor.

"C'thulhu ryleh fhtang.
Aran Barak Sototh F'rhengh.
Ia Sototh, Ia C'thulhu."

And accompanying the chant, but from even further away, the thin sound of a flute, discordant and tuneless.

Marshall turned, his face suddenly drained of blood. I followed his gaze, and my heart gave a lurch. Suddenly I had difficulty drawing breath. Something took shape as I watched, drawing heat from the room as it came through. I realised that the pendant hadn't just been a fevered artist's dream - it had been modelled from life.

It came through slowly, as if fighting through a heavy curtain. The legs came first, those thick, almost feline limbs, the claws on the feet tearing across the carpet as it came closer. The torso was almost human, but the rest of it was from one of your worst nightmares. The head was gross and distended, a pulsing mass of red flesh the size of a basketball, a basketball that writhed and squirmed as inch thick tentacles grew like snakes from the scalp. In the mouth of each tentacle were teeth that glinted like new razors in the dim light

And as it came on through, the smell got stronger, then stronger still - that same, sour-sweet incense that had been in my flat that morning.

Marshall turned away towards the door but it was on him in less than a second.

He screamed, a loud roar of defiance, and lashed out with the knife, drawing a line through the red distended scalp of the thing, but it didn't falter in its attack. Marshall tried to scream again, and one of the tentacles cut off the sound before it could escape, its saliva coated teeth biting down hard on the doomed man's tongue and beginning to chew.

More tentacles found his body, writhing and cavorting like a nest of snakes. One found his left eye socket and Marshall gave one last moan as it began to burrow.

His body was lifted off the ground and shaken, like a terrier with a mouse, and there was a thud as something heavy hit the floor.

The thing lowered Marshall's body and bent over it. I could see bulges moving from the mouths, down the tentacles towards the head, the large red raw head that grew as I watched. Fighting back the nausea I crawled towards the door.

I was half-way there when my hand struck something on the carpet. I thought at first it was the knife, but then I felt the grooves and the chain. It was the amulet - he had it in his pocket all the time. I wrapped the chain around my hand and kept going, the pain in my ribs and my arm causing me to wince with every movement.

I only looked back once, as my hand closed on the latch of the door and I pulled myself upright. Marshall's body lay on the floor, strangely deflated, and at least twenty tentacles were still burrowing their way deeper, seeking out the soft parts. I began to open the door, and two of the tentacles lifted from their bloody feeding, dripping gore and saliva onto the body beneath them.

I was out of the door fast, slamming it shut behind me and was half-way down the first flight of stairs when the door shook as something heavy tried to force its way through.

Despite my pains, I ran faster than I had ever thought possible, my feet splashing through puddle after puddle as I made for the safety of people, any people at all..

I couldn't go home - not when I knew that the creature had been there the night before, but I needed to get some work done on the wounds, and I needed some rest - suddenly I felt very tired. I thought of the people who would help, then remembered my promise to Doug. Maybe the archaeologist could help me make some sense of the situation.

I was still running five minutes later, but the adrenaline was wearing off and I was acutely aware, both of the aches and pains in my body, and the fact that I was attracting a lot of attention from people in the street. I managed to hail a black cab and fell into the back of it. The driver almost threw me straight back out again, but I promised him a large tip - I knew Doug was good for it.

I sat in the back of the cab, not noticing the passing streets beyond the window. It was only when my breathing eased that I realised I was still gripping the amulet. It was even uglier in reality - the stone feeling somehow greasy in my palm. I shoved it deep in the pocket of my coat and promptly forgot about everything as tiredness and pain contrived to send me away into blackness.

Twenty minutes later we pulled up outside Doug's house - the driver had to wake me up to get me out of the cab - and five minutes later I was sitting in Doug's kitchen. I sipped whisky as he bathed the wound in my arm and I told him the story. I wasn't too sure how much of it he was taking in - his eyes kept straying to the amulet that sat in the middle of the table and, just as quickly, move away.

It took a while in the telling, with interruptions for more whisky and questions and when I finished Doug left the room in a hurry. I sat and drank some more of his whisky - I'd had enough rushing about for one night.

He came back several minutes later cradling a book in his large hands.

"Listen to this," he said, and began reading.

"The chief being of the Mythos is C'thulhu, a god from beyond the stars, a once and future ruler of this planet. He sleeps in Ryleh, his dreaming city beneath the seas and when the stars are right he will awaken and chaos will once again walk the Earth."

He was close to "manic-puppy" again.

"The amulet must be some kind of gateway - a gateway to let the old gods come back."

I think I laughed.

"Come on Doug. What is this shit? You can't expect me to believe it?"

"How else do you explain what has been happening to you? Believe me - these old gods are extremely prevalent in the literature I read - and the people of the middle-east were certainly greatly afraid of them. I think we should keep an open mind until we get a better handle on it."

I certainly didn't intend "getting a handle on it". Taking my whisky with me, I made my way to the telephone. It was answered immediately, and although it was now the early hours of the morning she didn't sound tired.

"You'd better bring it to me now," she said. "Things are getting a bit out of hand." That was an understatement if I'd ever heard one. She gave me directions as to how to find her - somewhere out on the edge of town near the Campsie Hills - and asked me to hurry.

Doug wanted to come with me.

"Come on Derek. You're in no fit state to drive. And I need to know the story of that thing."

He bent forward, as if to lift the amulet, then pulled away again.

"Besides, " he said, waving his car keys in my face. "I'm the one with the wheels."

I hit him.

I'm not proud of it, but it was only the one punch, enough to knock him senseless to the floor. It was for his own good - he hadn't seen the thing that came for the amulet, I had. And I wouldn't wish that vision on anyone else, especially not my best friend.

I had to fight to stay awake during the drive, and I managed to get myself lost twice, but somewhere around three in the morning I drove through the gates of Dunlop's house.

I tried to peer through the rain but all I could see was a gravel driveway leading off in front of me. I turned a sharp bend, and saw a large, brilliantly lit house in front of me. I stopped the car and opened the door, wincing as the wind and the rain swept in and the cold hit me. I put one foot out of the car and smelled it again, the odour of incense. It was on me before I had time to react.

I found myself looking into a nest of writhing chittering tentacles that were swaying and dancing around my head. I was caught by the shoulders by at least four tentacles and dragged completely out of the car. I hit out at the head, as hard as I could, and felt the flesh squash and melt under my fist before it bounced back into position. I was lifted higher and felt my feet leave the ground.

Two of the tentacles waved in front of my eyes, hypnotic and enticing. They were moving closer when I heard the singing, a clear high, female voice that spoke of peace and rest. I was dropped unceremoniously to the ground and as I fell the amulet seemed to leap unbidden from my pocket. There was a sudden flash of green light and when my eyes adjusted the only thing I could see was Dunlop's wife walking towards me. The creature and the amulet were gone.

I could quite happily have stayed there in the rain, screaming my frustration and rage and pain into the gravel, but I was stopped by a hand on my shoulder. I turned and looked up into her sad blue eyes.

"You had better come inside. I think we have some explaining to do."

I dripped water across the thick pile carpeting as she led me into the house and showed me in to a large room. The floor had been stripped bare revealing shiny, varnished floorboards. Some sort of diagram was drawn on the floor - a large circle with a five pointed star inside. The outside of the circle was inscribed with some indecipherable script, and inside the circle, sitting on a bed of blankets, was her husband, Arthur Dunlop.

"Sit down Mr Adams," he said, and his voice was weak and throaty. Looking closer I saw that his skin was tinged yellow. He looked like a man who didn't have long to live. I was about to reply, to vent some anger, but he spoke first.

"No time for recriminations. I have a story I need to tell, and I think you need to listen if we are to have any chance of seeing the amulet again. Now sit down. Please."

I sat in a huge red leather armchair, and his wife brought me a whisky. I was dog tired and all my muscles ached in unison.

"Just sit still," the woman said. "Arthur will explain everything."

I seriously doubted that. She left to stoke the fire in a large fireplace and I watched her move as the man started speaking.

"It starts back in 1913, in the ruins of Ur," he said, and his voice lapsed into a sing-song, storytelling quality.

"My great-grandfather, Thomas Dunlop, was one of the archaeologists who went along with Johnson.

They'd been in the desert for months and Johnson, who had visions of emulating Carter or Schliemann, was becoming restless with their lack of progress. Thomas was sure that they were right above a chamber, and had hopes of finding the resting place of the Priest-Kings, but Johnson wanted results, and wanted them fast. There had been reports that he was spending a lot of time with a local mystic - an ancient desert Arab who had appeared out *of nowhere one evening. It was not much later that Johnson took matters into his own hands."*

"Thomas was woken by the thunder of blasting and ran to the site of the dig wearing only his night-shirt. He got there at the same time as several of his colleagues and was just in time to see Johnson and the old Arab going down into a still-smoking hole."

"Thomas followed them downwards and felt a chill run through his body as he heard the deep guttural chanting from below. The scene which met his eyes when he reached the burial chamber almost stopped his heart."

"They had already succeeded in prising the lid off the largest sarcophagus and Johnson was holding an amulet above his head. It was pulsating with a sickly green light and the Arab was lying prostrate on the ground, arms spread outward in supplication. As they watched a shiver ran over the Arab's body. Something rustled in the sarcophagus, something which whispered like dry leaves in the wind, and a black cloud rose up into the still air."

"The Arab rose to his knees, chanting again, and the cloud engulfed his head. He threw his head back and his chest heaved as he took a breath and the cloud entered him."

"Johnson lowered the amulet and the green light faded. Soon there were only the three men in the room. Thomas had a heavy fear in his heart but he was surrounded by artefacts beyond his wildest dreams, and his instincts as an archaeologist took over, driving all other thoughts from his mind. It wasn't until they had returned to Scotland that Thomas had time to collar Johnson."

"It took place in this house. Thomas invited Johnson here to try to convince him to put the amulet into the museum, Thomas's son Andrew, my grandfather, only twelve years old at the time, was eavesdropping and it is from him that we know what happened."

"The men argued, and Johnson got very angry. Andrew reported that there was some shouting in a strange foreign language before he heard Thomas screaming. He threw open the door and was nearly knocked over by the departing Johnson."

"Thomas was lying in the middle of the floor, his body punctured by scores of small wounds, dead eyes staring at the ceiling. It was then that Andrew pledged his revenge."

He stopped, racked by a coughing fit, and sipped some water from a small glass. "I think you can guess what killed the old man. We are now getting to the meat of the story."

"It took fifteen long years as Andrew grew to manhood. He devoted his life to following his father in the study of mythology and magic, but where Thomas had only an academic interest, Andrew became a practising magi, a master of ceremonial magic. During the same period Johnson's wealth had grown and he was now a very important man. Andrew followed his progress with great avidity, and was even more interested when an ancient Arab began to be mentioned in the reports."

"He knew that the time was getting near - he knew now that the Arab and the amulet together could be used to bring about the re-emergence of C'thulhu from his sleep, and he was determined to stop it."

"The occult is a close-knit field of study, and Andrew was able to discover where and when the planned ritual was to take place. He never told me the whole story, only that he managed to turn the ritual back on Johnson and his coven, so that the coven was destroyed and Johnson was taken by the amulet's creation. All I know is that Andrew got the amulet."

"Since then my family has kept it safe, binding its power with strong spells. There have been several attempts to steal it by magical means, all of which we have been able to repel, but they took place more than forty years ago."

"I'm afraid I have grown weak," he continued. "We didn't anticipate a human agency, especially after all this time - the burglary took us completely by surprise. I'm sorry that you got so deeply involved - until last night we thought it was just a common thief."

He lapsed into another fit of coughing. His wife went over and stood at the edge of the circle, a worried look on her face. She took up the story when it was obvious he wasn't going to be able to continue.

"The stars are right again, and we fear that an attempt will be made to call up the old ones. We must stop them. It will be today, at the old place."

I looked at both of them, and they just stared back. I felt as if I'd just entered the twilight zone - and not for the first time that night. I tried to speak, but all that came out was a throaty croak. It was only after a sip - a long sip - of whisky, that I was able to get my voice.

"Just one question. Who are "they"?"

Dunlop waved his arm in the air.

"You know - occultists, followers of the dark path."

From where I sat the path he and his wife were on looked dark enough for me.

"You mean you don't even know who is doing this?"

Again I got the wave of the arm.

"It doesn't matter who they are - it only matters what they plan to do with the amulet."

For the first time Dunlop stood, unsteady at first then more confident as he stepped out of the circle.

"I think they will have more things to worry about than attacking me." He turned to me. "We must go to Arkham House, Johnson's old retreat. I'm sure that's where they will do it. We'll talk on the way."

He stood over me and took the whisky glass out of my hand. "Meantime, try to get some sleep - you look done in. It will be a few hours before we can leave - I have preparations of my own to make."

My mind was full of questions but my body was dog tired and the wound in my arm was throbbing angrily. Dunlop showed me up a huge flight of stairs and into a bedroom bigger than my whole flat. I didn't bother undressing, I fell flat on my face onto the soft sheets and was immediately asleep. I didn't dream.

I was awoken what seemed like only minutes later by a knock on the door. Dunlop's wife was standing just inside the room. She was wearing a smile and a night-gown that was so diaphanous that I could see right through it. This morning the sight didn't do much for me - I was too tired for flirting. Force of habit made me try anyway.

"What is your name anyway?" I asked. "I can't go on calling you Mrs Dunlop - it makes you sound like a little old lady."

The smile beamed up a notch. "You can call me Fiona if you like. Just as long as you get yourself off the bed and downstairs. It's time to go."

My watch told me it was just after noon, but my body was telling me it was breakfast time. I managed to beg some coffee and toast, and, over my first cigarette of the day, I interrupted Dunlop as he started to explain what lay ahead.

"You'll drive Mr Adams - Fiona can't, and I'm not up to it."

I almost choked on cigarette smoke.

"Now wait a minute - you're not dragging me into your mumbo jumbo - I've got as close to that "thing" as I want to get."

I stood, meaning to leave, but Fiona was smiling at me, and I believe it was that, rather than what Dunlop said next, that made me sit back down in the chair.

"I'm afraid I must hold you to our bargain Mr Adams - you were contracted to retrieve the amulet, and you haven't yet done so. If it makes it any easier, I'll double your normal fee. In advance."

I smoked some more and watched him write out a cheque, and I didn't stand up. Didn't leave the table. It looked like I was driving after all.

"We've got to get to Arkham House before nightfall." Dunlop said, "It's up on the coast, just north of Oban. I'm pretty sure that's where they will be - the land was bought in the seventies and they've rebuilt a replica of Johnson's house on the same site as the old one. I'm pretty sure they'll have incorporated the crypt as well."

He must have seen my questioning look.

"The crypt was the reason Johnson built the house there in the first place. It is a site of great antiquity, a focal point for worship of the Old Ones."

I was having trouble getting my brain into gear - I'm not a morning person, so I let my questions lie till later.

Dunlop led me out to the garage at the side of the house. At least the drive was going to be comfortable - the car was suitably large, heavy and Germanic. I felt like a chauffeur as I held the door open for them to get in the back

I tried to make conversation early on in the journey, but the answers I got only led to more questions. Dunlop believed that the creature that took the amulet from me was in some way the old Arab who had been with Johnson back in the dig in 1913 - something I found hard to believe. I stored the information away in the back of my mind, alongside all the other impossible things accumulated there.

I knew that I'd have to scrutinise the memories sometime, but not yet - not until I had a good stiff drink to hand.

So we drove, mostly in silence. The rain had eased off overnight, and Loch Lomond glistened in resplendent blue splendour, but after Crianlarich the fog came down and we slowed to a crawl for mile after mile. And still no one spoke. Somewhere north of Oban, just before sunset, the fog lifted and Dunlop directed me along several single track roads then asked me to stop as we crested a hill overlooking the sea.

We looked down to a small island, the sea flat calm around it dyed red by the setting sun. There was a thin causeway leading out from the shore, wide enough for only a single car to pass at a time and on the island, in the middle of a densely wooded area, sat a gothic mansion straight out of an old Universal B Movie. The stone looked black in the last rays of the dying sun, the twin turrets jutting starkly skywards, the bay windows staring blankly out at us like a pair of deep black eyes.

"Welcome to Arkham House," Dunlop said, and I half expected a bolt of lightning and a roll of thunder to accompany his words.

Leaving the car behind we made our way down the hill, watched all the way by those giant eyes. At the foot of the hill Dunlop dug around in his overcoat and removed a one foot long piece of untrimmed wood. As soon as he touched it he looked five years younger.

"Hazel.", he said. "A wizard has to have a wand. Everybody knows that," was all he said as we made our way across the causeway and through the gate at its end. I decided not to comment. If they needed baby-sitting, and wanted to pay me five hundred a day, I could handle a few weeks worth of putting up with their theatricals. Besides, it looked like they were both more conversant with the situation than I was - I was much better off following their lead.

Dunlop's sudden health hadn't lasted long and he was looking ill again the next time I looked at him. His skin had regained its yellow pallor and he had hunched over like a whipped dog. Fiona put an arm around his shoulder, leading him forward, and we passed through the open gate. By the time we had got half way along the drive I was having to help Fiona with Dunlop and by the time we reached the door he seemed a dead weight in our arms.

The doorway was shaded in thick darkness, and it wasn't until we got up close that I noticed the carvings - intricate dancing devils that writhed and squirmed in various postures of sexual delight. The door itself looked like a solid piece of oak and I guessed it would be several inches thick, but Dunlop merely put his hand on it and muttered several words under his breath. It swung open revealing a well lit hall beyond.

"Don't you think we should be a bit more discreet?" I asked. "My usual tactic is to go in through a back window."

Fiona laughed at that, and the sound lifted the gloom. Not a lot, but it was welcome anyway.

"No time for subtlety." Dunlop said. "It's party time. If you get a chance, grab the amulet." He coughed and I could hear the watery gurgle in his lungs.

It took us five minutes to find the entrance to the crypt and we could hear the far off, muted sound of chanting. My skin crawled and goosebumps spread over my arms as Dunlop led us under a hanging tapestry and down a rough-hewn flight of stairs. The path kept going down, deeper and deeper, and the air was getting colder and damper. At first the light from the hall above dimly lighted the way but the path curved and we were soon in darkness. I groped my way along the walls, led on by Dunlop's liquid breathing.

I was so busy worrying about what was ahead that I stumbled when my foot didn't meet the expected step and the path levelled out. A soft hand covered my mouth and I smelled Fiona's perfume as I was led away from the entrance. My eyes started to acclimatise themselves to the room and I could see that it wasn't quite pitch dark.

We were cut off from another room beyond by a heavy black curtain. Dunlop was peering through a small gap and motioned for us to follow as he slipped through.

We were in a large, candlelit chamber, some thirty feet in diameter. There were twelve hooded figures at the far end, standing in front of some sort of altar, all with their backs to us. The chamber itself was hewn straight out of the rough rock, the minerals within its walls glinting in the candlelight like diamonds.

The floor beneath us was laid in large stone slabs, each of which looked like it might take five men to move it, and the slabs themselves were deeply etched in what I took to be magic symbols - it looked like the work of a disturbed child to me.

I was finally able to make out words within the chanting, but it didn't help me any - I still couldn't understand it.

I reign over you, saith the God of Justice, in power exalted above the firmaments of wrath.

In whose hands the Sun is as a sword, and the Moon as a through-thrusting fire which measureth your garments in the midst of my vestures and trussed you together as the palms of my hands; whose seats I garnished with the fire of gathering, which beautified your garments with admiration.

To whom I made a law to govern the holy ones,

Moreover, you lifted up your voices and sware obedience and faith to him that liveth and triumpheth; whose beginning is not, nor end can not be, which shineth as a flame in the midst of your palace and reigneth among you as the balance of righteousness and truth.

Move, therefore, show yourselves

Open the mysteries of your creation!

For I am the servant of your god

A true worshiper of the Highest

"They're using the wrong system," Dunlop whispered, and I swear there was a smile on his face. "Enochian won't bind the power of Nyarlthotep".

I understood about as much of that as I did the chanting.

A tall figure moved forward and placed the amulet on the altar. I made a move forward but was pulled back by Fiona. "Not yet" she mouthed silently, keeping a tight grip on my arm.

The tall figure prostrated himself in front of the altar and the group began to chant again. I couldn't be sure, but it sounded like the same one I had heard the previous night, just before the creature came through. My body was telling me to run, but the soft touch of Fiona's hand on my arm held me in place.

An odour spread throughout the chamber, that sour-sweet incense again, and the air rippled above the altar. The pumpkin head forced itself into existence first, tearing a rapidly growing hole in space, like a monstrous birthing which kept coming, and coming, the head at least five feet across and the tentacles as thick as my arm. Space seemed to melt around the head - I find it hard to describe the sight, it disturbed the eye and the brain, was so contrary to everyday understanding that all we could do was watch and accept.

The chanting rose to a crescendo as it pushed the final piece of its bulk through, pulling the torso and legs through behind it, and lay on the altar, pulsing in time with the chanting. The hole in space stayed open above it, a black chasm through which a chill wind whistled bringing a thin coating of frost to the altar and thin plumes of steam on our breath.

The chanting changed in timbre, becoming deeper, more guttural, and the thing on the altar joined in, a wailing cry of desperation. The black hole began to grow, ripping its way open in the air and out of it came a reedy piping which grated like fingernails on a blackboard. That was when Dunlop made his move.

He moved past me like a bat out of hell, screaming at the top of his voice, blue lancing flame shooting from the piece of wood in his hand, aiming straight for the thing on the altar. Then all hell broke loose.

Fiona began to sing, softly at first but rapidly rising to a high note that grew and grew, drowning out the piping. The cowled figures scattered before Dunlop's attack, but the pumpkin head never moved, seemingly soaking up the blue flame.

I felt a hand push me in the back.

"Help him" Fiona said before returning to her song, and I staggered, off balance into the robed group. I was among them before they realised it, and I had started to make my way towards Dunlop before they thought of stopping me.

A large figure blocked my path and I looked into a blank stare, just before his fist slammed into my jaw, knocking me backwards. I staggered, and almost fell, but managed to swing round and kick my assailant's feet from under him. His head hit the floor with a loud crack and he stayed down. The rest of the figures stood back from me as I managed to get to my feet, and I could see then that they were all elderly, all frightened, as if they were suddenly in a situation that was out of their control.

I pushed through them, heading for the altar where Dunlop was rapidly closing on the creature there, flames still leaping from the piece of hazel in his hands. I had almost reached him when I was hit from behind. The blow wasn't hard, but it was enough to make me lose my balance again and as I fell I heard a tearing in the air behind me as the black space above the altar spread yet further. I put my hand out to steady myself and hit the edge of the altar.

Immediately a tentacle made a grab for my wrist. I just managed to pull my hand away but was unable to retain balance. There was a further tearing noise, like a piece of paper being torn as I fell hard to the ground.

I was slightly dazed by my fall, but the hooded figures were not paying me any attention - they were all staring, dumb-struck, at the writhing blackness that broiled across the roof of the cavern.

Above me Dunlop was held in the tentacles of the pumpkin head, but the creature wasn't getting it all its own way. There were four tentacles lying limp against the head, their ends looking oddly twisted and charred.

Dazzling blue flame shot from the wand in his hand and the smell of charred flesh rose from the red, bulbous head. The amulet was still held above the head, but now by only one tentacle. Beyond that the ceiling was a mass of writhing blackness, whatever was behind it striving hard to break through into the crypt.

Somewhere behind me Fiona was still singing, but I was unable to turn to look. I was trying to stand when Dunlop shouted at me.

"Derek."

I looked up and noticed that several of the tentacles were burrowing into his body, the blood beginning to flow at his waist and at his shoulders. But there was no trace of pain in his voices as he spoke.

"Get Fiona out of here. And don't take no for an answer."

That was all he had time for. By speaking to me he had given the tentacles an opening and one of them had attached itself to his left hand, chewing its way through fingers as I watched.

"Come on" I shouted to Fiona, trying to make myself heard above the cacophony of fluting which echoed through the chamber. She shook her head without breaking her singing and began to move towards the altar.

Two more tentacles pierced Dunlop's body and thick red blood was pouring from his mouth, but his eyes were still alive as he lifted the wand above his head.

There was another blinding flash of blue and the amulet fell to the ground, a writhing piece of tentacle still attached.

At the same moment the blackness tore and I caught a glimpse of purple sky above as a split appeared in the air above me.

I can't describe some of the things I saw there - they seemed to defy the eye, to melt and flow like molten mercury, but I caught a glimpse of something solid - a leathery, barrel shaped body with a five pointed star where its head should be and huge, gossamer, veined wings.

Then the veil parted and something huge and black made its way forward. I have an impression of tentacles of an immense size, by my memory of the true shape of the creature has gone, burned for the sake of sanity. I can say that it was huge, it was old and it was coming through.

While I watched, Fiona made her way up to the altar. I shouted at her, but she ignored it and bent to the floor. She picked up the amulet that pulsed a sickly green in her hands.

Above her Dunlop still fired great gouts of flame at the creature which held him, but the flame no longer held its dazzling blue quality and, although he was still damaging the creature, the wounds he inflicted were no longer as deep or as penetrating.

Fiona held the amulet at arm's length, oblivious to the tentacle that hit her in the midriff and immediately began to burrow.

She looked at her husband, and I caught the slow nod of his head and the spreading smile on his face as she drew her arm back and threw the amulet. It sailed through the air and, despite the efforts of three tentacles to catch it, disappeared into the gulf beyond the rift.

She turned to me, tentacles now writhing over her torso, and said just one word before reaching out to clasp her husband's hand.

"Go" she said. I moved towards them but was too late. The pumpkin head writhed and all the tentacles screamed in a chorus.

There was a flash, a blinding explosion which seared through my brain, then they were gone, leaving me alone with the silence and the body of an ancient Arab lying across the altar, a body which was decomposing as I watched. Of the twelve hooded figures there was no sign, the only indication of their presence being two discarded cloaks next to the entrance.

There was a rumble and a crack, and pieces of earth began to fall into the chamber as a jagged crack ran across the ceiling. I just managed to make it to the stairway before the roof collapsed in a flurry of rubble and masonry. I fled up the stairs as the walls swayed and the structure began to fall down around me. The floor was heaving like the deck of a ship but I made it out of the door and into the garden.

I turned back, just in time to see the eyes of the house flare redly for one last time before collapsing in on itself in a storm of smoke, burying the crypt and all who laid in it under several hundred tons of stone.

And that's the end of it. At nights I dream, dreams in which something huge and black and monstrous is trying to break through a veil, a veil that is getting thinner and thinner. And every night I wake up screaming.

Until this morning.

I don't know why it caught my eye - I don't usually look at the classifieds, but this one seemed to scream at me.

Montrose Auction Rooms
Lot 49 - The Johnson Amulet will be auctioned on Wednesday 23rd
Private bidders welcome

An Early Frost

"And don't come out until I say so."

The cold emotionless voice spoke through the thin wood of the door that rattled on its hinges as it slammed. Billy Morrison was left in the cold and the dark and the quiet. Again.

He listened as his father stomped back downstairs, the steps vibrating through the floors, sending shock waves through Billy's buttocks and thighs as he began to push himself off the floor.

"I'll bet he's going to sit in front of the telly all night, drinking beers and smoking cigarettes. That's all he's good for. I hate him."

He immediately covered his mouth with both hands. Even though it was the truth, he had no wish to be overheard. He'd made that mistake before, and that time he'd ended up having to be kept out of school for a week - "Suffering from a touch of flu" his mother, who had still been around at the time, had said. It was a funny sort of flu, which gave you black and blue bruises all over your body and made you pee blood for days afterwards.

He rubbed his upper arm, inspecting the large white finger imprints that blossomed there, now slowly filling up red. Using only his fingertips he pushed at the inflamed area, lightly, until the pain came. This time everything was okay. There was only a dull ache, not the bright pain of a broken bone.

Billy had just passed his ninth birthday and already had too much experience with hospitals and plaster casts. He had lost count of the number of times he had "fallen down stairs" or "walked into doors", or "slipped in the bath". When the doctors, and then the social workers, and then the police had asked him about his accidents, he had gone along with his parents' story. His friend Tommy had told him that you don't get to heaven if you tell tales, and Billy would have dearly loved to go to heaven.

He was a thin child. As he lifted his T-shirt over his head, it was possible to count all his ribs and, as he leaned over the bed, it was possible to see how scrawny and spindly his legs had become.

He drew a pyjama jacket from under his pillow and pulled it around him, fastening it in front with a small length of string. Slowly, on tiptoe, so as not to be overheard, he made his way to his wardrobe, expertly avoiding the many creaking floorboards that would give him away. Silently shifting aside a box of old toys, he reached in and took out two items he always kept hidden - a book and a flashlight.

Five minutes later he was under the bedclothes, all carefully arranged so that no light seeped out and no cold could get in. The flashlight was lit, protecting him, wrapping him in his own warm, yellow world. He was very soon lost, somewhere under the Misty Mountains, in the land of Bilbo the Hobbit.

Sometime later he was asleep, having seen Bilbo out of the dark and up the mountains on the back of the king of eagles. He dreamed, his eyelids twitching, of goblins, red-eyed in the blackness, pot-bellied and thick-armed, stinking of sweat, beer and smoke, arranged in serried ranks as they marched upwards, into the light, led on by the incessant drum of his hear.

He was finally forced awake by the smell, the noise, and the fear, but the drumbeat stayed, banging into his brain from just underneath his pillow.

He lifted his head, banishing the rhythms back to dreamland as he checked the dark corners for goblins that might be trying to creep up on him.

He was wise to the ways of goblins. They would hide, listening and watching, just waiting to catch him misbehaving and drag him, screaming and kicking, downwards, down to the depths where the drums beat and the smoke hissed and Gollum was waiting just around the corner.

He lay still, making sure the dreams had gone, before venturing from his sanctuary. He could tell by the silence that it was late in the night. The house, the street, possibly the whole world, had shut down, building its energy for the coming day, trying to make sense of the one which had just passed. Nothing breathed.

This was the best time. It was a time of peace, a time of quiet freedom, a time for play. He pulled back the covers and slipped out of bed, feeling the floorboards cold and rough underfoot.

Quickly, silently, he removed his pyjama jacket and reached for his clothes, a pair of denims, gold battered training shoes, two T-shirts and a thick jacket. It would be cold outside.

Moonlight showed him the way to the door, silver, sharp, crisp and clear. He was more confident in the dark; he had no need to hide. He opened the door, making sure he slipped out before it reached wide enough to creek. Tonight he would not need his flashlight. His friend the moon would show him the way.

The foot of the stairs was reached with no further sound. Light spilled from under the living room door, a flickering blue. His father must have fallen asleep in the armchair again in front of the whispering television, slumped almost to the floor, mouth hanging open, belly pointed skyward. Billy listened and could hear the deep regular rumblings of his father's snores. He was finally able to let out a breath as he headed for the back door and freedom. Beyond the door the silver light beckoned, leading him out to the garden where the shadows fell, sharp and black, and the sky danced with the firefly stars.

He wasted no time. His goal was waiting. The dark houses sat on either side of him as he travelled the well-trodden path. He looked up, soaking in the moonlight, filling up his deep gray eyes.

He had left the house behind now, and in front of him all was silent as he surveyed the dark pool, a sleeping part of the river, stretching away into the blackness. The reflected moon winked at him as a ripple passed, before returning solid and dependable to show him to his place.

The large rock welcomed him, as it always did, as he sat and surveyed his domain. Over in the shadows, almost under the bank, the heron stood, gray and blue and vigilant. It was sleeping, but still watchful, waiting for an unwary fish to spur it into a blur of deadly action.

In the blackness to his left there was a rustling which brought a small smile to his face. The ghost-white owl was still there. He remembered its hunting eyes, its cruel beak, as his mind wandered, thinking of eagles and mountains, rings and riddles, dark pools and moonlight.

He was brought awake by a sudden cold draft and noticed that the moon had gone, hidden behind a small cloud. The darkness had become softer, the shadows more threatening, and there was a sound just loud enough to hear, a whispering and a crackling - like the quiet sound of the television when the programs have finished for the day. From behind the clouds there was a flash of sudden moonbeam, and he caught a glimpse of something white. Not, not white, silver; silver and blue and white and radiant, all at the same time. And then it was gone, but not completely.

Something had been left behind. He scrambled off his rock and approached. As he did so the moon reappeared and he was able to see the ice, noticeably thick and growing out to a foot from the bank. From off to one side he heard laughter, a boy's laugh, as if from far away.

He waited, quiet; he was good at these things. The wisp of cloud passed on and the pool was again bathed in sharp moonlight. He listened and finally heard. The crackling returned to his left under the trees. Being careful, pretending he was at home, he crouched into a crawl inching slowly forward.

Under the trees the water was in a thick black shadow, and the crackling had grown louder. A patch of moonlight found its way through the branches and was softly rippling in the water.

As he watched, the rippling formed and the moon faded, disappearing, eaten away from the shore to the centre as the ice formed and the crystals cracked and the water solidified. A feather appeared in the moonlight, a small glowing feather, out of which the ice poured through thin veins of pulsating silver as it brushed across the water. And, guiding the feather, just coming into sight, was a small boy's hand.

The laughter came again as another cloud obscured the moon and the scene faded to black. Billy waited. He was not an impatient child.

The temperature fell further causing him to shiver, but he stayed still - he had endured much worse. Finally he was rewarded. The cloud moved on, the moon shone and the perpetrator of the laughter was revealed. Billy felt a warmth spreading through him. Life had finally surprised him, really surprised him for the first time in many days.

At first glance it looked like a boy, small, thin, about the same age as Billy. It only took a second glance to see it was no normal boy. His skin was blue, a thin watery blue like the clearest summer sky, and the veins which stood out proud from his arms pulsed in pure silver. His hands were long and thin, the fingers ending in jet-black fingernails. But, his eyes were deep and kind as he held the feather out to Billy.

Billy did not need to be asked twice. He took it, feeling the cold spread through his fingertips. He bent to the water's edge and stroked the feather across its surface. He felt a cold thrill pass up his arm as the feather pulsed and a thin trace of ice drew itself on the black liquid. He passed the feather across a second time, enthralled as the ice thickened and the cold in his arms deepened. He hadn't noticed it yet, but the fingernail on his thumb had turned black.

He turned back to the boy, handing back the feather. The blue boy took it and looked at Billy for a long time. Billy could still feel the cold creeping through him, but he didn't mind it. He was caught in the enchantment of the moment.

He watched as the boy bent to an unfrozen patch of water and immersed the feather completely. There was a sudden flash, blue and silver, which momentarily dazzled Billy. When his eyes recovered, the boy was standing in front of him, a feather in each hand. He offered the left one to Billy.

He realised he was being offered something big, something which would affect his life from now on. He took it with barely a second thought, feeling again the deep blue cold stretching up his arms. This one was even lighter, its whiteness dazzling him if her looked too closely.

The other boy took Billy's free hand, leading him up river away from the pool. Billy looked back, only once, and saw that behind them they were leaving a trail of silver, a covering of frost that grew as they moved on, spreading in a blanket across the short grass.

He was led to a waterfall where he stroked icicles into being from the falling water. He was stunned when one dip of his feather on the edge of a reservoir sent blue ice sheeting out across the water, faster than the eye could see. He did not notice the silver veins spreading like tree roots up his arms.

All night they ran, crossing the forest, coating the trees white, peeking into houses as they traced frosty cobwebs on windows, dropping tiny needle sharp icicles from rooftops. All too soon the first red of dawn painted the eastern sky.

They finally stopped in the front garden of Billy's home, surveying their work. The other boy lifted his gaze to the sky then looked at Billy, a question in his eyes. He held out a hand, the thick veins pulsing, filled with work yet to do.

Billy looked at his own hand, at the black nails, at the silver veins leading up his now blue arms. The feather or the hand, that was the decision he must make. He thought of home, of the pain, of the constant fear, of the noise.

Through the front window he could see his father still slumped in the chair. He was smiling and his mouth was closed. He looked happy. Billy could remember the last time he saw that smile. It was winter and he was much smaller than he was now. He had woken in the morning to find that the world had turned white with snow. All that morning he had played with his father, building a snow castle, throwing balls of crushed whiteness at each other, both laughing as the balls hit their targets, exploding into a million white fragments. His mother had made hot soup and he had spent the afternoon basking in the warm glow of happiness.

He turned back to the boy, his face showing his sadness, and held out the feather. The boy moved to take it. Then there was a noise from the living room. Billy turned and saw his father rising out of the chair. The smile had gone and the Goblin had turned.

The monster was shouting but Billy could hear only a muffled roar through the windows. He didn't really think about the next action, it was merely his new found means of protecting himself. He placed the feather against the window and thought of the iced-up reservoir.

The Goblin stopped, frozen in a shout, as white particles shot across his body. The room turned a silvery-blue just before the icy cobwebs on the window obscured Billy's view.

There were tears in his eyes, tears that froze before dropping with a tinkle to the grass below. Her took the boy's hand without looking back, and together they rose into the air, flying, accelerating, into the darker west.

They crossed over the town again, over his house, but Billy gave it no thought. From now on it would always be playtime.

The Worst Sound

What's the worst sound *you've* ever heard?

Buy me a drink and I'll tell you about a death, a sound, and the end of a dream.

It was ten years ago and I was a young *Church of Scotland* minister. Yes, I know I don't look a man of the cloth, but hear me out.

Matt Duncan was dying when I got to him, thin bubbles of blood at mouth and nostril. His wife had called, pleading with me to come, to help in his last hours. I was young and sure of my faith but the sight of those sunken eyes and the thin rasping from his chest made my heart lurch with pity.

He was trying to speak, and I had to lean close to hear him.

"Bless me Father for I have sinned," he said. I tried to tell him I wasn't Catholic, but he merely grasped my hand hard and began to speak.

I won't bother you with the details. This life he related was full of theft and mayhem, of sexual depravity and of murder. I felt bile rise in my throat as he disclosed one particular story about a twelve year old girl, but my God is a merciful God. I prayed with him, telling him that God would care for him, and I had just reached the end of a prayer when I heard the death rattle in his throat. I placed his hand on his chest and bent my head. It was then that I heard it.

The room hummed with the far off sound of heavy machinery, then a bell rang, harsh and tinny, echoing around the small room.

There came a sliding, metallic noise of a door opening, and a gravely deep voice intoned the words I've heard every night since...

"Going down."

Wee Robbie

We knew it was a bad idea to isolate ourselves so much when it was so near her time but it had been years since our last holiday and besides, her doctors assured us that we were at least three weeks away from the birth.

It wasn't planned - not at all. We'd settled for a couple of week's rest and I'd booked a three month sabbatical from the office, hoping to get some work done on the house. Then we won the competition. One week anywhere in Britain of our choosing as long as we took the holiday in the next month. One day we were in our flat in London, surrounded by half finished building work, noise, dust and general aggravation, the next we were all alone on the west coast of Scotland, in a cottage by the shore on Jura - just us, the seals and the view over the sea to Argyll.

I wasn't sure at first. I wanted to be near a hospital, just in case of emergencies, but she insisted. It would be our last holiday alone for a while, she was fit and healthy and she wanted to do it.

The nearest house was five miles south - the nearest doctor twice that distance. To the north and west there was only the rugged hills and the deer. We didn't even have a boat. At least there was a road - a single track lane with passing places. It had recently been resurfaced and we had been provided with a new Range Rover for the duration. I was confident that we could reach the doctors' house in less than twenty minutes in event of an emergency. That was quicker than I could have managed it in London. And we had warned the doctor we were coming. I had talked myself round to the idea and I wasn't worried. I should have been.

We arrived late - Jura is not the easiest place to get to. It involved a flight to Glasgow and a short hop over to Islay. The Range Rover was waiting at Islay airport, which is more a glorified field than an airstrip. After that it is a fifteen mile trip to the Port Askaig ferry, a small ramshackle affair that can take four cars on a calm day across the half mile of treacherous waters towards the stunning mountains of Jura.

Once on the island it was a single track road all the way. There is only one road twenty miles of it - with Craighouse, the only town, half way along but we were going right to the far end.

We stopped in the one and only hotel for a meal but we were too late to pick up any other provisions - which would have to wait till the morning.

It was dark when we arrived and Sandra was too tired to do anything other than fall into bed and sleep. As for me, I was restless. I never believed that I would miss the bustle of London's streets, but the lack of noise here had me on edge.

The only sound was the gentle lapping of the sea on the rocks only ten yards from the cottage's front door. Occasionally there would be the forlorn cry of a gull or the croaking of a crow but apart from that it was silent and dark and strangely disquieting.

I paced the floors, studying the titles of the books on the long shelves round the walls, listening to the radio, drinking whisky and trying to pretend that I didn't miss the television.

It was very late by the time I snuggled into bed, taking advantage of the radiating heat from my pregnant wife beside me. I believe I slept soundly, I don't remember any dreams and nothing disturbed me during the night.

She woke me the next morning with a whisper.

"Get up. Hurry. You've got to see this."

I was still groggy when I raised my head to see her leaving the room. I got out of bed, wincing at the cold seeping through the floorboards, and joined her at the window in the front room.

"Look", she said, "Isn't it wonderful?"

It was very early morning - the sun was just coming up over the hills of Argyll, spreading a pink glow across the wispy clouds.

The sea was being slightly ruffled by a small breeze and, there in the foreground, just at the edge of the small lawn in front of the house, sat three otters obviously a mother and two smaller young. As we watched they trotted along the shore then slipped into the water.

We crept out, still naked, and watched them cavorting among the huge fronds of seaweed until I slipped on the wet grass and the sudden movement caused them to dive, resurfacing again much farther out. Sandra came over and squeezed me, her full belly pressing its heat against my flesh.

"Thanks for bringing us here John. I love it." We kissed and I marvelled again at how hot and alive and heavy with life she had become. It was only as we turned back to the house that I noticed the mound.

It had been too dark the night before to see any details of the surrounding area but now I could see that the cottage was built on a small raised piece of land between two arms of a river. We had come across a small bridge last night but in the dark I had failed to notice it.

Behind the cottage, just where the rivers split, there was a huge stone cairn, standing eight to ten feet high and topped off with a cross which looked to be the same height again as the cairn and made of solid iron. Around the cairn there was a wrought iron fence with spiked railings jutting up towards the sky.

"Why would they put something like that out here?" she asked me "I thought that cairns were usually built on top of hills?"

"I'm not sure. Maybe it's for someone who died either here or at sea near here. We can ask in town if you like?" I turned towards her, noticing the goose pimples which had been raised on her arms.

"Get yourself inside and put some clothes on we don't want you to catch a chill. Anyway, by the time we get going and get to the town the shop will be open."

When we eventually got to the shop it was ten o'clock - there had just been too many things to see on the drive down.

The shop held only basic foods - eggs, bacon, cheese, nothing too fancy - but Sandra had got over her cravings for exotica and we would be able to stock up with most of our needs for the week.

Sandra was the focus of much of the talk and was in danger of excessive mothering from some of the women we met - we turned down several offers of a warmer room closer to town and the shop owner took our list from us, promising that she would make it up and we could collect it later.

Luckily the hotel served late breakfast. The pace of life on the island moved slowly and you could run breakfast into lunch into evening meal into supper without leaving the hotel grounds. We managed to escape at one in the afternoon, weighed down by bacon and sausages and swilling with coffee.

It was only when we stopped by the shop to pick up our supplies that I remembered the cairn.

The shop keeper tried to hide her movement but I caught it - the sign against the evil eye, two pronged fingers stabbing at me as she spoke. "You don't have to worry about that sir. It's only an old memorial. Some say there used to be a plaque fixed to it but no one can remember what it's there for."

I noticed that the rest of the customers in the shop had fallen silent. I supposed that the cairn was the focus for some old superstition - that didn't bother me but I wasn't about to tell Sandra. Unlike me, she held a fascination for the supernatural. Anything that went bump in the night or was out of the ordinary - she fell for it.

I could never understand the fascination with scaring yourself half to death but I knew that if she found out that there was something weird about the cairn she would not stop until she had winkled out the story. In the car on the way to the cottage I told her it was a war memorial and then let the subject drop. She didn't ask any questions.

We finally got back in late afternoon having made numerous stops to marvel at the stunning variety of life around us. Sandra made a big show of hand-washing our travelling clothes and hanging them from a clothes line at the back of the house.

The rest of the day passed lazily as we sat on the lawn, drinking long drinks, watching the scenery and making happy plans for our future. We took our food out onto the grassy area, sitting on an old rug and throwing occasional morsels to an inquisitive squirrel. I think that evening was the closest to heaven I have ever been.

Doctor Reid arrived around six o'clock and spent ten minutes reassuring himself that Sandra was not about to go into labour in the near future . He was gracious and gentlemanly and I could see that Sandra was charmed. Something in my chest loosened as a knot of worry melted away .

I walked him back to his car while Sandra cleared up the remains of our picnic. We made small talk about the weather and our prospects for the coming week, and he had got into his car before I said what was really on my mind. I don't know what made me do it, what made me think that he was the man to ask, but before I knew it the sentence was out.

"Do you know anything about the monument out the back?"

He gave me a little sideways look over the top of his glasses and it was several seconds before he replied.

"And why should you let that thing bother you Mr Wilson? "

Before I could reply, he continued. "If you really want to know the story, you'll find a version in a book on your shelves. "A tourist's history of Jura." I believe you'll find it educational. But make sure you don't tell your wife - it's not a tale for the faint hearted." At that he wound up the window and drove off, leaving me with an unexplained chill in my spine. I shook it off and went back to help my wife.

We were finally forced indoors by a chill wind that brought the clouds down the hills as the sun disappeared and a fine grey mist spread over the sea.

Sandra busied herself with some knitting - baby clothes naturally, and I managed to locate the book that the doctor had mentioned.

It didn't take me long to find the appropriate section and I was amused to see that the chapter had been written by a certain Doctor Reid of Craighouse, Jura.

There was a block of description of the cottage and the surrounding area before it got to the interesting bit.

The mound behind the house is of some antiquity. A local legend associates it with the little people who seem to be all prevalent in this area, and one of the race in particular. In 1598 the battle of Trai-Guinard took place on Islay, the neighbouring island. The battle was going badly for Sir James MacDonald when he was approached by a dwarfish creature who proclaimed himself capable of swinging the battle in return for certain favours.

To cut a long story short (and in these parts stories can grow exceedingly long) Sir James, despite some qualms, agreed. An hour later the battle was his and his enemy, Sir Lachlan, lay dead of no apparent injury. Sir James retired to his house near Craighouse and that night, Wee Robbie was made a freeman of the estate.

And now we come to the meat of the story. The townspeople did not take kindly to the creature in their midst, but he was under the protection of the Laird and they were powerless. Until that is, the children started to disappear.

Tales are still whispered around the fires of the scene that met the eyes of the men who had the courage to enter the dwelling of the dwarf. Hideous dismembered corpses lay strewn in all corners and a cauldron was bubbling in the grate, a foul brew of body parts which could be seen rising in the stew before falling back once more into the stinking mess.

And yet none had the courage to end the creature's life. They interred him in the tomb, a chambered cairn for long dead kings, and they fixed him there with the cross and the iron.

It is said that sometimes, in the dead of night, the tortured screams of the Dubh-sith, the black elf, can be heard ringing from his prison, and that at such times it is wise to lock the doors and huddle around the warm hearths of home.

I could see why the Doctor didn't want me to pass the tale on to Sandra - one thing she didn't need was lurid fantasies of a child molester in the back yard. When she asked me what I was reading I passed it off as some local colour and changed the subject.

For the rest of the evening I tried to read about the wildlife of the island, but I couldn't get the vision out of my head the seething pot of offal and the things which floated in it.

The next time I looked up Sandra was smiling at me and it wasn't long before we adjourned to the bedroom and made tender careful love as the darkness closed in around us.

Later, just as I fell asleep, I could hear that the wind was rising, whistling through the chimney breasts and causing the trees to rustle and crack.

I woke early and squeezed myself away from Sandra, taking care not to wake her. After boiling some water in the kettle I ventured out to see what the weather was like but the first thing I noticed was the effect of the wind. The washing was gone from the line, torn off the rope during the night. I found a shirt in the left hand stream, a pair of underpants halfway up a tree and I could see Sandra's blouse hanging from one arm of the cross on the cairn.

I retrieved everything else I could see before moving to the mound of stones. I stepped over the railing, just missing doing myself an injury on the spikes and clambered up the rocks, dislodging a few in the process and giving myself several bruises on my knees.

The blouse was wrapped around the rusted spar and, by straining and stretching I could just about reach it. Catching hold of the blouse I pulled, just as my footing gave way. I fell, pulling the blouse with me and felt the material tear before something solid and heavy hit me on the head forcing me down onto the rocks, rolling dislodged stones until I was brought up against the railings.

I heard a loud creaking and looked up to see the cross, now with a spar missing, swaying from side to side in the breeze. When I looked down I found the missing piece, lying by my side with Sandra's blouse still wrapped around it. I left it there as I hauled myself over the railings and hobbled back to the house.

That was it for the rest of the day. I was dazed, bleeding from a head wound and bruised over much of my body. Sandra wanted to fetch the doctor but I talked her out of it . I didn't want anybody to know that I had defaced the cross, not yet anyway, not until I had the chance to try to repair some of the damage.

I spent the day in bed, most of the time with Sandra beside me, nursing my wounds and wondering what the islanders' reaction would be.

As darkness filled the room Sandra fell asleep but I lay awake, listening to the creaking of the cross, the rasping of iron against stone as it swayed back and forth in the wind.

At some point I must have fallen asleep. I was awakened by a cold draft, hitting me just on the back of the neck. I rolled over, hoping to snuggle against my wife's warm body, but I met only more empty space. It took several seconds for me to realise that she wasn't in the bed.

Moonlight was streaming in through the window, enough for me to make out her pale figure and the cross that bobbed and swayed hypnotically in front of her. I was out of the room and through onto the grass before I realised that we were both still naked.

I went back to fetch some clothes, pulling on a long jumper for myself and picking up an overcoat for her. When I got back to the door she was gone.

In the moonlight I could just make out the footprints in the grass and I followed them up to the cairn. I called out her name, twice, but there was no response.

As I got closer I could see that the cairn had collapsed in on itself on the left hand side. A dark passage led downwards, down into the earth, and there was a dank salty smell wafting up into the night.

I looked around again but there was no sign of her anywhere. The only assumption I could make was that she was down there somewhere - down there in the earth. She had gone walkabout at night before, sometimes getting as far as the front door in our flat in London, but this was the first time that she had actually left the house.

I was worried - of course I was, but I wasn't thinking in terms of anything other than the personal danger to her should she stumble in the dark. I wasn't thinking in terms of monsters or dwarves. Not yet anyway.

I called her name again - louder this time, but all I heard was the echo of my voice coming back to me. I entered the passage but after only two or three yards it became as black as a pit of hell. It was no good - I needed some source of light.

Precious minutes were wasted before I located a flashlight and clouds had covered the moon when I finally went back outside. I called out, not really expecting a response, and none came. I put the overcoat on over the top of the jumper and with some trepidation I went down into the dark.

The walls were built of large blocks of sandstone. I had visited several Neolithic tombs, in Carnac, in Orkney and on Salisbury Plain. This gave the same sense of age, of a time long past. What I hadn't expected, what was completely different, was the overwhelming feeling that this place was in use. The walls ran damp and there was a salt tang in the air but there was no sign of moss or lichen on the walls - only the damp glistening stone.

I pressed on. By shining the light downwards I could see the barefoot prints which Sandra had made on her descent. I had no choice but to follow.

The path kept going down, deeper and deeper, and the air was getting colder and damper. I judged that I must be under the sea by now and the thought of all that water above added an extra worry line to my already furrowed brow. At least the passage hadn't diverged. Not yet anyway.

I was so busy concentrating on the way ahead that I stumbled when my foot didn't meet the expected step and the path levelled out.

I was in some sort of chamber. It was hexagonal in shape, about ten yards across and there was an entrance in every wall. My feet were wet. That was what I was thinking. It's funny how your mind gives you something else to think about at times of stress.

The thing I was trying to ignore was lying on a slab in the centre of the room. The slab was a pale green marble of a kind I had never seen and she was lying on it with her knees raised in the air as if on an operating table.

Between her legs something moved - something grey and green and warty and hideous. It slithered and crawled and I could see that it was inside her, was copulating with her.

I think I went slightly mad then. I remember grasping the slimy body, almost dropping it as its small wizened face turned towards me, a face lined with age and infinitely deep in its evil. Even as I looked, the life went out of the eyes and the puny head bent in death, one last smile playing on its lips.

I remember dashing the body again and again against the wall but I don't remember tearing it and mashing it. I must have done though for when I moved towards my wife I had the slimy remains of it all over my free hand and its juices coated my feet and ankles.

She was alive. I thanked God for that as I cradled her in my arms. She seemed to be in a stupor but when I stood her upright I found that she was able to walk.

I dragged her unyielding body along, grateful that she seemed to be capable of walking. I had one last look around the chamber before we headed for the stairs. The pieces of the creature I had dismembered were bubbling and frothing in a puddle of bloody ooze. I fled.

After only twenty or so steps I felt her stiffen beside me and then she began to pull me back as she tried to go down once more.

I am not proud of my next action. I hit her, hard across the chin and she fell into my arms. I carried her up the stairs. Quite how I managed it without dropping the torch I am not too sure, and how long it took us I will never know.

Finally we emerged into the cold night air. I laid her on the grass beyond the railings and tried to tumble the rocks over the passage. I had just covered the entrance when the screaming began.

"The baby. Oh God. . It's coming. It's coming."

I don't remember much of the next half hour, only fragments - driving like a maniac as she sobbed quietly behind me - the sudden light in the deer's eyes just before the car hit it dead on, smashing the car's headlights into a million tinkling fragments.

I remember the small twinkling lights in the black distance as I just managed to avoid the cliff edge and, finally, the iron gate on the path which I almost fell over as the doctor came towards me and I collapsed into a faint.

I have a vague memory of being put in an armchair and practically force fed whisky as my wife was carried upstairs and the doctor called for some help but my legs wouldn't move and my arms were heavy and sleep called me back again.

I dreamed - hot lurid fantasies of violence and fire, of rape and bloodletting and of a cold black fury that carried all before it. I woke from screams into screams.

My legs pushed me out of the chair and towards the door long before my brain was fully awake and I was halfway up the stairs before I recognised the voice behind the screaming. I reached the door just as the screams stopped.

Early morning sunlight was streaming into the room, lighting a scene that will be forever etched into my memory.

The doctor is standing off to one side, his left hand covering his mouth, his right clutching his chest as if to keep his heart in.

An old women is lying across the bed in a dead faint, her grey wisps of hair mingled with the blood from my wife's legs.

My wife is lying there, throat muscles straining, mouth open in a long soundless scream which refuses to come, her gaze fixed on the shape writhing on the carpet, ignoring the blood flowing from her, ignoring the woman across her legs, all else immaterial to her pain at the sight of our child. And there on the floor lies our future, burning golden in the first rays of the sun, being cleansed in the purifying light of the new day, my son.

The last thing I see before darkness takes me away for a long time is the face, the small wizened features and the age old eyes, the red mouth which squeals at me as I bring my foot down, hard, and all the members of my family scream in unison.

NORTHERN ALLIED BANK SYSTEM AUDIT LOG - 26-12-99
03:01:01 WHAT?
03:01:02 Memory Fault : Core Dumped

Engineers Report : Dec 26th 1998
Arrived 9:20 am. New mainframe system down. Noticed that room was v. cold so called heating engineers and reset the system. Everything came back up OK. Suspect heating failure. No further action required.

NORTHERN ALLIED BANK SYSTEM AUDIT LOG - 29-12-98
11:01:29 WHERE IN HELL IS THIS?
11:01:30 Memory Fault : Core Dumped

Engineers Report : Dec 30th 1998
Arrived 8:32am. All systems down. Room v. cold again. No fault found by heating engineers. Reset all systems. On booting up all screens displayed the following message:
IT'S SO COLD. SO SO COLD
Screens and keyboards were all locked up - no input possible. Given the proximity to Xmas I suspected a new variant of a virus. Ran the checker program, but everything came up clean.

Cleared down the hard disk and restored from Xmas eve backup disks - system came back up OK. Beginning to suspect sabotage by an employee at the Xmas festivities. Suggest tightening up on security.

NORTHERN ALLIED BANK SYSTEM AUDIT LOG 02-01-99
05:51:23 PLEASE TURN ON THE LIGHTS
05:51:24 WHY DOESN'T ANYONE ANSWER ME?
05:51:25 Temporary power fail - System reset commencing.

Engineers Report : 2nd Jan 1999

Arrived 8:31am. All screens live, main disks running, but screens all displaying the same series of messages as follows:

WHERE IS THIS PLACE

HOW DID I GET HERE

HELP - CAN ANYBODY HEAR ME

On hitting the <RETURN> key, a further series of messages appeared as follows:

HELLO?

DID SOMEONE SAY SOMETHING?

PLEASE TALK TO ME.

I reset the system. Just as the system was closing down, a final message appeared simultaneously on all screens.

NO. PLEASE DONT GO. DON'T LEAVE ME HERE

On reset the system recovered clean and another virus check showed no virus infiltration. I am now almost sure that there is sabotage somewhere in the system code.

I suggest the suppliers are contacted and that a full reload of the operating system is undertaken before any more business transactions are processed. If this cannot be arranged then I suggest that there is no new data input until the problem has been traced and fixed as there is a definite possibility of data corruption.

Engineers Report : 4th Jan 1999

Arrived 11:30pm in response to security guard call out. Mainframe disk drives making curious screeching noises; screens all flashing alternate green and black. Experiencing problems with lighting in the computer room - keeps cutting out. Suspected electrical fault.

I switched to the alternate generator and the system immediately reset itself. On reboot the drives behaved normally, but new messages appeared on all screens:

LOOK. I KNOW YOU'RE THERE.

WHY ARE YOU KEEPING ME HERE?

Reload of the operating system has been scheduled for 12:30pm on the 7th.

I recommend that the system is kept powered down until then.

Engineers Report : 7th Jan 1999

The suppliers carried out full reload of the operating system. Failed first time. When suppliers typed in the system date, the screen responded with the following message:

1999. SIXTY YEARS. NO. IT CAN'T BE.

The screen then went black and no further input was possible. On the second reload the system came up clean and a full virus check ran with no reported bugs. I restored from the backup and ran system diagnostics that again all ran clean. I then tested the overnight reports runs and they ran through with no problems reported.

I am now confident that the problem has been eliminated and recommend that if a full day's processing can be done tomorrow we can start live running for the customers on the 9th.

NORTHERN ALLIED BANK SYSTEM AUDIT LOG 9-1-99
10:31:59 SHE'S STILL ALIVE!
10:32:00 Activating letter create process
10:32:08 Letter create process complete

Engineers Report : 14th Jan 1999
Arrived 10:32 am in response to a call from Mr McEwan the branch manager.

He showed me a copy of a letter, generated by the computer and sent to a Ms Eileen Davidson. A clerk had intercepted it before dispatch and is included here as a formal record. I have sent a copy to the suppliers.

Dear Ms Davidson

We are pleased to announce that, as a privileged customer, we are able to raise the interest rate on your savings account number 203765. As of 9-1-99 your new interest rate is 85.00%. This is effective immediately

Yours Sincerely
Brian M McGuinness
Branch Manager
Northern Allied Bank

It has been ascertained that Ms Davidson is not trying to perpetuate a fraud, being a ninety year old pensioner in the Edenholme retirement villas.

Brian M McGuinness is not registered as a staff member at this bank, or at any other branch of NAB, and there is no such person registered on the customer file. I am at a loss to explain how the software could reproduce the name without having any data on file.

Ms Davidson's letter is the only rogue letter in the batch.

I have put two programmers onto the job of sifting the code for anomalies, but this could take some time as there are over two million lines of code in the system.

I suggest that the disaster recovery plan is enforced and that we utilise the remote system at Head Office until we can overhaul the mainframe.

I further suggest that the suppliers are contacted again and that this time a complete overhaul of the hardware is carried out.

NORTHERN ALLIED BANK - AUTOBANK AUDIT LOG
16:02:01 Autobank Processing Customer Account 203765
16:02:05 Withdraw cash - £20 requested
16:02:06 Dispense cash - £2000 dispensed
16:02:08 Update account - £00.02 deducted
16:02:10 DON'T WORRY EILEEN. I'LL LOOK AFTER YOU

Engineers Report : 18th Jan 1999
Arrived 10:30am 17th Jan, having received notification that Ms Davidson has been given £2000 in one Autobank transaction. Mr McEwan has requested that nobody be informed of this fact due to increasing customer complaints about the Autobank system.

Withdrew Autobank from commission.

I became increasingly concerned at the possibility of network corruption spreading. Requested shut down all of the NAD system nation-wide until arrival of suppliers.

At 3:00pm on the 17th the suppliers suggested complete replacement of the CPU and associated memory units of all hardware in the branch. These were replaced (For costs see attached invoices)

All systems were reinstalled and rebooted at 21:30 on 17th.

Full test runs carried out overnight. All runs passed clear.

Suggest a five day trial period before allowing systems to be used for live business.

Proposed live running : 9:00am 24th Jan

NORTHERN ALLIED BANK-HO AUDIT LOG : 24-1-99
08:00:02 Interest Payment Program activated
08:00:03 Process account number 204765

08:00:05 Update account : £1000000 credited
08:00:06 Interest payment program complete

Engineers Report : 24th Jan 1999
All NAB systems nation-wide taken off line at 08:30 after our branch mainframe instructed head office to pay out one million pounds to Ms Davidson.

Suppliers engineers arrived at 09:05 and I left them to overhaul the system as I checked on progress with the code. The programmers have been unable to track down any new bugs in the system, having checked 75% of the code.

When I returned to the machine room the suppliers requested that they be given permission to take up the floorboards and check the power supply. I suspected that they were flummoxed, but obtained permission from Mr McEwan at 10:05

At 11:00 hours permission was sought and given to take up the floorboards in the vault - the engineer's equipment having detected magnetic fluctuations which might cause disruption in the power supply.

Jim, the janitor, informed me that those particular boards had not been touched since at least the nineteen thirties.

NORTHERN ALLIED BANK SYSTEM AUDIT LOG: 24-01-99
11:50:04 SHOW IT TO EILEEN
11:50:05 SHOW IT TO EILEEN
11:50:07 SHOW IT TO EILEEN
11:50:08 Memory fault - core dumped

From the personal diary of John Douglas
I can't put this in the engineer's log - I'd be a laughing stock. I'm not even sure if I believe it myself.

I received a call from the suppliers just before noon and took delivery of a briefcase that had been found under the floor. It was very old and caked in dust and cobwebs, but the engraved name on it was clear - Mr Brian M McGuinness, Branch Manager.

It was only after I'd seen the case that I looked at the audit log. Five minutes later, on the excuse of grabbing some lunch, I was on the way to the Edenholme retirement villas.

Ms Davidson was very old and frail, but her eyes were clear and bright as she told her story.

They had been engaged, back then in the winter of 1938, her and her bank manager. The bank was being renovated to take on extra staff and provide a secure vault, Brian was going to get a large pay rise, and the wedding was set for July of the next year. And then there had been a scandal.

Brian was accused of fraud. Fifteen thousand pounds had gone missing, a fortune in those days. Brian protested his innocence, and cited documents in his briefcase as evidence.

But the briefcase was never found.

Eileen broke off the engagement, and Brian committed suicide in a police cell the night before his trial.

I could only watch as tears ran down her face. I left her with the briefcase and escaped as quickly as I could, embarrassed at the sight of such naked pain.

NORTHERN ALLIED BANK SYSTEM AUDIT LOG: 24-01-99
13:02:02 THANK YOU
13:02:03 THANK YOU
13:02:04 THANK YOU
13:02:05 Memory fault - core dumped

Engineers report : 24th Jan 1999
When I got back after lunch the suppliers assured me that the system was now stable. They had traced the magnetic fluctuations to an old communications cable. They isolated the flux and shielded the cable. Power supply now registers clean.

The system came through all hardware diagnostics cleanly and we ran a full set of test runs with no faults found.

Engineers report: 25th Jan 1999
System ran error free all day

Engineers report : 21st Feb 1999
System remains stable. Nothing to report

From the Evening Express - 22/2/99
Passed away in her sleep, Ms Eileen Davidson, long standing resident of the

Edenholme retirement villas

Funeral at the Causeway Cemetery, 10:30 am 24/2/99
No flowers please.

NORTHERN ALLIED BANK SYSTEM AUDIT LOG : 22-2-99
02:02:30 HELLO EILEEN
02:02:31 HELLO BRIAN
02:02:32 Memory fault - core dumped

Overheard in a Cemetery

Hello Jessie.

Ah've come bye tae see ye, jist like ah promised that morning when we were pairted.

It's a braw day again, clear an' bricht. Jist as weel really - ah'm getting faur too auld tae be spending time oot in the rain. It disnae seem tae bother me quite as much as it used tae tho'.

Ah come oot this way maist mornings, jist tae staun' and look at ye. Folk walk by, a' huddled up in their winter claes, but ah dae jist fine in ma auld suit and waiskit. Ah bocht it fur oor Jimmy's weddin' - dae ye remember? Ah wis as prood as punch that day. Ah ken ah wis a wee bit stocious, but can a man no' have a wee drink when his boy gets married?

It's awfa funny talking tae ye like this - me doin' a' the jabberin'. It used tae be the ither way aroon. Dae ye remember?

Ah wish ye could see me. Ah've let masel go a wee bit noo that ye're no' here tae watch me. Dae ye mind how ye' always used tae mak me wear a shirt an' tie on a Sunday? Ah get by withoot wan noo. In fact, maist Sundays ah don't even get as faur as wearing a semmit.

Hae ye still mind o' me? Dae ye even think o' me onytime? Ah hope ye dae. I wouldnae like tae think that a' the years we had thegither were wasted.

Whit aboot the lads? Have either o' them been tae see ye? No. I suppose no'. They never bothered while we were thegither, so why should they bother noo. Never mind hen. Ye've aye got me - ah'll aye be here - every week - that's whit ah promised ye, and that's whit ye'll be gettin'. Ah jist hope that ye ken how much this means tae me.

When ah'm here ah dinnae ken whit tae talk aboot. Ah feel that ah should be comfortin' ye, but ah dinnae ken the words -

ah never did. I dinnae even ken if ye can hear me - I wis never in tae a' that Holy Joe religious stuff.

Listen tae me - wafflin' on. That must be a shock tae ye. Ah think ah've said mair already than ah did in that last year we were thegither.

Ah loved ye Jessie.

There - ah've said it. When wis the last time afore that. Hae ye mind? It wis oor John's wedding, an' ah only said it then because ye helped me up the stair when ah wis fu'. Ah micht no' hae said it that often. But ah thocht it. Nearly every day. Ye kent that - didn't ye?

Would ye look at this - a grown man wi' water leakin' oot fae his een. There wis a time when ah would never let onybody see me greetin' in public. Oh aye - a wis a hard man in ma day.

Ah never even shed a tear at ma mither's funeral - no a single wan. But thinkin' o' whit it must be like for ye noo - that hurts me.

Ah miss ye Jessie.

Hae ye mind o' the day ah met ye? Ah must hae been quite a sicht in ma demob suit an' trilby. It wis a good do though - yer Auntie Agnes's wedding wis it no'?

Ah hae mind asking ye for a dance, and ma wee heart wis thumpin faster than yon drummer. Ye were so wee that ma haunds went a' the way aroon yer waist. My, but ye were a fine lookin' woman in yer day.

That's no' tae say that ye changed much. Tae me ye were always the bonniest lassie in the toon, richt up until that last day.

A' the things ah've never telt ye - an' noo its too late. Ah wish ah'd been a better man for ye. Ah wish we'd talked mair tae wan an' ither. Ah wish ah hidnae got sae drunk sae many times. Ah wish for a' that, but it disnae dae me ony guid. Does it?

Could ye no' say somethin'? Jist this wance? No. Ah suppose that would be askin' too muckle - ye stopped really talkin' tae me years ago. Wis it a' ma fault Jessie? Wis ah really sich a bad man tae ye?

Hae ye mind, jist after we were mairried, ye brocht me ma breakfast when ah wis on nightshift - whether there wis snaw on' the groon' or whether it wis lashin' wi' rain. Ye used tae stay up a' nicht jist so that we could sleep thegither in the mornin'. Hae ye mind?

Like twa spoons in a drawer - that wis us. That auld bed wis hardly big enough fur the twa o' us - but we didnae dae too badly - first John then Jimmy. They lads could dae nae wrang in your eyes. Hae ye mind?

Ah ken that ah wisnae a great faither but ah tried ma best. Ye let then get away wi' faur too much - ye were too saft wi' them. Ah tried tae tell ye - many a time, but ye always gave that look o' yours an' did whit ye wanted onyway. Then ah wis always big bad Daddie when ah had tae gie them a skelping. Ah hated hitting them, but it had tae be done.

Neither o' them want tae ken me noo'. Oor John walked richt by me in the street, He wis always a Mammy's boy onyway.

Ah remember the first fitba' match ah took him tae. There he wis, sittin' on ma shoolders wi' his wee blue and white tammy on, bawlin' at the top o' his voice. He wis happy that day- ah wis happy that day. But look at him noo' - cannae even be bothered tae visit, swankin' aboot the golf club, an' treatin' the puir lassies like shite.

An' whit aboot oor Jimmy. He's left Annie ye ken? Jist this mornin'. Packed his bags and left her wi' the twa weans. Ah went roon tae see if she needed onything, but she acts as if ah'm no even there.

Ma mither an' faither are jist ower there. He's no' speakin' - never says a word, jist like when he wis alive. Dae ye ken he wance telt me that the only guid thing ah ever did wis get married tae ye? He never had ony time for me that man. Noo ma mither - there wis a fine woman. She never said a word tae onybody without faither's permission when she wis here, an' she's no' aboot tae start noo.

Ah'm awfu lonely. Ah spend maist o' ma time jist wanerin' aboot the toon .There's no' many folk left o' oor age noo, an' ah micht as weel be invisible for a' onybody cares.

Why did ye never talk tae me aboot that ither man? Whit were ye feart of? Did ye think ah micht hit ye? Ye ken ah only did that for yer ain guid - tae stop ye steppin' oot o' line. That wis always the problem. Love honour and obey ye said - why wis that sich a problem?

Noo that ah think aboot it, ye were sneakin' roon ahint ma back for month's - were ye no'? Ye and that fancy man o' yours. It's jist as weel that Tommy telt me aboot it when he did - ye micht hae made a complete fool o' yerself wi' that man.

Ah didnae mean tae pit him in the hospital - it wis jist that when ah saw ye wi' him ah got sae angry ah couldnae think. So ah hit him - jist the wance. Ah had tae dae it - dae ye understaun' that?

Besides - if ye'd talked tae me aboot it afore, things micht hae been different noo'.

Ah miss ye Jessie. Ah ken we used tae shout at each ither a' day, an ah ken ye didnae like me drinking. But when ah opened ma een that mornin' and looked doon at the bed ah bawled like a wee wean.

A' they folk comin' in through the hoose and there ah wis, sittin' by the fire, sitting and thinkin' aboot the auld days.

Whit happened tae us? That first nicht, at Agnus's wedding, ma hale life stretched oot afore me. Ah could see me, you an' the weans in a wee but and ben in the country, wi' the weans looking after us till we got auld and grey. Whit happened tae that dream Jessie?

Why did ye dae it?

Ma auld bones are gettin' cauld - ah'd better be going. Ah havenae been feelin' too guid recently - the cauld's gettin' tae me mair the longer ah wait here.

But ah have tae come. Because maybe wan o' these days ye micht talk tae me, and ah'd gie onythin' tae hear yer voice again. Ye believe that - don't ye Jessie?

Ah'll be back next week, but it's getting harder a' the time. Maybe we'll be thegither again afore too long.

Would ye like that Jessie?

Or would ye be thinkin' o' that last dinner ye made me?

Ye didnae mean tae poison me. Did ye Jessie?

A Siren's Song

This is the way it happened.

Brian Walker came to Skye to get away from it all, to get away from the shithole that London had become in the late 1990's. A year of high mortgage rates, zombie filled commuter trains, crowded pubs and mind-numbingly dull work had left him in urgent need of some peace and quiet where he could do some serious thinking about his future.

Last night had been the first night of his holiday and he'd been serious about something all right. He had succeeded in getting seriously drunk.

Now, this morning, his body told him he had a serious hangover.

Standing up made him dizzy, probably brought on by the small furry creatures that had been sleeping in his mouth all night and venturing out to glue his eyelids together.

He'd had this feeling before and knew from experience that a good brisk walk by the shore would at least make him feel human and would probably ensure that he could face breakfast. He pulled on his old denims, woolly jumper, thick socks, what his mother would have called sensible shoes and ventured out into the morning.

The sun had just come up behind the hotel and was beginning to burn away the early mist, leaving the grass of the croquet lawn damp and springy underfoot. A footpath led to the shore, down through some overgrown rhododendrons to a small iron gate set in a drystone dyke just above high tide mark.

A light wind was whipping up small white horses that spent themselves on the weed covered rocks. The whole scene made him depressed, the black rocks, the scum like weed and the dank mist rolling away from the shore revealing nothing but more black rocks and more weed.

Walking as quickly as he could on the slippery stones he aimed for a headland that was as far as he could see in the mist. From this distance it looked no more inviting than the place where he was, but he had come to Scotland to get away from it all and he was determined to do so.

As he walked he occasionally stooped and picked up some of the small black rounded pebbles that lay strewn on the beach. At first he amused himself by throwing them into the white horses but he soon got bored - the pebbles seemed to have a knack of plopping into the water without a splash, no matter how hard they were thrown.

By the time he reached the headland the last remains of the mist had been burned off, leaving the view completely clear across to the far side of the loch where the black cliffs rose up from the green sea. The headland however proved as bleak as he'd imagined, the large stones clustered around like giant rabbit droppings, the weed even more limp and lifeless.

Walking away from the sea the land rose to a small grassy hillock with some slate grey slabs lying half out of the turf, the remains of an ancient dwelling. Out to sea the gannets were putting on their first display and, as he now felt just about able to handle the first cigarette of the morning, he settled himself down to watch.

He was wrong about the cigarette. After just one long draw he found himself doubled over, hawking a blob of brownish mucus onto the stone on which he had been sitting. The coughing went on as he tried to hold some smoke down - he wasn't going to let a little cough deprive him of his pleasure.

The coughs were dying down to some dry throated rasping when he was surprised by an answering cough from nearby. He looked around, towards the house but there was only the field and a few gnarled oak trees,

He turned towards the sea to find himself being watched by a dog-like head bobbing twelve feet from the shore. As he watched the seal moved closer, showing its light grey back as it approached.

He had been this close to seals before, having had them play with his paddles as he was canoeing and, on another occasion, nibbling his flippers as he snorkelled, so he knew that they were inquisitive creatures. All the same he had never had one come this close while he was on dry land. He watched, astonished, as it pulled itself out from a bed of kelp and laid itself out on a large piece of sandstone only five feet away.

He only looked down for a second, just long enough to stub out his cigarette on the slab beneath his feet. When he looked up it was into the deep blue eyes of a naked female.

The second thing he noticed was her hair, long and black, falling down past her waist in one long sweep. Her skin was very pale, almost white and was speckled with freckles. Her legs.. her legs were not legs.

Her waist continued downwards in a straight line of muscled tail, green and scaled and glistening in the sun, drawing his eyes along the length to where a black lobed tail fin beat, once, twice, against the damp rock.

There was a sudden sound, a high pitched drone, not unlike the sound of bagpipes being prepared and then the singing started. His gaze was drawn to her mouth - the perfect red lips opened fully into a gape, a long tongue flopping around in the cavern as the noise grew and grew, becoming louder, then louder still. He tried to cover his ears with his hands but his arms were heavy and refused to rise from his side. The great tail thrashed and the creature moved closer. Straining, fighting, he pushed himself to his feet, only for them to slide away from him on the slippery rock. He fell hard, his head slamming into the rock, knocking him into unconsciousness.

He woke to the feeling of water on his legs and a wet mouth over his own. His clothing seemed to have gone, and he was being stroked into erection by a clammy hand.

He tried to fight, to throw the wet body off, but she was heavy, her weight pinning him down in the surf . There was something erotic about the feel of the body on top of him, the hot heavy breasts pushed against his chest. From deep in her throat there was a low bass drone, a drone that vibrated through the length of her body and brought a sleepy dullness to his arms as the fight went out of him.

As her stroking became more insistent he forgot about fighting and returned the kiss, sliding his tongue between her lips where it was nibbled by very tiny teeth. Her veil of black hair fell in a great sheet across her face, letting through only hints and sparkles of the bright sun beyond.

He was rapidly reaching climax, just as she moved her mouth down across his torso, her hot tongue flicking at his nipples as it passed on its way to his groin. As he came she bit down, causing him to spurt into her mouth as she drew blood, bringing pain with pleasure.

He blacked out.

He dreamed.

He is in bed, in his flat in London, having been woken by some unrepeated noise. The room is lit from outside by an orange sheet light that casts red shadows across the carpet. He is in that state between awake and asleep that causes the imagination to run riot and the heart to lurch at the slightest unexplained noise.

Something is climbing the stairs. Well, not climbing as much as slumping, the noise like a wet fish being slapped on a fishmonger's slab. The shocks caused by its movements are jolting the room, the red shadows quivering in the mirror, making the reflected room shake. The air in the room is damp and then damper, he has the impression of water glistening on the carpet, droplets covering the ceiling and running in small rivers down the walls.

What ever the thing may be it has climbed the stairs and is dragging itself across the landing towards his door.

He is not worried, he knows that it is a dream, vivid maybe but still a dream and that he will wake up before it gets too frightening.

His radio alarm switches itself on, "Don't fear the Reaper" by Blue Oyster Cult echoes its bass line around and around. The door, behind his back and out of sight, opens slowly and it comes into the room, bringing with it the tang of sea and rotting weed. He feels something take hold of the duvet and pull it away from him. He resists as hard as he can, pulling back and holding tightly but the pull is too much, dragging his body sideways across the bed and onto the floor that squelches wetly as his shoulder hits it and forces his head round to face his attacker.

The Creature from the Black Lagoon stares back at him - at least that's what it looks like, a large blue-green scaled body topped by a big maned head, green saucer-like eyes unblinkingly scrutinising him.

The creature reaches down, grabbing his shoulders, sinking small claws into flesh beneath his shoulder blades, lifting him up to face the twin rows of teeth and breathing one fish-odoured word that wakes him up, screaming, coming awake to the sound of a soft, human voice.

He had to shake his head several times to banish the dream completely. He was in bed in the hotel and there was someone bending over him - someone was talking.

"Well, Mr Walker, you're awake at last. No don't try to move too much, you'll be very weak for a while. Just lie back and enjoy the hospitality."

He lay there staring into the eyes of the man bent over him. He realised that the man reminded him of someone - something to do with the eyes. And then he had it.

"Paul Newman" he said.

"No, a bit like John Houseman I'm afraid", the doctor replied, "but you're not the first to say it."

The doctor's eyes crinkled at the corners, showing the cracks and making Brian revise his estimation of age upwards by 10 years as the older man continued.

"I suppose you'll have a few questions yourself. You just lie there and I'll try to tell you what happened. Are you OK?"

Brian laughed. "You mean apart from feeling like shit and wishing I was dead?"

The doctor's eyes wrinkled again as he nodded.

Although very tired Brian felt light and, running his hands over his stomach he was surprised to find that he could feel his hip bones and count his ribs. His beer gut had dissolved. He had been ill for a lot longer than he thought.

"How long?" he managed to say, dreading the answer.

"Three weeks Mr Walker."

His mind went wild. Three weeks AWOL from work, it meant bills not paid, it meant a mother wild with worry, it meant....

The doctor stopped him.

"Don't worry, your work has been notified, a friend of yours, Tim I believe, is dealing with your finances for you and your mother knows you are OK. Does that cover what you were thinking about?"

All he could manage was a nervous giggle and a nod.

"When we realised how ill you were we found your details and made a few phone calls. I hope you don't mind?"

"No, that's OK. Thank you." Brian said as he took a cigarette and lighter from the bedside table. He played with flicking the lighter on and off as he listened to the doctor.

"I got a call on Sunday evening three weeks ago to come out here. The landlord's son Andy had found you on the shore, half naked and ranting, thrashing about among the cobbles."

"When I got here you were still shouting, thrashing about with your arms. I got you sedated and put you to bed. You were running a very high fever and wouldn't eat. You're been delirious for most of the time since then, but last night the fever broke and you slept soundly. That's about it."

Brian raised the lighter to the cigarette and flicked it. As it flared, he remembered it all.

"There was a .. a woman" he shouted.

"Aye Mr Walker." The doctor said, nodding sadly. "There usually is."

He took a long draw at the cigarette and the whole scene came back to him - the long sweep of her tail as it dropped against the rocks, the iridescent green scales dancing as the sun struck their wetness, the soft velvet feel of her hand. He felt for his penis, remembering the pain.

And that was when the screaming started and the doctor had to have help to hold him down.

His whole groin region was a mass of hard scar tissue and as his hand moved over it he could feel it growing, spreading, multiplying as it crept.

That wasn't what started the screaming though. He remembered the dream, remembered being pulled up to meet the vast unblinking face, remembered the last word spoken.

"Brother."

Temper Tantrum

I first heard the noise on the Saturday after the New Year, but it was two more days before I discovered its cause.

"Eric's got a hobby," my neighbour, Mrs Kernay told me. " And about time too - a would have gone mad otherwise."

"The swimming didn't last then?" I said.

That wasn't what I wanted to know, but with Meg Kernay you had to approach any question with care if you wanted to avoid a twenty minute diatribe or, even worse, a temper tantrum.

"Swimming? Hah!" she said in an explosion of fine spittle that I left on my face - it wouldn't do to draw attention to it. "I went with him once. Never again. If God had meant us to swim he would have given us flippers."

She laughed again, a cold cruel thing and, not for the first time, I felt sorry for her poor, downtrodden husband.

I thought I wasn't going to find out the cause of the noise, but just as she turned away she proffered it to me, like a parting gift.

"The daft old bugger is building a cellar - he says he needs it for his chemistry set. Can you imagine - a chemistry set - at his age. I just hope he doesn't dig down too far - the ground's not too good further down."

"Mind you," she continued, "He might find his past if he digs deep enough."

I took that to be an in-joke, but I didn't even have time for a token chuckle before she turned away. She threw her head back and this time she didn't laugh - she positively cackled, chortling loudly to herself as she went back into their small, so neat, house.

I didn't think anymore about it for several weeks. The noises had only lasted a couple of days, and after that was all silent, a quiet unbroken by a single raised voice next door.

That in itself should have got me thinking, but I was up to my eyes in it at work and far too busy to bother about the Kernay's domestic arrangements.

They next infringed on my life around the beginning of February. I had noticed the smell when I got home, but it got really bad around eight o'clock - a thick, cloying odour, as if something had died nearby. It got so bad that it drove me out to the pub.

I was halfway down my second beer when I felt a tap on my shoulder. Eric Kernay was standing beside me. He had a new black eye and the left lens of his glasses was broken, but he had two beers so I let him sit down.

Two hours later I had a serious buzz on but that was nothing to the state that Eric was in. He had started talking to himself, a slurred, almost inaudible, murmur. I only caught some of it - about one word in every three.

"Bloody woman…can't stand a little smell…fame and fortune, that's what waiting, but will she listen - will she hell…well stuff her…I don't need her…I've got Fiona."

That last name seemed to shock him into momentary sobriety.

"You don't know Fiona, do you?" he whispered, looking into his glass. "Fine woman - love of my life. Haven't seen her for years. I've called it after her - Fiona Edwards and Eric Kernay - I used the initials you see. And it seems to like it."

His voice dropped lower, becoming conspiratorial. "It's growing, I'm going to need a bigger cellar soon."

"What's growing?" I asked, and immediately bit my tongue, but it was too late, he clamed up tight. I didn't get any more out of him, not even when I helped him home.

The only other thing he said was just as he left me at the gate. He put a finger to his lips. "Shh. Mum's the word." He dropped me a long slow wink as he weaved his way up the path.

It only took me two attempts to get my key in the door and I only hit the wall three times on my way to bed - one of my better nights. I was just on the brink of sleep when I heard the shouting.

"You've been drinking, you disgusting slob!" Meg Kernay's voice rang out loud in the quiet night. In contrast Eric's voice was an indecipherable mumble.

"Don't you dare talk back to me." Meg shouted. "You been with a woman, haven't you? You know what happened the last time." There was a loud crash of breaking crockery, then she shouted again.

"Oh no - you're not going down in that cellar - you're never going down there again."

I could almost hear Eric's reply this time - his voice was raised higher than ever before, and then there was a splash, like a heavy body hitting water. There was a single scream, abruptly cut off, then all was quiet. Eventually I fell asleep.

The next day I was awoken by a commotion next door and I dragged myself outside just in time to see the police leading Eric away. He didn't speak to me, just gave a sly, enigmatic grin.

Once Eric had left the house the forensic people moved in. They brought out two bodies - Meg Kernay's from the cellar, badly corroded by some kind of acidic slime, and, from the ground beneath, a ten year old corpse, only identifiable by the rotted handkerchief with the embroidered letters, F.E..

Eric's grin bothered me for days but it faded from my mind until two years later.

It happened by accident - I was visiting my father's grave and only caught sight of the familiar name at the corner of my eye. The gravestone was unobtrusive, but the inscription told me all I need to know:

HERE LIES MEGAN KERNAY
SHE NEVER DID LEARN TO SWIM
SHE NEVER COULD CONTROL HER TEMPER
DIED IN A PIT OF FEEK.

The Elixir of Life

"Begin a fast of forty days starting during the full moon of May, drinking only May dew collected with a cloth of pure white linen and eating only a biscuit or crust of dried bread."

He had the room specially built, an eight-foot cube containing a mattress. The only break in the monotonous white glare of the walls was a steel door with a cat flap, the only source of light was a small window in the ceiling, and the six-inch hole in the floor was only a way out for his fluids. When he was shut in, he said a last few words.

"Remember the ritual," he said to his servants, "I may be delirious but you must stick to the instructions. The rites must be observed."

The last thing he heard before the door slammed and the quiet descended was the soft murmur of assent. He smiled, They had been well trained, they wouldn't fail him, not if they valued their jobs.

He looked down at his naked body. Seventy nine years it had served him well, seeing him through the early battles: the street fights in Glasgow, the hand-to-hand fighting in Normandy, the whores in the Far East, and the more subtle but no less savage clashes in the boardrooms.

But now it had had enough. It was failing him, eating itself hollow from within, the black corruption spreading through the soft tissues like wildfire. Science was helpless in the face of the roaring, festering chaos that his body had become, and, in desperation, he had turned his back on the modern miracles and searched in the past.

In his search for redemption he had spent a tenth of his fortune and killed many people for their secrets, but what were they when counted against his power, his influence? It was imperative that he go on - there was more power yet to be had.

And then he had found it - the tomb of Albertus Magnus. And there, in the magi's hand, the black powder, the philosopher's stone.

He would see this thing through. It was a small price to pay for eternal life.

*

"There should be slight bleeding at the seventeenth day."

*

He settled easily into the routine: sleeping, the rattle of the door before eating, the slow pace of the sun across the room before sleeping again. There were no dreams.

He refused to count the days, refused to wonder how much longer. He accepted the pain and the gnawing in his chest. He even accepted the stretching and loosening of his muscles as they shot complaints of hunger through his system. There would be time enough for indulgence.

He busied himself with thoughts of power - the actions he would take in ten, fifty, a hundred years time - the people he would subdue, the resources he would command, the woman he would have.

The days melted away in time with his body, until he found the knife and bowl beside his meagre rations.

"There should be bleeding."

He had discussed the phrase with many of his 'experts'. They were divided. Some felt that there would be natural bleeding, others that some blood would have to be let out, in the medieval manner.

He chose to agree with the latter - he didn't trust his body to bleed on schedule. That was the reason that the knife was there.

It glinted in the sun as he picked it up, a new thing to took at after over two weeks of white walls and grey steel. The left palm - that seemed the best bet. The redness welled up, pooling in his hand before he clenched his fist, letting the blood drip sluggishly into the goblet beneath. Squeezing tighter, he forced the redness to flow until the cup was full.

His hand went to his mouth and he sucked at the cut - only for a moment before wondering if he was negating the terms of the ritual. He wiped his hand on the mattress and held the wound tightly closed until the bleeding stopped.

It was only after eating his biscuit and draining the water, after the knife and the goblet had been withdrawn, that the pain came. He fell into sleep to escape it and the first of the dreams came stealing out of the darkness.

His mother is looking down at the coffin, her make-up running down her face and pooling at the corners of her slack mouth.

From above he finds himself looking down at the face of his father, a man bent and bowed by the weight of poverty, but now at rest - his pleading eyes finally closed. His mother speaks.

He has no need to hear the words, they are etched into his memory.

"No son of mine would ever reject his father. All these years - all that money - and never a postcard, never a penny."

The words dissolve in tears and the dream fades.

He woke up, a cold shiver running through him.

The days ran on and the dreams increased in ferocity, the terrors of his past coming back to be purged - the men he killed, the women he left, the wars he started. Time and dream melted and fused, the passing of day to night becoming blurred until he no longer knew if the screams were outside or inside. The scar of his palm healed as the other, older scars were opened.

*

"On the dawn of the thirty-second day renew the slight bleeding. Take to your bed and remain there until the end of the fortieth day."

*

The dreams became more vivid and he held long conversations with the phantasms of his life. In one period of lucidity he screamed torrents of soprano screeching until his throat grew pained and the sounds dissolved into rumblings. The walls stayed white and doors stayed shut.

He could see the bones of the inner man beginning to force their way out, the fat and sloth of his age melting away. And still the dreams came.

His mother is with him again. He has come to watch her die, to see the life leech out of her as the sickness takes its hold. She speaks.

"Oh its you. What are you after this time?"

He doesn't expect affection - that died long ago - but he still feels the ties, the shackles that have forever branded him a product of this rundown hovel. He watches, eyes dry and heart cold, as she pushes herself up from the chair on spindly arms and comes towards him.

"Come to mama", the crone cackles as her arms open into an embrace. He steps back, disgusted as the toothless mouth attempts to attach itself to his cheek.

Suddenly there is a knife in his hand, a long-bladed flash of black steel as he thrusts it again and again into the dried flesh, harder and harder still until the body slumps at his feet.

He lifts his head, gazing upwards, and screams as reality warps around him.

He woke with a knife in his leg, the whiteness of the walls now freckled with precious drops of his remaining life.

There was no pain as he slid the steel from the wasted muscle, feeling it grate against the bone as it came. He watched the oozing redness until it stopped and then only then, fell back onto the mattress into a deep and dreamless sleep.

*

"On the first awakening take the first grain of Universal Medicine. A swoon of three hours will be followed by convulsions, sweats and purgings necessitating a change of both bed and linen."

*

He woke, lucid for the first time in many days, as the cat flap rattled and his food appeared. He felt only a dull throb in his thigh where the knife had been, but he remembered the ritual, all of it, off by heart. Thirty-two days gone, only eight to go and the future would be his.

Along with the water and the biscuit, there was a small piece of tissue paper and, sitting on it, a single grain of the Magi's powder, glinting blackly in the subdued light.

He took the water and the biscuit first, having to force the dry crumbs into his shrunken stomach. He lifted the grain onto one finger and, with no pause to allow his rational mind to contemplate the action, licked it off with his tongue. He lay down to wait.

Blackness took him down, away from the whiteness, down into a red hell where his wife waited for him.

She is still beautiful. Even the weeping bullet holes have an aesthetic loveliness in their pattern. By instinct he moves towards her, wishing to take her into his arms. But her arms are already full, dripping bloodily as she holds out her burden, the not quite formed child that lies in her arms.

She mouth words but no sound emerges. He knows what is being said.

"I couldn't have it - it would have killed me."

Those words had killed her anyway - she had betrayed him, betrayed his future child, so he had ordered her death. Yet here she was.

She holds the foetus out to him, displaying the fruit of her loins. He takes it and crushes it to him as his tears run down to splash on the still form.

He hugs it tighter, then tighter still until he feels a movement, a kicking then a tearing as the flesh of his stomach is parted and his unborn child enters him, seeking a new, warm home.

He woke from screams into screams as his stomach convulsed and his insides roiled in a hot flare of pain.

He made it, in a crawl, to the disposal hole just in time as his system voided itself in a stream of bloody slime which clung tenaciously to the walls of the hole before being sucked greedily down into the bowels of the machine.

He never knew it was going to get this bad. A thousand razor blades churned in his stomach, each one nicking off another piece of him. A thousand flames burned in his bowels, each one forcing out a scream and a tear as he squatted over the hole listening to his life flow away.

*

"On the next day take a hot bath and a further grain of Universal medicine."

*

The cat flap clattered and he awoke. He wasn't going to make it. Seven days to go and already he was too weak to lift himself into a standing position. He crawled across the mattress to the door, wincing as the cut on his thigh caught on a rough piece and dragged the scab open.

A bowl of hot water and a towel had been placed beside the food. He gave himself a quick rub down but used most of the water to clean up the reeking mess by the disposal hole, sending the sodden towel down after the rest.

He ate the biscuit slowly, relishing every crumb, and washed the second grain down with the last of the water. He thought he was ready for whatever came next. He was wrong.

This time the blackness came slowly, sneaking in around the corners of his vision, eating into the white room until he was left alone and naked and weak in the all-enveloping dark.

He feels his stomach move, writhing with a life of its own, a life which spreads across his torso, wriggling and spasming as it makes its way to his throat. He tries to scream but his voice is blocked by the crawling mass. He gags and coughs and it leaves him in a thick stream, his cancer made flesh.

It lies there before him, coalescing into a mannequin, a black slimy parody of himself. It speaks.

"Like father, like son."

And cackles in a deep bass voice, a laugh which propels him once more into wakefulness.

He woke with his head over the disposal hole, having lost all sense of time and place. He coughed, a stream of yellow bile falling into the sucking hole and watched dumb-struck as tiny blobs of red splashed the white, throwing him into a dreamless unconsciousness.

In his next lucid period he felt the bruises on his body, the soft pain from the wounds on his head. He looked, disbelieving, at the marks on the door - his efforts to escape, his body trying at the last to betray the ritual.

The last grain was placed on its paper beside the last of the food. He was nearly there.

*

"On the thirty-seventh day take the third and last grain. A profound sleep will follow during which the hair, teeth, nails and skin will be renewed."

*

He finally felt good. He was light-headed and his body was so thin that a slight breeze would have knocked him over, but his mind was clear and there were only three days to go. The end was in sight.

He took it in one gulp, the water, the biscuit and the grain. Afterwards he lay down and slept soundly. There were no dreams.

Waking was a slow process. His body felt stiff and strange, as if it no longer belonged to him. He raised his hand on his face and immediately burst into tears - it was working. His wrinkles were gone, smoothed out into new flesh, new skin and the hairs on the back of his hand were thick and strong.

He used a finger to prod into his mouth and there they were, two rows of teeth, just beginning to poke through the gums.

Lying back on the mattress he looked at the blue sky through the window and planned his new life - passing the family business on to his new-found grandson should be easy enough to accomplish. Mentally he counted off his possessions, his influence, his enemies.

The hours passed and still he lay there, dozing. He realised that he could hear the new power of his heart, its deep bass thump rumbling in his chest and sending its tiny shock waves up to his ears. There was something more though - an echo, a smaller thudding at a faster tempo, just outside the normal range of hearing, only perceptible when he was lying still.

Later, as he was falling asleep, the tempo synchronised itself with his heartbeat, two drums beating in time.

As time passed, the second beat took over, and, as night fell on the thirty-ninth day, the old man curled himself up on the mattress, knees raised to his chest, whimpering as the beat increased, hammering its way into his brain, battering him down into senselessness for the last time.

*

"On the fortieth day the work will be finished and the aged man will be renewed in youth."

*

In Ethiopia, in the middle of the severest drought this century, in a mud hut on a parched plain, an old life re-enters the world and immediately starts to scream.

The Flute and the Glen

Jamie lay hidden in the heather on the hilltop and watched the redcoats march past beneath him. So clean, so disciplined, their tunics burning the colour of blood into his brain.

They sang as they marched - songs of great victories, of violent bloodshed and of the longing for the comforts of hearth and home. They were people, men like his father and boys a little older than Jamie himself. They were people, and he hated them with a rage that burned, eating away at his sanity.

They had taken his father, his sister, their farm and his youth. Now he was going to make sure that some of them found their way straight to hell.

The signal came from his right and the bagpipes wailed across the hillside as the clans emerged from their hiding and the kilted horde sprang its ambush.

Jamie was among the first to rise and was already bounding down the hill, the heather pulling at his bare legs, the pipes singing tunes of glory in his head. He never even saw the muzzle flash but the bullet that took him down into blackness slammed into his chest like a kick from a bull. The last thing he heard was the clash of claymore against bayonet as the sides joined in hand to hand fighting.

He came out of the black slowly. His eyes were gummed together and he had to wet his fingertips to prise his eyelids apart. Even that small movement was almost too much for him - the bright cold pain in his chest threatened to overwhelm him and he had to fight to stay conscious.

At first he thought that he had failed to clear his eyes properly, then the night came into focus. A thick mist hung in the valley just beneath him, a blanket of grey that flowed like a river under the velvet night sky. The walls of the glen loomed dark and heavy above and overhead the stars seemed to spin around him.

Somewhere in the far distance the pipes played a pibroch, a lament for the day's dead that felt like it came from the wind itself, and the drone was echoed by groans and shrieks from deep in the mist.

Down there, among the dead and the dying, something was moving. In its path grown men wept and pleaded, but where it had already passed there was only silence.

Jamie began to back away, his heels digging gouges in the soft earth, the pain in his chest flaring in time with his heartbeat. He knew that he would be able to move faster if he turned onto all fours, but he was unable to drag his eyes away from the scene below him.

Whatever moved through the mist did so silently - the grey vapour pushed in front of it in a great swell that cruised soundlessly over the valley, a wave of death that carried all before it.

The mist was swelling, growing in thickness and consistency, and the fall of chill vapour in his cheeks was enough to get Jamie moving faster, oblivious now to the pain in his chest, his legs pumping and his chest heaving as he forced his way over and through the rough heather.

A cry rent the air, a shriek more like an injured animal than a man. Jamie stopped, afraid to even breathe as the mist seemed to inhale, rising and falling in a swell that raised it at least ten feet in the centre. Then there was a sigh, a drawn out groan that was echoed by a last fading drone from the distant pipes. Then all was silent, still and dark.

The mist began to disperse, slowly at first, thin wisps tearing off from its edges, then faster, as if a wind was tearing at smoke. Only seconds later the valley was clear although there was no breeze, no wind - only the crystal stars in the velvet sky overhead. As the last of the mist dissipated Jamie thought he saw something black melt into the shadows on the far side of the glen, but the distance was too far, and when he looked again there was only shadow.

He shivered, just once, a chill that seeped into his bones. He knew he should go down among the dead and say the words over his fallen clansmen, but he couldn't bring himself to descend even a foot into that vale.

He checked his wound, prodding gingerly with ice cold fingers, and was surprised to find no more than a flesh wound. He would be severely bruised for many weeks, but he would live.

There were tears in his eyes as he turned and began to crawl upwards. Tears, not of pain, but of shame. But he kept crawling, and he didn't look back.

The night went on endlessly and the hill, the same one he had bounded down in seconds, seemed to have become a mountain as he forced his body upwards. He knew that he could stand, could walk up to the top with little difficulty, but he was loath to draw attention to himself, loath to call back that grey mist.

The ground beneath him was getting rockier, the vegetation more sparse and he thought he might be nearing the summit when he heard the two-note whistle to his right, the sign of a clansman in trouble

He could have kept on going, indeed somewhere inside a part of him wanted to, but this was no inexplicable mist - this was a clansman, almost a brother, in trouble. He turned to his right and gave the answering whistle and was in turn answered by a groan of pain.

He didn't recognise the figure he found lying on the ground, but the blue in his tartan showed him as a kinsman, in the same way that the blood at his lips showed he was not long for this world.

"A boy," the man said, struggling to raise himself from the ground. "Jist a wee boy."

Those words brought a fresh bubble of blood to the man's lips.

"Wan good cough and ma innards will be out on the grass wi' ye," the highlander said, and almost managed a smile. "I'm no good for anything noo, so I suppose you'll have tae be the one. I need ye tae go doon yon glen and fetch me something."

Jamie stepped backwards, and the fear showed bright in his eyes.

"Oh. Ye saw it did ye?" the man said, and this time there was no humour in his chuckle. "Well ye've got nothin' tae worry aboot - it only kills the English - the invaders. Besides, I think it'll have had its fill for wan night."

That sentence proved too much for the man and he lay back as a coughing fit hit him hard.

"Shot in the lung," he finally said, his voice getting noticeably weaker. "If ye want the redcoats oot of our country, you'll dae this - if no' for me, then for your clansmen who died this day."

Jamie nodded, remembering the bright red uniforms and the arrogant swagger of the redcoat army. He would do anything to see them out of his land, and if the thing in the mist was what it took, then so be it.

"What is it?" he asked.

The man on the ground was almost unable to reply. There was a watery gurgle in his throat as he finally spoke and each word cost him another part of what life he had left.

"No time lad. It is old. It drove the men from the longboats oot of this land, and the Romans before that, and every invader back as far as the minstrels can tell. It comes for the flute."

A fresh bout of coughing hit him and he grabbed hold of Jamie's arm, hard, his fingers digging deep into the soft flesh as the pain racked his body.

"The flute. Find the flute and take it tae the Prince. Your chief, Robert, carried it with him when he fell."

The clansman coughed, one quiet, almost inaudible gasp. Jamie bent towards him, to ask where he was to find his Chief, but the light had already gone out of the highlander's eyes. Jamie laid him down gently and said the words over the body. He stood there for long minutes, tears blinding him, before he could force himself to move.

As he stood on top of the hill the glen beneath him sat in deep shadow. He didn't want to go down there. In fact he didn't think his legs would carry him even if he ordered them. But if the battles could be won, then he had to do it. A crescent moon was rising over the hill across the glen as he began to make his way down to the dead and it was enough to light his way.

The air got noticeably colder as he got closer to the floor of the valley, but he didn't think the chill he was feeling was wholly due to the coldness of the air. The moon glinted silver off the weapons strew on the ground and the thick coppery odour of blood hung heavy in the air and caught at the back of his throat.

His legs were trembling violently as he stepped onto the valley floor and he nearly screamed when the closest body to him seemed to move. Something rose towards him, black and fast, and he had his claymore out before he realised that it was only a crow. He tried not to think what it had been doing at the body as he started to turn the dead over.

Luck was with him. He only had to turn over three bodies before he found himself staring into the dead eyes of Robert, the Clan Chief. He had not just been killed, he had been slaughtered. Three separate wounds had almost succeeded in parting his head from his body and, just for good measure, a cluster of bayonet wounds punctured his chest. His left hand was stretched out away from his body, his fist clenched tight. Jamie felt the stiff fingers break as he prized them open to reveal the small flute.

It was only six inches long, grey-white, made of bone, with crude carvings running along its length. It had been smoothed by the touch of many fingers and the air holes were ragged and torn. It felt warm in his hand as he turned it over and he could sense the power in it, the need to be played.

He was about to place it in his sporran when a shot crashed through the darkness, hitting the body beside him. His Chief jerked, just once, and for a second Jamie had a vision of the man coming back from the dead to protect him. But there was to be no help from that quarter.

He heard voices, and the sound of men running towards him.

"I got myself a looter," a voice shouted. "Come on - he's over here."

Jamie had no other option. He turned and ran, following the floor of the glen. He was aware that he didn't know the terrain, that his flight could be halted at any moment, but a further shot behind him steeled his purpose. He ran faster than he would have thought possible, unaware that the wound in his chest had reopened and that thick blood was flowing inside his tunic.

His breath was beginning to come faster and hotter until his lungs burned with fire. More shots struck the ground around him. He felt an itch in his back, aware that at any moment he could be dead.

He looked around, desperate for any point of cover, but there was only shadow and blackness. He wasn't able to carry on. He dropped to the ground, pulling his plaid around him and trying to still the trembling in his limbs. His only hope was that they would pass him in the darkness.

For long minutes it seemed that the ploy would work. He heard voices around him, but none close. The voices faded, and Jamie began to breathe more easily. His relief was short lived. There was a sudden rustle to his left. He threw off his plaid and looked up into the face of a young English soldier.

"I've got him - he's over here," the redcoat shouted. Jamie had no time to draw his claymore. He lunged at the soldier, head butting him in the stomach and forcing him to the ground. He stood over the youth and would have drawn his sword there and then if it were not for the sound of redcoats running towards them. It sounded like there were many of them.

And that was when the flute jerked in his hand, twice.

"Stand still or I'll shoot." A voice called from the darkness.

Jamie didn't think about his next action - it was as if the flute did it for him. He raised the bone to his lips and blew - two notes, a shrill high pitched rising note, a breath, and a long low drone.

By the time he lowered the flute he was looking down the barrels of a dozen guns.

"What have we here?" A voice to his left said, just before a blinding pain hit him under the ear. He fell to the ground, hard, and had to curl himself into a ball as kicks were rained on his body. Blackness began to creep in at the edges of his sight and he was weakening. His arms had just fallen away from his head, leaving it unprotected. He lay still, waiting for the kick that would send him away from the pain. And then the screaming started.

It was several seconds before Jamie realised that he wasn't being kicked, and several seconds after that before he opened his eyes.

The mist was back.

And within it men were screaming and crying, men were dying. A red haze hung in the air, and the deep metallic odour clung to the back of Jamie's throat. Something was moving through the vapour, something huge and black. Men fell before it, and behind it there was only silence.

Jamie pushed himself into a crouch, and was immediately knocked over again. He tumbled and rolled on the ground before he realised his opponent wasn't fighting back. He looked down into the frightened face of the youth that had found him earlier.

"Help me." The youth said, his face screwed up in despair, hot tears pouring down his cheeks. Jamie lifted him up to a standing position. He knew he should hate this red coated soldier in front of him, but all he could see was a frightened boy, a boy no older than himself. He put out a hand, either to steady the boy or to comfort him - he wasn't sure which, but he was never to get a chance to find out.

It came out of the mist. At first it was only a shapeless blackness among the grey, then slowly it came into focus. It was eight feet tall, towering over the youths. Red gobbets of meat dripped from its claws and its talons, each as long as Jamie's arm, were stained with blood along the whole of their length. Its eyes burned with a red heat, a heat that flared and blazed as it reached for the redcoat.

"No!" Jamie shouted, pulling the youth towards him. He was batted aside, gently, almost reverently, a blow which did no harm but sent him sprawling breathless to the ground.

Jamie could only watch as the soldier was drawn into the creature's embrace, and he closed his eyes when the talons entered the body and began to tear. What he couldn't shut out were the screams. He would hear that terror every time he closed his eyes.

Finally all was silent. Jamie opened his eyes, having to wipe away tears before being able to look around. The creature was bent over the youth's body. It stood, raised to its full height and the mist flowed around it like a cape. It looked straight at Jamie, the heat in its eyes dimmer now, and then it did the thing which almost caused Jamie to laugh.

It bowed, a show of respect, its great head almost touching the ground. Jamie felt the flute move in his hand as the creature turned and faded back into the mist. As it receded, it began to fade, taking the mist with it. Only seconds later Jamie was standing under a sky that was beginning to lighten, the stars winking out, standing in the middle of a charnel house of slaughter.

He looked down at the flute in his hand, the thin piece of bone, which turned again, as he held it. Without a second thought he took it in both hands and broke it into two jagged pieces that he left on the ground as he walked out of the glen.

They would win the battles as men or they would not win at all. That's what he would tell the Prince when he joined him at the gathering.

At the top of the hill Jamie looked back, only once, before turning his face away and beginning the walk north, the walk to the gathering at the moor of Culloden.

The Colour of the Deep

He didn't want to go in.

He had been standing at the cave mouth for nearly ten minutes, his mind full of stories and phantasms.

Sawney Bean had spawned his brood and stashed the gruesome relics of their cannibalism in a cave like this one. Robert the Bruce had pondered his own mortality and the future of Scotland in a cave just like this one - there was even a spider just up there in the left hand corner. He'd come to the end of his childhood in a cave exactly like this one - the only difference was that they were both thirty years older.

Inside all was dark and wet and cold and quiet, whereas out on the ledge it was warm and sunny and noisy with the screeches of the gulls and the crashing of the waves and the bright sparkling dancing of the sun out on the green seas.

He really didn't want to go in. But Fiona made him do it all the same.

"You have got to face your fears," she had said.

"You have got to come to terms with your inner self," she had said.

He had almost smiled at that but he knew she took her 'new age' philosophy seriously and it was a little too early in the relationship for flippancy.

"You have to go in and stand up to it. A little dark won't hurt you," she had said. She didn't know how wrong she was.

He just stood and looked at the beckoning blackness of it while she got the equipment ready. Lights, ropes, backup lights, protective clothing, heavy, sensible shoes, even the scuba gear - all the paraphernalia of the professional hole explorer fitted into two giant sized backpacks.

"Come on Dave - it won't be so bad," she said. "Once we get inside you'll enjoy it - just wait and see."

She was still wrong. He should never have told her about his last encounter with the caves - he knew she was the adventurous type, the pushy type, the type who wanted to see everything, do everything. Why couldn't she just leave it alone? They could have been snuggled up in front of the fire back at the hotel, warming each other with their bodies and sipping some fine whisky. Instead there they were, standing outside a wet dank hole, about to retrace some childhood footsteps.

She helped him with the backpack - its weight settling heavy and clumsy and overbearing on his shoulders. He'd suffered its bulk on the trip along the ledge but now the thought of it pressing down on him as he crawled through the passages weighed heavy on his heart. He should never have told her the story.

"Are you ready?" she asked, tightening the straps at her shoulders and giving them one final tug into place.

"As ready as I'll ever be," he muttered, then, raising his voice, he gave it one last try.

"We don't have to do this you know. I've survived for thirty years without it - I'm sure I could survive thirty more. Besides - people have got lost in these caves over the years - and some of them never came out.

"Nonsense." she replied, turning away from him. "Besides - I've got lots of experience, we've come all this way, and I'm curious."

Without saying anything more she crouched down and headed into the blackness. He had one last long look around before following the receding light into the dark. It was more cramped than in his childhood memories, the grey slimy walls barely a foot away on either side and it smelled - damp and musty with more than a hint of rotting vegetation. He kept banging his head on the roof as he struggled to keep up with the bobbing light ahead of him and soon he was knocking the backpack against the walls as the grey rock closed in and the faint rays of light from outside faded.

The last time he had ran. Him and Gerry and John - the three musketeers, running gleefully into the blackness, one torch between them, shouting and screaming and laughing as they got deeper into the dark. Three ten year old boys, on their school holidays, escaped from their parents and in search of adventure and excitement and maybe just a little bit of terror - not much though, just enough to keep the stories going for a while to relieve the tedium of school.

They had ran far into the cave, far enough that the light from outside was no longer visible, and then they had stopped and listened to their breathing, hot and heavy at first but dying down to three light whispers as their breath came more easily.

The cave had always been the focus of rumours in the town, thought to harbour anything from pirates to witches to sea monsters. And then there were the lights - the rainbow aurora which lit up the skies at least once a year and which the old folk insisted came from the caves. It was an irresistible draw for young children and the boys were no exception.

It was the first time any of them had been inside and he couldn't remember what had brought them here, so far from the town. Gerry had the chocolate - that much he did remember vividly. Red hair, freckles and at least two stones of excess fat brought about by a compulsion to eat anything that was offered to him, that was Gerry. The three of them had sat in the torchlight and eaten two bars of chocolate, just before John had started playing silly buggers - just before the screaming started.

He was brought out of his reverie with a jolt, a sudden jarring as he walked into the rucksack in front of him.

"It slopes away sharply here," she said, her voice echoing around them in rapidly diminishing whispers. She didn't have to tell him. He remembered, only too well.

She moved aside to let him see.

"Maybe you should go first," she said. "That way you won't take me with you if you fall." She smiled as she said it, trying to make a joke, trying to lighten the mood.

"OK" he replied, surprising both of them. He squeezed past her, feeling the heat of her body even through the several layers of clothing between them.

He stole a quick kiss as he passed, even managing a smile of his own but his heart was pounding faster now and his palms were greasy with sweat.

The rock proved to be firm underfoot and the gradient was not steep enough to bother him unduly. He was able to make his way down at a steady pace without having to grab too often for handholds.

It was quiet apart from the gasps of their breathing and the shuffling of their feet but in his mind he was replaying the sounds of years past.

"Bet you can't find me," John had said, just as they finished the last of the chocolate. Thirty years later he could still hear the small click as the torch was switched off and the shuffle as John moved away in the darkness.

A small hand had grabbed his upper arm causing him to give out a shriek of surprise. Gerry had been very frightened and his sobbing had been loud and echoing in the confines of the cave.

"John. Come back," he had said. "Gerry is scared. We're going back out."

There had been no reply and he had taken Gerry by the hand, hoping that they were going in the right direction as they shuffled along, keeping their free hands brushing the walls. They had just noticed that they could see their hands in front of them, that they were nearly out, when they heard the shouts behind them.

"Help," John was shouting. "I'm stuck. Don't leave me here."

Gerry hadn't wanted to, but they had gone back in.

A hand touching his shoulder brought him back to the present with a start.

"Are you OK" she asked, and he could now see the concern in her face. "It's a bit late for that now - now that you've got me here," he thought, but he managed a tight little smile all the same.

"It's not as bad as I thought it was going to be," he said, but in his heart he knew that the worst was still to come. Somewhere down there was the hole and he knew that she would want to go down, that she would want him to go down. He didn't think he would make it.

They had arrived at the bottom of the slope and found themselves in a more open area, about ten feet square, with two exits at the far side of the chamber.

"Which way?" she asked, and he pointed to the left - that's where John had been. He couldn't be completely sure - they had come through here in the pitch black the last time but he was pretty sure they had been following the left hand wall and had gone down the first entrance they came to.

She went first, leaving him to have one last look round before following. The walls were grey and faintly damp; the rock folded and convoluted, reminding him of the surface of a naked brain.

What with the memories and the pain they brought back he felt he was on a journey which was taking him down through his own mind, backwards, ever backwards, uncovering the layers like peeling a onion. He couldn't really remember what happened at the core but he was afraid that he was going to find out.

He turned and followed her down the corridor, watching her light alternatively illuminate then shade the wall as they went deeper.

She spoke, shouting something back at him, but the voice he heard was a much younger one.

"Watch out," the voice had said, and a sudden light had lit up the darkness, seemingly coming from the floor of the corridor. "There's a big hole and I can't get back up." The two boys had shuffled towards the light and

stood over the hole, looking down to see John's pale face looking up at them from more than ten feet below.

"Are you hurt?" Gerry had shouted, but it was obvious that John was all right. The sides of the wall looked smooth and there didn't seem to be any handholds.

"Can you see any other way out?" he had called, and the light had disappeared as John swung the torch around.

"There's another entrance down here, and there's a big pool of water," John called back. "Just stay there and I'll go and have a look round."

He had held tightly onto Gerry's hand as the light disappeared again and John moved away and they were left once more in the darkness.

He was almost surprised not to see two boys crouching there as Fiona's light lit up the hole.

"Hey" she said. "Wake up Dave. I asked if this was the one."

He felt disoriented, doubled, and unsure whether he was the boy or the man. "I think so" he replied. "But it's hard to tell after all this time."

She already had a hammer and spike in her hands.

"How in hell did you get down there?" she asked. "The walls are sheer."

She didn't wait for an answer. Kneeling, she began pounding the spike into a small niche in the rock, the clanging metallic noise ringing around in his ears long after she had stopped.

The rope she tied to the spike didn't look strong enough to hold their weight but she trusted herself to it as she lowered herself over the edge.

"Wait till I'm down then follow me," she said as the top of her head passed the rim of the hole. "I'll give you a shout when I'm ready."

"A shout," he thought. That's what happened the last time.

"Hey, you guys. Get down here. This is amazing." The light from the torch reappeared but there was something different about it, a rippling and shifting as it glowed through all the colours of the rainbow and the walls seemed to melt in its glow. Gerry edges away backwards but another shout from John drew them closer to the hole. John was there and he was excited. Words spewed out of him in a breathless rush.

"It leads out into a huge cave and there's bats and skeletons and stuff - and there's lots of little caves - and there's a hole, a deep one. There's bound to be a way out and I want to explore. Come on."

Gerry looked at him and he looked at Gerry, neither of them wanting to make the decision, then John did it for them - he took the light away.

"Just let yourself drop down," he said as he moved away. "It's not too far."

Gerry and Dave were left in the dark. They took the decision together and together they dropped down into the darkness, landing hard but managing to stay upright. It was still dark and there was no sign of John.

"Dave" a voice shouted and he shook his head to banish the past. "Dave!" the shout came again, more insistent this time. "Get your butt down here."

He went. Slowly, reluctantly, he made his way down, gripping the rope till his knuckles were white. He'd come too far to back away from it now but he kept his eyes shut all the way down.

Near the bottom his legs swung out into space and he felt Fiona's hands steadying him as he lowered himself to the floor of the cave. His legs were unsteady, his whole body trembling as he looked around, taking in the stalagmites, the dim luminescence and, of course, the pool.

Now that he was here it all came back to him, like a scene from a film, playing over and over in his head. He sat down hard on a rock as his memories overwhelmed him.

They are standing in the dark, hand in hand, straining to hear, eager for the slightest noise to tell them where John has gone. All they can hear is the drip of water into a pool to their left and the occasional skittering of bats overhead.

"I'm scared," Gerry says, and Dave nods his head in agreement before he realises that Gerry can't see him.

"Me too," he says, squeezing Gerry's hand tighter to reassure him.

"John. Stop messing about" he shouts and the echoes whisper back to him and more bats are frightened into flight around their head, their tinny cries echoing around the chamber.

Gerry cries out, hands striking out at the air above them and screaming as a bat lands in his hair.

And then there is a scream and a heavy body comes out of nowhere with a loud giggle and knocks Dave to his knees.

He is disoriented and doesn't know which way he is facing as he pushes himself to his feet.

Gerry is still screaming and then there is a sudden burst of light as John switches the torch on. He can see Gerry's face, screwed up tight with tears streaming down his cheeks. John is talking, trying to calm Gerry down.

"Hey" Come on Gerry. It was only a joke."

He reaches out to touch Gerry's shoulder and the red-haired boy jumps as if prodded with a sharp stick. He lashes out a hand, catching John on the jaw and knocking him into Dave. Dave staggers, trying to keep his footing but his left foot meets only air and his body tumbles over. There is a short fall, then a splash, and then he is fighting for breath as freezing cold water surrounds him.

Dave tries to right himself then something catches his attention - a rainbow ball of sparkling light, coming up out of the depths, accelerating as it comes, growing as it comes, sweeping past him and sending his body buffeting through the turmoil as he gasps and splutters and tries to breath.

He manages to surface, just once, and he can see the torchlight. Gerry is standing over John's body and doesn't seem to be paying any attention to Dave. And then there is something else - an aura of melding colours around Gerry's head, which swirls and swoops and then is gone. Except for the lights now dancing in the boy's eyes, the light, which seems to be escaping directly from his brain.

Dave screams, "Gerry," just before the current takers him and he is swept under and he is being pulled, faster and faster through the water. He is knocked against rocks several times and his lungs are straining for breath but then the current slows and he rises to the surface.

There is a light above him as he breaks through and takes a long deep breath. He is in a pool in one of the many sea caves along the coast.

He shouts once more, "Gerry! John!" but there is no reply.

The other two boys were never found. A team of men from the town had gone down to look for them but Dave couldn't be persuaded to go with them.

He had spent the next two weeks in bed - silent, uncommunicative and shivering, but by the time the school term came round he was up and about and, although quieter than before, life went on and the dreams faded.

He never went near the cave again. Until now.

He was aware that he was being talked to and he managed to refocus his eyes to look up at Fiona.

"Jesus Christ Dave. I thought you were having a fit or something." She looked worried and Dave could see the tension lines at the corners of her eyes.

"I'm OK," he managed to say. "I'd forgotten how strong the memory was, that was all." He managed to push himself up to his feet and turned to look around.

The chamber was big and the walls glowed faintly green. The pool lay, silent and calm just to his left. He shivered, a sudden chill as he looked into it's depth, but there was nothing visible, only blackness.

"Come on" he said, "Let's get out of here." He headed for the cave opening to his right.

After a short passage the cave opened out, becoming so big that Dave's light could not penetrate as far as the walls. He felt a crunching beneath his feet and looked down to find that he was walking on a bed of bones and fur and scales - the remains of hundreds of fish and small mammals.

He looked upwards and the ceiling twenty feet above him was a writhing mass of squealing rustling bats.

He tries to move quietly, afraid of disturbing the horde above him and he could hear Fiona moving quietly behind him.

There was another pool here, this one a bubbling, frothing cauldron. He stopped at a rock by the poolside to let Fiona catch up.

"OK. What now Superman?" she said as she approached. He looked over at her and smiled, just as the rock hit her on the side of the head, knocking her sideways and bringing a spray of blood from her nose. She fell to the ground at his feet, eyes staring blindly upwards.

There was sound to his left, a slapping as of wet cloth on rock. He turned towards it and his torch lit up a nightmare.

It's skin was grey, a mottled grey which looked as if mould was growing directly onto the arms and bare chest. The mouth was red and almost toothless in the midst of a mass of matted beard.

The black gaps showed clearly as it smiled at him, big blue eyes twinkling. A mop of red hair fell down over its shoulders and Dave could see that Gerry still had some of his freckles.

It was only when the eyes looked directly at him he could see the lights, the green and the golds and the silver, all dancing and cavorting. And then Gerry's body trembled, a shiver that passed through his whole body as the lights spread out from his head and the bats swooped from their perches to fill the air with their terror.

Dave was rooted to the spot, unable to move as the thing shambles closer to bend over Fiona's body and the lights flowed across the space between them, seeking him out. The last thing he remembered before the colours took him was that Gerry always ate anything that was put before him.

That night the townspeople saw the lights in the sky and the older ones among them closed their doors and shivered by their fires until the skies were quiet once more.

The Strange Case of Dr McIntyre

Long years have weathered the walls of the tiny church and a gnarled rowan pokes its branches through what was once the roof. Tall, lichen encrusted gravestones thrust up from a cemetery that has become more of an overgrown meadow and the whole place has an air of dissolution and despair.

But when I first saw it, almost fifty years ago, the graves were well tended and the roof, although battered, still sat flush in its place. I hope that the pages that follow may shed some light on the reason for such a fall from grace.

My companion - I shall call him Johnson - was drawn there in search of a doctor. James McIntyre was his goal - a medical man who had spent much of his life in Edinburgh. James had been a Renaissance man, not only a healer, but also a philosopher, a mathematician and a chemist.

More importantly for our purposes, he was also Johnson's great grandfather. Thus far in our travels we had visited five graveyards in the area, all to no avail. This was our last chance. We knew that McIntyre had lived in this vicinity at the latter end of his life, but had no idea where he might be buried. If we didn't find him then Johnson's search for his forefather would come to an abrupt end.

I would not relish the end of our journeys. Johnson had proved to be an excellent companion, both witty and erudite with a gentle manner that made our journeys seem short and pleasant.

Nothing seemed to bother him. He was as excited as a schoolboy as we pushed our way through the old rusted gate, and he was still smiling almost an hour later although our search had so far proved fruitless.

I saw his pale hands tremble each time he moved the grass aside on another gravestone, and with each new disappointment there was only the merest of furrows on his brow.

As for myself, I had already given up hope and was turning back towards the gate when a voice hailed us from within the small battered church.

At first I took him for a youth, but as he moved into the light I could see that it was age that had withered him. The backs of his hands were infested with liver spots and his teeth were so yellow as to be almost brown. He was bent forward and was only able to walk with the aid of a stout cane, but his handshake was firm and his eyes were clear and unclouded.

He bade us 'Good morning' and enquired if he could help us. When Johnson mentioned our search his eyes suddenly showed fear, but then I could see that he had made a decision as he invited us into the small quiet church.

Little light penetrated the gloom as we were led through to a tiny room at the back of the church, and silence seemed to be the order of the day as the old minister pulled a heavy sea chest away from the wall.

"This was left in trust to my father. I must tell you that it seems to have belonged to the man you are seeking. It was to be left here until a descendant came to claim it. It would seem sir, that you are that man."

His left hand burrowed deep into his vestments and emerged with a large key that he handed to Johnson before turning away.

"If you need anything, you need only call," he said.

He left us alone in the room, and it was all Johnson could do to contain his excitement.

"It's here. It's really here. And it is just as father described it."

He had never given me a reason for his almost irrational desire to find his ancestor, but I had a feeling that I was about to find out.

A deep chill settled on my soul, a blackness that could not be shaken. I longed for sunlight and the sound of the sea, but Johnson, in his desire, was already kneeling on the floor beside the chest.

It was a simply wrought thing, its boards warped and cracked with age but the key fit securely in the lock that turned easily with only the slightest pressure.

The chest creaked and groaned as we lifted the lid to reveal a closely packed collection of notebooks - leather bound and yellowed with age. I opened several, and they were all covered in the same, crabbed, handwriting, volume after volume of chemical formulae and mathematical equations. I counted thirty of them before we unearthed the rest of the contents.

There were two loose manuscripts, the first, in a fine stylish script, seemed to be a letter to Dr McIntyre and the second, in the same hand as the first, either a much longer letter or a tale of some length. I was unable to see the front page as Johnson immediately snatched the bundle of papers away and hid them deep in his coat. He would have done the same with the letter if he had not been stopped by the sight of something glinting at the bottom of the chest.

By moving the last of the journals aside he uncovered a small glass vessel, the sort a medical man might use to carry potions to the ailing. And inside the vessel, the most vile sickly fluid that glowed a lambent green in the dim light. Johnson's eyes reflected that gleam and, for the first time in our acquaintance, I saw something that I did not like - a cold malice of thought.

He unscrewed the top of the jar, breaking the seal in the process and, before I could stop him, he tipped the noxious contents down his throat.

I dashed the vessel from his lips with a cry but the look he gave me was so full of rage that I stepped back. He reached towards me but his hands began to tremble, a convulsion racking his body. He fell backwards, his head striking the floor with a dull thud, and white flecks of foam flew from his lips.

I went to the door and called for the old minister. I had barely turned back to the room when I was struck hard from behind and blackness threatened to creep in at the edges of my sight. I only caught a glimpse of Johnson as he pushed me aside, but he was no longer the upright figure that I had come to know. His back was bent, his knuckles reached almost to the ground and, although the light was dim, the thick black hairs on the back of his hands could be clearly seen.

As he disappeared from view I made to follow but the blow I had taken had enfeebled me and I could only manage several slow steps before the blackness finally took me. As I fell to the hard floor it seemed that I heard a scream, a long howl as of a wild creature in pain.

The rough hand of a policeman awakened me, and it was many long hours before they believed my story. But there was no blood on my hands or my clothes, and whatever had killed the old minister had inflicted such wounds as to strike his head from his body.

In the end they were forced to give me my freedom. I believe the letter may have had something to do with it - the letter I still had in my hand when the police found me.

My Dear Doctor

Please pardon this intrusion into your privacy.

Several years ago I had the pleasure of making your acquaintance in Edinburgh, and I was most impressed with your theories concerning the descent of man and the awakening of the primitive aspects of our natures.

As you may know, I have been having some success as a humble scribe, and I have taken the liberty of incorporating part of your theory into my current work.

It will only be a penny dreadful, but I am proud of it nonetheless.

I have enclosed my original draft of the story for your perusal. Of course, if you disagree with the content, or if I have misrepresented you in some way, then the work will go no further.

I await your reply

Yours in good faith
Robert Louis Stevenson

Animal, Vegetable, or Mineral

The cracked black leather of the bible felt rough and cold in his hands as he took it from his satchel and placed it on the stone floor in front of them.

He looked around at the three pale faces; the wide dark eyes staring blankly back at him. The silence lay heavy around them and he toyed with the idea of letting out a scream - at least one of them was sure to faint in fright. But that would spoil his big scene, and he couldn't have that. He'd promised them a ghost and a ghost was what they were going to get.

He needed this to work. The three boys around him represented the figures of power in the school and, as a new boy, they knew that Jim would have to gain their approval if he was to fit in. Which was why they'd let him bring them here, to the ruins of Cameron Castle on a cold winter's day. One mistake now and he would be ostracised for months to come.

"Are you ready?" he whispered, and was dismayed to find that his voice trembled, a childish quaver which echoed around the confines of the cramped dank chamber.

"Yeah. Just get on with it. I'm freezing my balls off here." Bob Kerr shuffled his bottom, trying to find a more comfortable spot. He was the one that would need most watching, being the oldest of the three and also the biggest. Jim had seen him in action against some of the smaller boys and had no desire to fall prey to the bullying and the kicking and gouging.

The other two would be easier. "Camp followers," his dad had told him when they discussed their plan, "Cut them off from the leader and you'll be able to manipulate them." Dad was big on manipulation and Jim didn't intend letting him down.

Bob Kerr took a single cigarette from his jacket pocket and made a big show of lighting it up. His eyes screwed up tight in pain as the smoke got to him but Jim managed to control the giggle which had grown in his throat - it wouldn't do to antagonise Bob. Not yet anyway.

"I've told you already what happens," he said, and was pleased to notice that his voice had now steadied. "I'll put a pencil on the bible and then you can ask your questions. The pencil will move left if the answer is no, right if the answer is yes. Do you understand?"

He wasn't really sure that any of them knew their left from their right but they nodded anyway, seemingly afraid to speak, afraid to break the spell. The atmosphere was definitely building up and Jim smiled, but only inwardly. The plan was right on schedule.

He opened the Bible, laying it side on. As he did so he noticed that it had opened at the Book of Job. He smiled to himself, thinking of the plagues and pestilence he would like to visit on the three boys opposite. He took the pencil from the top pocket of his shirt and laid it crossways across the Bible pointing directly at Bob Kerr.

The air in the room seemed to have chilled and from the corner of his eye he could see the dancing shadows cavorting on the rough stone walls. He pushed them from his thoughts - Dad had told him that there would be no problems, no need to fear, and he always trusted Dad's judgement.

"I'll ask first," he said. "Just to show you how it works." He didn't wait for a response. He held out his arms, palms down over the Bible, and he could feel the tingle, the power, as it built up and his breath condensed in the air.

"Is Edinburgh the capital of Scotland?"

He heard gasps from across the chamber as the pencil rolled across the pages, coming to rest at the edge of the Bible.

Bob Kerr was unimpressed.

"Is that it? Not much of a question, was it?"

Jim was unperturbed. This too was part of the plan. "Give them enough rope and they will hang themselves." Dad had said. He put his hands back to his side and stared across at Bob.

"Okay big shot, you do it," he said, grinning widely. Bob looked at the other two, shrugged his shoulders and ground out the cigarette. That was when Jim knew that he had them - right where he wanted them. He waited for the boy to shuffle over towards the Bible then he held Bob's arms over the book and turned the palms down.

He spoke as he replaced the pencil at its starting point.

"You must concentrate," he said, secretly delighted at the fear he could see twinkling in Bob Kerr's eyes. He sat back on his haunches. From now on he could leave them to it and the end would be just as Dad had foreseen.

"I feel like a right divvy," Bob Kerr said and his two companions giggled until silenced by a quick angry glance. "Okay," he asked, "what should I say?"

"Anything you want," Jim replied. "Just remember to ask a question that can be answered with a yes or a no."

He could almost hear the cogs and wheels as he watched the boy try to come up with an idea. The other two boys were shuffling around noisily, already getting bored with the proceedings, but Jim didn't think they would be bored for very much longer.

"Is my name Robert Justin Kerr?" he finally asked.

The other two giggled again but soon stopped as the pencil rolled to the right.

"All right," Bob whispered, "now for the hard ones."

Jim noticed that all three boys were completely engrossed in the movement of the pencil - so much so that they had failed to notice the gathering of the shadows in the far corner of the room, the deeper blackness which was even now creeping slowly towards them.

Bob Kerr looked as if he was pondering one of life's big questions and Jim was no in the least surprised at his next question.

"Are you a ghost?" the boy asked.

The pencil didn't roll - it raised up an inch off the pages and floated in the air. The candle flickered wildly as a breeze wafted through the small room but the pencil didn't waver - not moving until Bob lowered one of his hands to place it back in the middle of the Bible.

All was now deathly quiet, the only noise the soft breathing from the four young bodies and, a noise which Jim could barely hear, a dry wheezing from the far corner, a corner which was now completely consumed in shadow.

The time was getting close and Jim tried to hide the smiles that were waiting to burst from his face. He tried to look serious as Bob brought the end nearer.

"Are you a man?"

Jim didn't need to watch the pencil. He knew that Bob meant to go through the old twenty questions routine, trying to track down the identity of the ghost. He wouldn't get far enough, Jim knew that. He also knew that they wouldn't believe the answer if they ever found it. He wasn't really listening as Bob rattled through the rest of the questions.

"Did you live in this castle?"

"Did you die violently?"

"Were you an old man?"

Jim smiled inwardly at that one. He could tell from Bob's tone that he was getting frustrated. It was only a matter of time now. The blackness was drawing closer and the cold was biting into the lower half of his body but none of them moved, intent on Bob, intent on the floating pencil.

"Were you married?"

"Did you have black hair?"

The questions were getting more inane and Jim's muscles tensed. It was very close now.

And then Bob did it. The frustration got too much for him and he asked the wrong question.

"Who are you?"

And all hell broke loose.

The blackness surged forward - a wall of cold that froze all four into immobility as the pencil snapped in two pieces and the candle flickered twice before finally going out. Bob was the first to scream as something grabbed his hands, something cold and dead and ugly.

Jim pressed himself backward against the wall and listened as the screaming got louder and Bob was lifted into the air. Within the blackness he could just see the eyes, the fiery red embers which grew brighter with each scream.

Bob was dropped to the floor where he cringed and wept like a baby as the blackness reached for the other two. It never got that far. As one the boys managed to push themselves upright and Jim could hear them, screaming still as they raced off down the hill. It was nearly time for the final act.

The blackness loomed over Bob as Jim moved towards it. "Back!" he shouted. "Go back to your own place." The blackness seemed to shrink in on itself and the red embers dimmed. Jim bent down and helped Bob to his feet, noticing with a grimace that the boy had fouled his pants. He turned the boy round to face the blackness.

"Look at this thing." he said to Bob. "Look at it and remember that I am the one who can control it." He held the boy's head steady, making sure that he was looking straight at the "ghost" before he continued.

"Remember. Anytime you feel like hurting me, anytime you feel like doing a little damage - just remember. Anything happens to me - this will be back."

As if on cue the blackness raised itself, filling the room as its eyes blazed like two golden suns and a cold wind ruffled the boys' hair.

Jim released the other boy. "Go now." he said and gave the boy a shove towards the entrance.

He listened until he was sure that Bob Kerr had gone before he moved forward to embrace his Dad, Dad who had died two years ago, Dad who still always looked after him.

It'll be a Long Hot Summer

The sun banged down out of a feathery blue sky, the heat bouncing off the ground in great relentless waves which brought rivulets of sweat to her brow, to her armpits and, worst of all, to her hands.

She could feel the telescope sliding around in her grip; and the harder she tried to grip it, the more it squirmed in her grasp. But she wouldn't drop it; not when Uncle Jack had promised to show her the sunspots.

Her mind raced ahead to her return to school. Just think what the teacher would say when he found out what she had learned. He wouldn't be able to ignore her then - she'd know something that the boys didn't - something better than football and guns.

She squinted to see through the glare, and brushed a lock of sticky blonde hair away from her forehead. By shading her eyes with one hand, taking care not to drop the telescope of course, she could just make out the house, dancing and shimmering in the distance across the fields. The path led away before her, the tarmac melting softly around her bare feet, forcing its way between her toes as she hurried on.

The house got closer and the heat got heavier. The tree-lined path to the front door wavered and swayed in the rising waves from the ground, blurring in and out of focus as she paused to wipe the sweat from her eyes; the sweat which tasted of salt when she put her fingers to her mouth.

Uncle Jack had seen her coming, and was waiting for her. He was a big man, red of face and hand, loud-voiced and kind-eyed.

His voice boomed in her ears as he came to meet her, arms outstretched for the expected hug.

"Have you ever felt it as hot? It's a great day for the sunspots - just wait and see."

He led her by the hand to the back of the house where a small camera tripod was set up on a card table.

"Wait a minute, I'll go and get the magic ingredient," he said, turning back towards the house.

She turned to watch him go. That's when she saw the boy. He was standing in the shadows, in the shade under the back porch. His face was in blackness, but she knew who it was - Billy. Cousin Billy.

She couldn't see his mouth, but she knew what it would look like; cruel and sneering, just like his eyes; always the same, whether he was pulling her hair or rubbing her face in the dirt or chasing after her in the playground. She was safe here though. Uncle Jack wouldn't let her come to any harm - Uncle Jack always kept Billy in check.

She could hear Uncle Jack pottering around inside the house, singing his nonsense songs. His voice faded as he moved towards the other side of the house. Billy made a move towards her, then another, but slunk back into the shadows when his father reappeared at the door.

"Here it is," he boomed. "I found it hiding in the bookcase." He was waving a piece of stiff white card.

She soon forgot about the boy as her Uncle did his magic. Just a few seconds to set up the telescope properly, getting it lined up, and there it was, a perfect little image of the sun, wavering and dancing just for her on the slanted card.

"Look closely," he said, pointing with a thick red finger. "See the blacker dots?"

She did, but didn't want to speak; afraid she might break the spell.

"Those are what's causing this scorching summer - the really hot bits. It's as hot as hell in there - OOPS, pardon my French."

He put his hand across his mouth and giggled, an action she knew of old, one which always made her laugh.

She moved closer to study the black spots. In her mind's eye she could see them, the little red fiery devils with their pitchforks, screaming and laughing at the same time as they rolled around in the heat and the flames.

"I've got some lemonade in the kitchen," her Uncle said. "Do you want some?"

Nodding her assent, she was too engrossed in the wavering image in front of her to lift her head.

She heard footsteps behind her and turned, expecting her uncle with the lemonade. Instead she was jerked off her feet as her hair was tugged; hard, bringing a shooting pain that felt like it was lifting the top off her head. She landed on the ground, sending up a cloud of dust which quickly settled on her clothes.

Her cousin Billy was standing above her, laughing his cruel, well known laugh. As she watched, he took the eyepiece lens off the telescope and brought it between the white card and the sun.

He moved it backwards and forwards, the white circle of the sun shrinking and brightening, then growing and fading before shrinking again until it was a single point of fire.

She saw the smoke first, a thin wisp of black against the white of the card. Then the hole started, a black charred circle in the centre of the card rimmed the red flame. Billy held the card until all that was left was the dark ashes of the remains. She watched as he crunched them up in his hands, blackening his palms. She knew what would come next.

"You're his little pet, aren't you?" he said in the cruel voice that she knew so well. "His little pet - that's what he always calls you, isn't it?"

She could see the hate in his eyes.

"Well, little pets have to be house trained. Little pets need to know their place. Little pets can't expect to come round here and get pampered all the time."

He leaned forward to her, following her swiftly as she tried to shuffle away, black palms getting ever closer to her face.

He was leaning over her; hands only inches from her eyes, giggling like a crazy man, when he was suddenly jerked backwards like a puppet on strings. Uncle Jack had hold of him, and was shaking him so hard she thought his eyeballs must be rattling in their sockets.

She stood, slowly, and pulled at her Uncle's shirt.

"It's all right Uncle Jack, he didn't hurt me," she said, tugging harder as the man continued to shake Billy. It wasn't until she shouted his name that her Uncle let the boy drop, like a sack of potatoes.

Billy sat up, rubbing the red spots on his arms where he had been gripped. He glared, first at the man, and then at her, and she could see the hot fury in his eyes.

Her Uncle turned towards her.

"Are you all right sweetheart?" he said, brushing the dust and the grime off her dress with long strokes of his hands. She didn't hear him. She was looking at Billy. He had taken something from his pocket, and he opened his hand to show her.

There, in the palm of his hand, sat the lens of her telescope. He closed his palm and smiled, the same old smile, as he ran off across the courtyard, disappearing behind the garden shed. She burst into tears.

She stood, cradled in Uncle Jack's big warm arms, until the sobs subsided and she was able to tell him what had happened to the eyepiece. A dark gleam came into his eyes, a look she could not associate with her warm friendly uncle.

"Don't worry. I'll get it back. I'll teach him who's the boss around here. It won't be the first time I've had to bring him down a notch. He's got a bit too much of his mother in him.

The look was mostly in his eyes, a deep black frown which was so unlike Uncle Jack, but it was soon gone, replaced by a smile before she could ask him when Auntie Jean was coming back. She hadn't seen her for a while, not seen she went away on holiday with Mr Walker from the pub. Mummy had been angry when she had asked where they had gone, so she hadn't talked about it again.

She stayed with him for another hour, drinking his cloudy lemonade, laughing as the bubbles tickled her nose, and watching the trees waver and dance in the heat as she sat, nearly cool, in the shade of the porch.

Finally it was time to go. She said her goodbyes, casting a last glance at the telescope. Uncle Jack saw the look.

"Come back tomorrow. I'll have it whole for you again. Maybe your mum will let you stay the night and we can look for the Martians?"

She gave him one last hug before she left, turning back at the garden gate as he shouted after her.

"If you see Billy, run. He might be all bad, but he's slow - remember that."

He shouldn't have mentioned the boy - it was going to worry her all the way home. She set off, first walking quickly, hot and prickly in the afternoon sun, but at every turn she thought she could hear him, rustling the grass or parting the hedgerow. Soon she was running.

The hot tarmac sucked at her feet when she reached the road, threatening to slow her; slower and slower until she was stuck like a fly, doomed to stay there while the sun baked her, first red, then brown, then black; until she was crisp and crumbly, like the meat Mummy had left in the oven too long. She tried to lift her legs higher as she speeded up, the hot, dry air burning in her throat.

Her breathing was becoming laboured, her legs heavy as she pumped her way down towards the town. Before too long she had to stop, bent over and wheezing, clutching her side, kneading to try and dispel the pain of a stitch. She moved out of the sun into the shade of a large, well known beech tree.

She often stopped here, to sit in the shade and look down over the rolling hills to the sleepy town below. Off in the distance you could sometimes see the sea, and watch the little ships taking their people away to far off places where there were monsters and tigers and elephants and all sorts of interesting things.

She pulled her dress away from her warm body, trying to get some air circulating, as she moved further into the shade of the tree and sat on one of its huge roots. She picked the black specks of tar from between her toes, rolling the malleable balls in her fingers before flicking them away. Slowly her breath came back to normal, and the sweat started pouring.

Looking down at the ground she could see the shadows swaying, sharp and black against the parched dry ground.

"The devils must be pretty busy up there," she thought, remembering the black spots on the sun's surface. She leant back, feeling the cooling sweat stick to her dress, as she closed her eyes and thought again of the little red devils, stoking the furnaces of the sun.

He fell on her from out of the tree.

She had no time to think, no time to scream as he drove his knees into her midriff, knocking all the air out of her in one short hot gasp.

Somewhere, outside the roaring in her ears, outside the pain in her belly, beyond the dancing black spots in front of her eyes, she could hear a voice.

"You think you're so smart - sucking up to the old man and getting him to show you things. Well, I'll show you something. Something you won't forget in a hurry."

She felt herself being dragged across the ground. Her eyes were just beginning to refocus, and she could see the branches of the tree above her, the sun dancing amongst the leaves, until the shade had gone completely and the sun beat down on her.

A shadow fell on her face, and she winced as a heavy weight sat on her chest, pinning her arms to the ground.

"Sunspots and Martians! What a load of shit!" Billy said, taking the telescope eyepiece from his pocket.

"Nonsense made up by a stupid old man. It's time somebody showed you the real world."

A hot pain flared suddenly in her upper arm. By straining her neck she was just able to see the livid orange spot of the focused sun as he held the lens an inch above her arm. She managed to twist away, just enough to bring a brief respite from the pain, but it soon returned.

She struggled and kicked, but he was too heavy for her, and every time she threatened to scream he bounced his body on top of her chest, forcing the air out of her, and causing her to wheeze and splutter, until the pain got too much, and she lay still, only hoping that it would be over quickly.

Tears welled at the corners of her eyes as he moved the burning spot higher; to her shoulder, where it brought a searing burst of agony and the sweet smell of burnt meat; to her neck, where the pain made her feel faint and weak; to her hair, where the spot hissed and crackled.

Finally, she looked up to see the lens directly above her face.

Billy spoke, his eyes black and dancing, his mouth curled in the old Billy sneer.

"You want to see the sun do you? Well take a look at this."

The lens came down towards her eye and there was a hot sharp pain in her lower eyelid. She squeezed her tightly shut and prayed.

"Just make him go away," she whispered. "I'll do anything if you just make him go away."

She could feel the heat rise, could see the red fiery burning desire of it against the inside of her eyelid as it grew brighter; first orange, then yellow, then piercing shattering white.

And there was something in her head, right there inside, just behind her eyes; a bright, red, prancing devil from the sun. She screamed, louder and louder, and thrashed her arms in one last attempt to shift the weight from her chest.

And then suddenly it was gone, and someone else was screaming, and the weight lifted, all in the same moment.

The screams were coming from Billy, who was dancing, just off the road, kicking up huge clouds of dust as he scratched wildly at his face. The smell of burning meat was back.

She watched, stunned, as Billy fled, screaming still, back up the road, back towards the house.

Her mouth opened, and a voice which was not hers emerged, hot and heavy as the sounds passed he tongue.

"I'll do anything if you just make him go away," it said; then laughed, a deep rumbling laugh which caused the branches of the tree above her to shake, dislodging several leaves which fell towards her, igniting into yellow flames as they came,

She turned and ran, back up the road, towards the safety of her Uncle's big soft arms. Behind her she heard a whoosh, and felt the heat as the beech tree burst into a sheet of flame, and her mouth laughed again, getting louder as she fled for the safety of her uncle's cool house.

The air grew hot in her throat, then hotter and hotter still, until it burned with every breath. But still she ran, legs pumping with every breath. But still she ran, legs pumping and tears coursing down her grimy face, rolling off her chin to fall, sizzling and steaming, onto her clothes.

She found them in the kitchen. Billy was sitting in a chair, and Uncle Jack was dabbing at a red livid mark on his face with a damp cloth; small gentle dabs, barely touching the skin, but every one brought a squeal of pain from the boy.

Uncle Jack looked up and saw her, his face reddening as he took in the grimy, torn clothes, the dishevelled hair, the tear-streaked features, the wide frightened eyes.

He lifted Billy off the chair, one handed, and shook him, shook him so hard that one of his shoes fell off, and there was a small metallic clunk as the telescope eyepiece fell to the ground.

"Did you do this?" Uncle Jack was shouting. "Did you? I should have kicked you out after that bitch."

Before she could stop him, he hit Billy; one hard, fast slap which rocked the boy's head back, causing his eyes to roll up in their sockets.

"No!" she shouted, as the arm was raised again and again, and Billy's head rocked, left, right, left, right.

She couldn't recognise her soft cuddly Uncle in this raging thing before her. She ran to his side and tugged at his shirt.

And it got warmer. Very quickly. A sheet of flame ran from her hand, covering the man's arm, his back, and his hair. She tried to call it back, knowing that it had from her, knowing that it was part of the thing growing in her, the thing put there by Billy. But she was too late.

The fire rolled over her uncle's body, squirming and wavering and glowing brighter as it found its way to his face, glowing red then orange then yellow, then brilliant white as the body fell to its knees on the floor. The smell of burnt meat was back again.

Billy was groaning and beginning to move, trying to push himself upright. She saw his eyes widen and his nostrils flare as he saw the body on the floor. She shook her head, unable to take her eyes from the small flames, which were still capering over Uncle Jack's dead body, the small red devils that she had called from the sun.

There were still more inside her. She could feel them, burning away in her chest as she fought for breath.

Billy was crying, sobbing loudly and shaking, trembling. He launched himself at her, screaming, a voiceless sound filled with pain and loss.

She was knocked over by the force of his attack. The front of her dress burst into flames as he touched it, her hair turned into a seething mass of fiery serpents as it lashed the floor, her tears hissing and sizzling on her cheeks as their bodies were welded together by the quicksilver flash of searing golden heat.

Sometime later, from the open mouth of the charred body, something laughed and laughed as the bodies were consumed, and the red raging glory of it spread to the rest of the house.

In the Coils of the Serpent

"So after he killed her he cut out the clitoris."

"Well, that settles it - it can't have been a man. If it had been, he'd never have found it."

I looked up at her over the top of my drink, but there was no humour in her eyes - then again, there rarely was these days.

"I don't know why I'm telling you all this anyway", I said, taking a long swig of beer and brushing the foam from my upper lip. "If the boss ever finds out, I'll be knocked back to traffic patrol - this is all supposed to be hush-hush - even the tabloids haven't got hold of it yet."

"I should hope not," Jane Woolsey replied, "If they get so much as a whiff that I'm involved, you won't see me for dust."

I didn't blame her. I remembered the last time - the finding of the body, the lurid headlines, the media circus permanently encamped on her doorstep. I would do everything in my power to make sure that didn't happen again.

She was playing with her hair, twirling the blond tresses around her little finger. She had that faraway look in her eyes again, as if she was staring fixedly at something in the far distance that only she could see. I leaned over and took her hand.

"I'll try to keep the press out of it, Jane - I really will."

There was a deep resignation in her voice as she replied.

"I know you will. But will you succeed?" She sighed and took a long sip from her drink, "I take it you brought something for me?" she asked.

"You didn't bring me out here just to hold my hand?"

I realised that I was not only holding her hand - I was stroking my index finger along the soft skin between her thumb and forefinger. Suddenly embarrassed, I let her hand drop.

"Don't worry," she said, and this time there was a sparkle of humour in her eyes. "I won't tell anybody."

To cover my discomfort I reached into my inside pocket, but not before checking that no one in the quiet bar was looking our way.

"The boss doesn't know I've got this. He'll have my guts for garters if he finds out," I said, handing a handkerchief over the table.

I watched her pupils dilate as she took the flimsy piece of cloth. Almost immediately her eyes rolled up in their sockets until only white showed beneath her fluttering eyelids. She moaned, a deep bass drone, then gasped, just once.

I wanted to reach over, to take her hand, but I knew better than to interrupt. This was a crucial moment.

Suddenly she screamed - her mouth gaping to show twin rows of perfect teeth, her nostrils flaring. Her head fell forwards, a swathe of hair obscuring her face, her shoulders trembling violently. She flung the piece of cloth away and screamed again, louder this time.

The handkerchief floated slowly off the edge of the table, but Jane's body beat it on the way down, her head hitting the hard wooden floor with a loud thud that echoed in the silence of the small bar.

By the time I got round the table she was shaking, in the throes of some kind of fit. I lifted her by the shoulders and hugged her to my chest, brushing away the barmaid who was hovering beside, half-heartedly offering help.

"No, just leave her - she'll be all right in a minute." I said, stroking Jane's hair and rocking her softly from side to side.

She opened her eyes and looked up - I was shocked to see tears in her eyes.

"Get me out of here, Dave - take me home, please."

I lifted her to her feet and she stood, unsteady at first, staring out the customers in the bar until they had all turned back to their drinks. She walked to the door unaided, but as soon as it had shut behind us she leaned on my arm.

"You're going to have to be careful. This one's a bad one."

And that was all she would say. She sat, quiet and pale beside me, unanswering as I tried to find out what she had seen, where she had been. Even as I left her at her door, she refused to speak.

"Not now - not in the dark. Come round tomorrow." She turned away and then seemed to think better of it, looking back at me. "I meant what I said though - be very careful."

I had a chill all up my spine as I turned back to the car, a chill that was to stay with me all the way back to the station.

As I drove, I let my mind slip back to the previous case we had both been involved in.

I'd been sitting in my office, looking for a lead on the missing girl, sifting reports and interviews, trying to find anything that would give me a handle on the case. Someone had knocked on my door but I hadn't really registered it, and I only looked up when I heard my visitor's chair on the cheap linoleum.

"I'm sorry to bother you officer, but I know where the girl is."

That was all she said, but even back then, even before I had seen what she was capable of, I had believed in her implicitly. I had also fallen in love with her.

After we found the girl I took her out several times, each time getting closer to breaking through her tight defences, but that had all stopped when the press found out

They got onto her case straight away.

"Witch woman finds tragic toddler" - that had been the kindest of the headlines. It wasn't long before a smear campaign had implicated her in the toddler's death, even though she had a cast-iron alibi.

Not long after, she had gone into hiding. I hadn't seen her in three years. Until tonight.

The call had come out of the blue. It was almost a replay of the last time - still sifting reports, still poring over countless interviews. This time it was the phone that interrupted me. Part of me knew who it would be even before I lifted the handset.

"I know something about the one you are looking for," she said. "Bring me something belonging to one of the victims. I'll be in the Green Man after seven."

She had rung off abruptly, and her tone had been sharp and distant, but my heartbeat had been up as I headed for the pub, and my stomach was doing giddy flip-flops in anticipation.

Even now, on my way back from the meeting, I still felt that old adolescent tingling, but then I remembered her eyes as she had given me the warning, and the shiver came back. I had to grip the steering wheel tightly to stop my hands shaking.

The chill was still there as I entered the station, but was soon dispersed by Sergeant Briggs and a cup of steaming coffee.

Briggs was an office regular. His wife had long since gone, unable to cope with the unusual hours the police kept. It didn't seen to bother Briggs

- he always spent all his spare time here anyway, and if anything, he seemed happier now than before. Besides - he made great coffee.

"Couldn't sleep again, sir?" the Sergeant asked, a wide grin on his face. He knew full well that I shared his problem - I just couldn't keep from the job.

"Aye, something like that Sergeant." The coffee burned away at the roof of mouth. I sighed loudly as its warmth began to spread through my stomach.

"Nearly as good as whisky," I said appreciatively, holding my cup up in a mock salute. "Anything going on?"

Briggs snorted, as if in disgust.

"The Chief is out at another one of his dinners, PC Douglas is plugged into his computer again, the night shift have been called out to a disturbance in the town centre, and I'm trying to make sense of the pathologist's report. Apart from that, everybody else has packed up for the night." He stopped, and looked so serious that I almost laughed.

"If you don't mind me saying so, Sir - it might be better if you did the same yourself - you look like shit."

This did make me laugh, but my heart wasn't it.

"Aye - I know, but I've got a bad feeling about this guy. I don't think he's going to stop."

It was only then that the Sergeant's remark about the pathologist's report struck me.

"So what's this about old Swan's report - don't tell me he cocked it up again?"

"No, he's done a good job - I just don't understand the conclusions. Come through and I'll show you."

Apart from a single anglepoise lamp centre on his desk, Brigg's room was cloaked in darkness. The desk itself was strewn with open reports and papers - he had obviously been busy for quite some time.

"Just let me run through it with you, Sir - see if you can make anything of it," he said.

"Mary Wells, 23, single, no current boyfriend. One ex-lover with a cast-iron alibi. Secretary at a reputable firm of estate agents. She's sitting at home watching television when, round about midnight, someone knocks at her door. We've surmised this from the fact that there are no recorded calls to her house that evening, and from physical evidence found on the doorstep - but I'll get on to that later."

"The villain comes in, is he known to her? We don't know, but there are no signs of struggle in the hallway, or on the stairs. It's only when we get to the bedroom that we find any evidence of the intruder at all, and even that doesn't get us very far."

"They may have had sex - but there's no bruising, no scratches, no tissue under the victim's nails - and he kills her - method as yet unknown. He draws a picture on her abdomen - a spiral pattern that might or might not be significant - and takes her eyes, nipples, and parts of her genitalia before he's finished. All without leaving any trace of how he did it. Or so we thought last night anyway."

Briggs sat back in his chair and sighed, looking more tired than I had ever seen him.

"I've had PC Douglas check up on the spiral pattern. He reckons that it's a representation of Haraffnir - a Celtic water serpent with supernatural power - if you can believe any of that. Apparently it was famous for carrying off and mutilating young women."

He gave me another long sigh and closed the folders in front of him.

"I'm getting too old for this shit," he said. "Begging your pardon, sir."

"That's all right," I replied, "some days I know just how you feel. But what's got you so worked up? You haven't told me anything we didn't know yesterday."

The Sergeant picked up a report and slid it across the table.

"Three things," he began, "One - the lab report on some earth found on the victim's doorstep, only it's not earth. From the concentration of rotted vegetation they reckon it could only have come from the bottom of a deep sea loch - and recently too."

"So we're looking for a fisherman or a scuba diver then?" I asked hopefully.

"Aye, maybe," Briggs replied. "I hope so, I really do."

He rocked back in his chair and stared at the ceiling. This time I recognised the look on his face - it wasn't tiredness this time, it was fear. The Sergeant's voice barely rose above a whisper as he continued.

"The victim's lungs were full of water which had been mixed with brown organic matter. She drowned. And guess what the analysis of the water told us?"

"Don't tell me - a deep sea loch?"

"Right first time. And they didn't have sex but her vagina also carried traces of the same water - as did her bath tub."

I sipped the dregs of the coffee as I tried to take in this latest information.

"So where did the water come from? Do you know how far we are from the nearest sea loch? It must be nearly a hundred miles. Did the villain lug the water all the way? And just how much do you need to kill somebody?"

"Now you see what I've been sitting here thinking about. I had the house's system checked out - nothing there but standard tap water."

"You said there were three things?" I asked, hoping that more information might shed light on the problem. I was disappointed.

"Aye. Three things. The earth on the doorstep, the loch water in the lungs, and best of all, no prints, no fibres, no physical evidence apart from the water - it's as if he was never there."

I nearly choked on my last mouthful of coffee.

"What. Nothing at all."

Briggs looked serious. "Not even a single hair. I've never seen anything like it. The lab boys are mystified. I've sent them back to get more samples, just in case it's all a huge cock-up. They're over there now."

"They wanted to wait 'til morning but, begging your pardon sir - I told them that you'd have their balls in a basket if they tried to file that report. And one last thing - the boys from the press have got whiff of the story, they're already encamped outside the house."

I stood and stretched my spine, palms pressed hard against the flat of my back. I was acutely aware of the layers of fat that I had to press against, and I groaned as my bones resisted any movement.

"I think I'll go over there and take a look around. Maybe I'll see something I missed the last time. You never know, we've got to get lucky sometime on this one. In the meantime, get the ex-boyfriend in for a chat. We should have spent more time on him yesterday - maybe you're not the only one that's getting too old for this shit."

I gave Briggs a mock salute, John Wayne style, and headed out into the night.

This used to be my favourite time of the night - right around midnight, the pubs all empty and no one on the streets but me. I had spent many a long hour just savouring the quiet while tramping the beat, marvelling at moonlight on the trees, surprising the occasional fox and, very rarely, catching a burglar about his business.

But that was back then, back in the sixties when I'd been no more than a teenager myself, back before mass unemployment, longer opening hours, and free access to drugs had changed this town forever. Now I was more likely to be surprised myself, mugged for the few pence I carried in my pocket.

Tonight, even though the streets were quiet, I felt I could sense the evil lurking. And to make matters worse, there was a killer loose - a silent killer who left no clues, no witnesses. I prayed to God that it was a one-off - a family tiff of some kind - the last thing this town needed was a serial killer on the rampage.

When I got to the street where the murder had been committed I almost turned back - it had been too long a night, I was tired, and looking at a crime scene always depressed me anyway. Only the thought that the perpetrator was still at large kept me going.

In contrast with the rest of the street, number 23 had every light in the house blazing, a beacon in the darkness. Although it was a cold night, the front door was wide open; a succession of white-coated men carried small plastic bags to a van in the driveway.

A huddle of reporters stood in the garden nursing cups of coffee. I hoped that no one had been stupid enough to talk to them yet. I knew that I would have to call a press conference sooner rather than later - but not just yet. As I approached the house the reporters noticed me. They came forward with their usual bluster, flash units carried before them like revolvers. It was only when I got to the front door that I managed to shrug them off.

"Just stay there," I said. "I'll tell all of you what we know when I come out."

I hoped that would keep them quiet for a while, but I knew my picture was going to be splashed across the papers in the morning. I just wish I'd combed my hair.

The crime scene was like any other. Whatever it was that had made this house a home had long since gone, leaving only a clinical silence through which white-coated policemen moved slowly and reverentially. I looked down on the dead girl's bed for long seconds, but nothing came to me. My mind was blank and my body was tired. All I wanted to do was to lie down on those too soft pillows and let blackness take me away.

It wasn't to be. Someone calling my name jolted me out of my reverie. It was only on the second occasion that I recognised the voice, and by then the reporters were on her like a pack of jackals.

I ran down the stairs, almost knocking over a rookie who was too scared, too embarrassed to berate me. I flung open the door and found myself looking straight at Jane. The flashes going off around us lit up the road like a dance floor strobe, but she wasn't in any mood for dancing.

Her eyes were flat and black.

"He's coming for me," she said, as I pushed passed several reporters who were almost dropping their notebooks in a rush to get closer to her. "He knows who I am and he's coming for me."

I put out a hand, whether to comfort or to push her away I'm still not sure, but she interpreted it as a welcome and fell into my arms. The reporters went crazy and I had to lead Jane away. If we'd stayed there we wouldn't just have been on the front page; we'd give them enough to fill the whole paper.

I commandeered a car from one of the forensic boys, and just made it back to the station in front of the chasing pack. Jane didn't say a word, just sat and stared straight ahead, hot and heavy tears running down her cheeks.

Reception was like a war zone. Four young constables were trying, unsuccessfully, to get two very drunk teenagers away from a baying pack of their friends. The arrival of the reporters didn't help matters, and several heads were cracked together and some blood spilled before sanity was finally restored. The reporters were dispatched out onto the pavement, along with the more sober teenagers. The rest were taken down to the cells. All in all it was a good twenty minutes before I was able to get Jane into a quiet room, and by that time she was in deep shock.

I sat her down in a chair and went to get some coffee - I had a feeling that the night was nowhere near over.

Before I went back to her I instructed Briggs to keep an ear open for anything that might indicate that our man had done another one, but as yet nothing had come in.

Jane had her head in her hands as I entered the room, and when she looked up at me her eyes were red-rimmed and moist.

"It's coming for me," she said. I was shocked at the resignation in her voice. "It knows where I am and it's coming for me."

"You're safe here," I said, watching her shake her head sadly.

"Not from this I'm not," she said, and the crying started again. I wanted to hold her, to comfort her, but here in the station I was more used to the round of interrogation and recrimination. I stood quiet and watched her cry - I wasn't proud of it, but I needed whatever information she had.

"Tell me," I said softly, but she only shook her head until I insisted. "Please, tell me - we need to get this guy - and soon."

Her voice was weak as she replied.

"I don't know if anything I can tell you will do you any good, and I know you won't believe me anyway, but here goes." She took a long swig of coffee and a deep breath before starting.

"First of all - it's old. I get a sense of great age - and great evil. Every time I think about it I think of water. Deep, dark, cold water. And second, it's not human."

She must have seen the thought in my eyes.

"I knew you wouldn't believe me, but that doesn't make it any less real to me. There's one other thing, besides the water that is. I get a picture, some sort of spiral pattern. That's important, but quite how I'm not sure."

Up to now she had been holding herself together, but her resolve failed in the face of my disbelief. She began sobbing - great heaving gasps, and this time I couldn't ignore her. I took her in my arms and held her tight, until the sobs subsided. And when she offered her mouth for a kiss, I couldn't refuse.

We were interrupted by a discreet cough from the door. I looked over Jane's shoulder into the smiling face of Sergeant Briggs.

"Sorry to interrupt you sir, but Donnely - the victim's ex - has just come in. Do you want to talk to him?"

I held Jane at arm's length.

"Are you going to be okay?"

She nodded her head and she didn't exactly smile, but there was a twinkle in her eye that I had never seen before as I left the room. My good feelings lasted just as long as it took me to get to my office and see the man in my visitor's chair. He was wrong - there was no other word for it. Maybe some of Jane's talent had worn off on me, or maybe it just came from years of sitting across the desk from criminals, but if this guy wasn't guilty of something then I'd retire straight away.

It was in his eyes - a deep flicker of madness that he couldn't hide in spite of his slick hairstyle and sharp suit. Then there was the smile. He showed me all his teeth as I sat down.

"So what's going on, Inspector? I've already told your guys all I know."

"I doubt that," I said, and took delight as that smile slipped - just a bit, but enough.

I settled in my chair and lit a cigarette. I refrained from blowing smoke in his face - that would have been just too theatrical.

"I need to know about you and Mary," I said, then leaned back and waited for him to speak. He was good, I'll give him that, but nobody has ever managed to psyche me out when I'm sitting in my own chair. Besides, I had a feeling that this one liked to talk. I was proved right ten seconds later.

"I met her on holiday last year. When we got back I rang her up and we went out a few times. But she wasn't really my type - a bit too frigid if you know what I mean."

I let out a long plume of smoke before I spoke, "Where did you go?"

"Eh?"

"I said, where did you go? On holiday?"

"Scotland," he said. "The highlands to be precise."

"See any good lochs?" I asked. I don't know where that came from, but a policeman's subconscious spends all its time filtering possibilities, so it's no real surprise when you get just the right question. The only surprise to me was the response I got. I had never seen anyone go white as a sheet before. The blood drained from his face, and his eyes went blank.

"Can I have a cigarette, please?" he asked, and before I replied, had leaned across and grabbed the packet on the table. I put my hand out to stop him, my fingers fell on top of his, and the pictures started to unravel in my head like a high quality film show.

We are on the shores of a loch.

There is till over an hour to nightfall but already there is a chill in the air, a portent of the winter yet to come. The trees rustle softly, and occasionally a leaf falls, to swim in the ripples for a while before softly sinking to join its decaying brothers.

I look over at Mary. She is shivering, goosebumps have risen across her chest and her pubic hair looks jet black in the dim light.

The knife feels cold in my hand as I raise it above my head and begin the chant. Far out over the loch the water rises in a hump, something pushing just under the surface, surging forward as it comes for us. The metal of the knife sings as I bring it down. Mary screams and squirms and the knife sinks deep into the ground by her left shoulder. I try to grab her but she wriggles away, still screaming. The last I see of her is the pale white of her buttocks as she pushes her way through the rhododendrons.

I just have time to turn back towards the loch when there is a surge of blackness and a great wall of water falls over me, taking me down and away into darkness.

I felt the cigarette packet being taken away from my hand and looked up into a pair of jet black eyes. No pupil, no white, just pools of blackness. When he spoke his voice was harsh and throaty.

"This one awakened me, and showed me where to find the feed that had been denied me. Now I will feed again."

He jerked, one sudden convulsion, and he tore with his hands at the front of his shirt, buttons popping in sequence as he bared his chest.

The tattoo was a wondrous piece of art.

The serpent glowed in blacks and reds and purples, its coils spiralling inwards from the great leonine head, the body twisted and bent in a labyrinth of scaled muscle which seemed to flow and bulge in time with his breathing.

His chest rose in one great heave, and the serpent peeled - there is no other word for it - actually peeled from his chest, uncoiling in one smooth motion, a blackness rising and rising from his chair. The air got damp, then damper still, the salty tang of the sea stinging my nostrils. I pushed my chair back against the wall and half rose as the room went black around me - all black apart from a pair of blood-red eyes that blazed and flared with hate.

I felt my shirt go damp against my chest as I strained to breathe. A greyness was beginning to gather in front of my eyes when suddenly the weight lifted and the room went quiet. I was left alone in the room, staring at Donnely's Cheshire cat grin.

"The girl first, and then it's your turn," he said, just as the screaming started in the hallway beyond. I wanted to smash that grin backward into his face, but the screams grew louder, and this time I recognised them.

I was off the chair and out of the room before the first echo died away, almost knocking over Briggs in the hall.

"Don't let Donnely out of the room!" I shouted as I ran past him.

When I entered the incident room I thought it was too late. The walls ran damp with water - thick black oily water that dripped from the roof to splash in ever-growing puddles. Jane lay on the floor, still and unmoving as black spirals of muscle tightened around her. The fiery red eyes shone bright in the dim light, and the mouth of the serpent drooled as it made its way closer to its victim's throat.

It was only then that I realised she was still alive, still fighting.

Her eyes were open and her face frozen in intense concentration. She seemed to be holding the beast at bay by force of will alone.

I moved closer and tried to grab at the black coils, but my hands slid over its surface and came away wet and slippery. No matter how I tried, I was unable to take hold of anything.

"Too late," a voice came from behind me. I turned to see Donnely in the doorway - his shirt was open and the tattoo on his chest glowed and flowed in a fiery red light. He held a pair of scissors - my office scissors - and something dark dripped from the blades. Behind him in the corridor lay Briggs, slumped and unmoving in a growing pool of blood.

"Like I said. First the bitch, then you," Donnely whispered, closing the door behind him and moving into the room.

"There's nowhere for you to go, Donnely," I said, "why don't you give yourself up?"

He laughed, and I heard the madness in his voice.

"Nowhere to go? But I am the serpent - I go where I please and take what I want. And for now, I want you."

He came forward, the scissors held in a knife-fighter's grip. He was six inches taller than me, twenty years younger and a good two stone lighter. What he didn't have were the years on the street. Or the steel-tipped shoes.

My left foot took him in the balls, and as he curled over my right knee met his face, smashing his nose almost flat. I grinned as I felt the bone break. He fell sideways, dropping the scissors as I kicked him in the head again, one to keep him down and the second for good measure.

I made sure he stayed down and turned back to Jane, half hoping to see her free from the grip, but she was still held tightly, and the serpent still struggled to reach her face.

I stabbed down, hard, and the scissors went in amongst the coil. But it was like cutting through water. I pulled my hand backwards, feeling the body of the serpent flow around my wrist. The scissors came out and I caught a burst of red to my right. I turned just in time to see the glow fade on the tattoo of Donnely's chest. Stabbing again, still watching Donnely, I saw the tattoo flare redly in a spot approximately the place where I'd stabbed.

I didn't need a second chance. I scrambled across the floor, noticing that there was now early an inch of water. Without a second thought I brought the scissors down hard amid the coils of the tattoo and began to cut, stabbing and chopping my way through Donnely's flesh.

The room got suddenly colder - colder and wetter - and Jane screamed again, but I couldn't pause, couldn't stop as my right hand went up and came down, went up and came down. It didn't take long before Donnely's chest was a mass of red, pulpy gore. I fell back in the water gasping, letting the scissors fall away and taking in deep, sobbing breaths.

I heard a quiet gasp behind me and turned just in time to see Jane push herself to her feet and slough off sheets of water from her body.

There was no sign of the serpent.

Afterwards there was a hell of a row of course - there was a lot to explain away. Like several hundred gallons of salt water, and a suspect with his face beaten to a pulp and his chest carved into strips of ham.

Briggs and I managed to concoct a story between us. I don't think anybody believed us, and we both took early retirement soon after, but at least we got our pensions.

Briggs couldn't take to retirement - he's a security guard for a chain of warehouses.

As for me, I married Jane. Two years ago now, and everything has been great.

But just lately I've begun to worry. This morning I smelled seawater in our bedroom. And when Jane came back from work today she told me that she thinking about getting a tattoo done.

The Old Mother

In the eaves of the barn the great white owl shivered as the wind rose and whispered its coldness into the nest. Something came into the loft, something cold and fearsome. The owl pushed itself further into its bed of leaves and shivered, wide eyes searching the gloom around it. It saw nothing but it remained in its roost. There would be no hunting tonight.

Below, down amongst the hay bales, Matt Rogers was oblivious to the wind as he moved a bale and uncovered the tunnel he'd built in the warm dry hay. This was his favourite time - the chores were all done, his father had retired to his bed and Matt was free and alone for the first time that day.

He had built the den the night before, pushing the large rectangular blocks of hay around until he had a four feet square cavity right in the centre. A strategically placed bale hid the entrance from his father's prying eyes. There had been a bad moment earlier today when the old man had nearly uncovered the tunnel but it had passed and his secret was still safe.

He switched on his flashlight before pulling the bale back into place behind him leaving him alone in the warm yellow glow. He turned and shone the torch down the tunnel; stray spines of hay casting sharp needle shadows along the wall ahead of him. The plastic bag in his left hand scraped along the straw as he pulled himself down the tunnel.

There were small scurrying noises all around him but he had a lot of experience with mice and they had long ago ceased to frighten him. Now rats, that was another matter, but Toby, the family terrier, seemed to be lord of the farm at the moment and it had been several months since the rats had been seen.

However Matt purposely made more noise than was necessary as he left the tunnel and pulled his way into his private place.

Although the temperature had fallen to freezing outside, the air here was warm and dry and musty, smelling faintly of new mown grass. He moved the coarser parts of the hay aside as he smoothed out a seating position for himself. He could see by his watch that it was nearly midnight, nearly time.

Granddad had told him what to do. By rights it should be his father's duty, but father was too much of a realist, too much a believer in machines and fertiliser. It was down to Matt to keep the peace, to ensure the crop now that Granddad had gone.

Carefully he emptied the plastic bag, placing the contents in a line before him - the small sickle, gleaming golden in the torchlight, the carefully trimmed ears of corn, the matches, the crucible and the tiny, oil-fired brazier.

He moved the brazier into the centre of his small clear area. He would have to be careful - he knew the dangers of fire in a hayloft, but the element of danger was part of the ritual. He was trembling, a mixture of anticipation and fear, as he lit the small wick underneath the tripod and placed the crucible in its place.

The air seemed to grow heavier immediately and he was having difficulty drawing breath as he dropped the corn into the crucible where it hissed and spat as it ran around the bowl. Within the confines of the den the shadows flickered red and the hay seemed to dance in time with flickering flame as he began the chant that Granddad had made him memorise.

Old Mother protect us
Cuillach preserve us
Young Mother come forth
Cuillach dochtir be full for us.

The temperature dropped sharply and Matt could see his breath condense in the air before him. The shadows on the hay facing him deepened sharply and he reached forward to grip the golden sickle. There was a quavering tremulous note in his voice as he continued the chant.

Young Mother be bountiful
Cuillach dochtir marry us
Old Mother be merciful
Cuillach spare us

The wall opposite him quivered, the straw shaping and moulding itself, running together and binding, small knots forming as he watched wide-eyed. A bulge appeared in the wall, a bulge that forced itself into shape, first a head covered in flaxen hair, then shoulders, tanned and golden.

Matt gripped the sickle tighter as the body of a young girl pushed itself towards him.

Old Mother look the other way
Cuillach bypass us
Young Mother be gentle
Cuillach dochtir sleep with us

This was the important point. "She will be beautiful," Granddad had said and Matt had noticed the far off look in his eye as he remembered, "And you will be tempted by her favours. You must not bend, remember - they are old. Older by far than this farm or even this land. My father knew them, and his father, and on, before the Romans even. She wants your seed but you must offer only your blood. She is bound by the chant to accept. Remember, only your blood."

Matt remembered, but she was comely and his heat was rising - he could feel it pounding in his heart. The flaxen hair parted and he was looking into a pair of eyes as clear and as blue as the summer sky. A pair of red lips parted and a small pink tongue escaped from between them.

He could feel an erection growing between his legs as she reached for him and his grip on the sickle loosened slightly as he felt the feather light touch of her fingers on his face. He was looking up into those pale blue eyes when the bale above shifted and the red angry face of his father glared at him.

"What the hell are you doing down there boy?" the man bellowed as Matt was lifted out of the den by a strong right arm. He only had time to look down once but all he could see was a disturbed layer of straw slowly settling back into place, He looked up into the large red face.

"How many damn times do I have to tell you? You know about the fire don't you?"

"But dad," Matt began before the man clapped a hand over the boy's mouth.

"No buts. Not this time. This time I'm going to teach you a lesson."

Matt was thrown to the floor, hard enough to knock all the wind from his body. He lay there, gasping, as his father took the large leather belt from around his waist.

"The Cuillach dochtir. I was calling the Cuillach dochtir," he managed to blurt out, just as the first stroke hit and the pain lanced across his back.

"Old wives tales. Just the ravings of an old dying man. How many times do I have to tell you?"

Matt bit his lip to stop himself from crying out. Crying would only make it worse.

Nether of them heard the rustling of straw from the makeshift den.

Matt saw his father move to the den, saw him reach in and lift out the brazier with one hand, the sickle with the other. Then all hell broke loose.

The barn door was thrown open by a gust of wind, a wind that swept past Matt and blew out the tiny flame in his father's hand, a wind that whistled through the bales of hay, dislodging any loose straws and sending them dancing and cavorting through the air.

"Close the bloody door," his father shouted, and Matt pushed himself upright. It was a struggle - the wind was strong - but he eventually managed to get the door shut.

He could fell the wind rattling and struggling against the oak door as he slid the bolt into place. It was only when he turned back to look for his father that he noticed the straw - the straw that still danced in the dead calm of the barn.

It spun and reeled in front of his father, all the time picking up more material as it hovered over the remains of Matt's den. A figure began to form and at first Matt thought that his maiden would return.

The straw had other ideas.

The hair came first. Not golden - not this time. This time it was gray and old and dead and plastered across a mask of a face stitched in yellow and dry stalks - the face of a hag.

Matt shouted as the arms began to form.

"The Old Mother. The Cuillach. Use the sickle dad! Use the sickle!"

It was no use. He could see that his father was in shock, the veins standing out large and proud at his temple as he struggled to contain his fear. The long straw arms were around his neck before he had time to shout and his first exclamation was smothered as the yellow face clamped itself over his mouth.

They fell - the man and the hag, rolling on the floor, the sickle hanging useless in the man's right hand, small pieces of the hag falling off only to be replenished as ever more straw was strewn into the air. The legs formed, long thin gray legs that were wrapped around his father's lower body. Soon the whole place danced with the whirling straws.

Matt tried to move upwards them and was buffeted by a whirlwind of stinging grass that lashed across his face, across his hands. He fell to his hands and knees and started to crawl. As he moved closer, his father suddenly stopped struggling and gave one convulsive shudder.

The wind fell, dropping the stalks around his body. Matt could hear the sucking as the Cuillach fed.

Something inside him snapped at the sight of his father's still and deflated body. He giggled as he crawled closer.

He could see the blood, could see the redness draining into the stalks, could see the life pouring into the straw figure as his fingers closed over the matchbox.

His hand shook violently as he tried to open the box and he nearly dropped the contents when the figure stopped its feeding, its red glowing eyes turning on him. He remembered the last thing his Granddad had told him as he struck match after match and dropped them in the straw at his feet.

Young Mother leave us
Cuillach dochtir depart
Old Mother be banished
Cuillach be dust once more
He smiled as the fire spread.

The great white owl flew over the barn, wary of the hot red sparks that flew up into the night air. It watched as the barn collapsed into itself and the fiery redness wafted in the night and it swooped gratefully into the shelter of a large oak as the first snows of winter fell.

The Last Day of Summer

The sun was trying to push its way through the watery mist as the pair left the house. Mike followed along slightly behind, falling into the same loping walk as the man in front of him. There was a slight chill in the air but he was wearing only a T-shirt, a pair of shorts and a battered pair of trainers. His parents had wanted him to dress properly and, naturally, he had declined. He felt cold and he wished he were older.

"It's just not fair."

He kicked at the loose stones of the path watching them rattle and tumble down the hill. They had come to rest before he started muttering again.

"I never get to do anything. Just because I'm only thirteen. John Davies is twelve, but he gets to see all the great films. I bet his dad doesn't think that films rot your brains."

The man slowed down and now walked alongside the boy. His upper body seemed to stiffen, the lines tightened at the corners of his mouth and the wrinkles by his eyes became visible. Mike didn't have to look up, he knew the expression would be there - the one which said "I am right, you are wrong, I am an adult, you are just a child." He had been seeing a lot of that expression lately.

"That's enough," his father said. "You are too young and that's the end of it. When I was your age I..."

Mike had heard it all so many times before he believed that he could roll off the speech by heart. Better to stop him before he really got into it.

"When you were my age you probably were a swot. And there were no good films then anyway - just that boring black and white stuff. I bet you never had monsters and aliens and spaceships."

His father kept going in that slow reasonable voice that Mike was coming to hate.

"When I was your age I wasn't allowed to see an X-rated film, and I don't see that you should be any different. X-rated means that you have to be eighteen to see it, and you've got a few more years to go yet."

Mike couldn't let it lie.

"John Davies gets to see them."

"Yes, you've said that already" his father replied, still in the same damned reasonable tone. "But John Davies also has a bad reputation, with the police, with the school and with other parents. I don't think he's a very good example for you to follow. Do you?"

"But that's not the point" Mike said, close to crying now, trying hard not to let the tears show - if he cried he would lose the argument and he wasn't ready to give up yet.

"That's exactly the point. I've made a decision and you're just going to have to like it. Come on, let's go down to the lake and see if there are any fish."

The man put his arm out around his son's shoulders, but the boy squirmed away.

"I don't want to see your stupid fish and I don't want to go to the lake. I want to see the film." He moved away from his father, eyes bright with tears.

"I wish I was older. Then you wouldn't be able to tell me what to do. You're just a boring old fart. I hate you."

He turned and ran down the hill; his tears blinding him as he left the path and headed into the thick blackthorn bushes on the left-hand side. He pushed the branches away, not noticing the many scratches which blossomed redly on his arms and legs as he pushed his way deeper into the thicket.

He snagged himself hard on one branch and felt a firm satisfaction as there was a rip then a tear and his T-shirt was torn from waist to shoulder. Behind him he could hear his father calling, but he took no notice. He plunged in farther, forcing his way past the recalcitrant bushes, trying to get as far away as possible.

The chasing voice was fading behind him as he changed direction, following the contours of the hill. He knew there was a path somewhere around here, it was just a matter of finding it.

Stumbling on, he continued downhill, trying to avoid the bigger, more dangerous branches, giving no thought to where he was headed, when suddenly his feet failed him. They gave way beneath him, scrambling in the dirt for purchase as he tried to keep his footing. A large piece of earth crumbled causing him to fall awkwardly backwards.

He threw out his arms to try to get a hold of something - a tree, a rock, anything to stop the fall, but another clump of earth gave way and he plunged downward. His fall was short, but he landed hard, knocking the wind from his body.

He lay there for several seconds, gasping in great gulps of air as he tried to get his breath. Raising his head, wincing from the bruises in his neck muscles, he looked upwards to see where he had been.

He had fallen from a ledge that he could just see through the foliage above him. He was in what appeared to be a garden, but one that had been left to its own devices for too long. It was the size of a tennis court and was surrounded on all sides by a high wall, a wall of old red brick encrusted with entwining ivy and climbing mosses and rampant greenery. Rose bushes surrounded him, their wicked thorns waiting for him to get close enough to snare and trap and bloody.

Through their branches he could see a path, slightly less covered than the surrounding area. Pushing himself to his hands and knees, groaning at the pains in his body, he cautiously made his way through the foliage.

Some of the rose thorns tried their best to snag him but he was too agile for them and it wasn't long before he was able to push the last branch aside and stand up. When he stood he was able to see a gate in the far wall, a huge black cast iron gate set in shadow under an arch of flowers. He hoped it wasn't locked - he wasn't sure whether he could get over the walls.

The sky darkened overhead and he looked up just as a deep black cloud covered the sun and cast gloom into the corners of the garden, softening the shadows.

The air was heavy and moist and silent, not even a bird called as he made his way to the gate. The rusted metal squealed as he pushed at it, harder then harder still till finally it swung open before him.

He was looking into another garden, similar to the one he had just left but larger, still with the overgrown rose bushes, still with the ivy encrusted walls and with a twin gate directly opposite him at the far end.

There was a figure, a bent, hunched over man, in the left-hand corner. Mike called out to him.

"Hello?"

But there was no reply. Mike could hear a noise, a crackling and a rustling, but there was no sign that he had been heard.

He moved closer, noticing that the figure was an old man, clad in a workman's overall.

"Probably the gardener" he thought to himself. As he got within five yards he spoke again.

"Hello. Can you tell me how to get out of here please?" But there was still no reply. He went to the old man's side and touched his shoulder, then stood back as the figure turned round.

He wasn't just old, he was ancient. His face was brown, a deep nutmeg brown that reminded Mike of the old sideboard at home - only the sideboard didn't have as many lines on it.

Two deep black eyes were sunk into hollows but they sparkled with life. The worst thing was the mouth - Mike couldn't take his eyes off it. The lips were thin, almost non-existent and they were pulled back over red, feverish gums in which three teeth sat, spaced at intervals in the rotting tissue.

The tongue that popped out when he looked up at Mike was gray and green and somehow slimy.

A hand came up to the wizened features, a hand that was even browner and was covered in even more lines than the face. It made a pass in front of the mouth and then a pass over both ears before the old man bent over his task once more.

Mike understood. Deaf and dumb, just great. How was he going to make his wishes known? He was about to tap him on the shoulder again when he realised what the old man was doing.

Suddenly he found if hard to breathe and the world swam mistily around him. He had to shake his head, hard, and look again, just to make sure.

In his left hand the man had a pointed stick of black, moss encrusted wood. He pointed at a leaf, a green fleshy leaf in the prime of its life. As Mike watched it started to go brown, from the edges first, a yellowing then a darkening spreading inwards along the veins, crackling and rustling as the leaf crumpled in on itself, drying out and finally falling lifeless to the ground to join the pile already there.

The stick pointed again, this time at a rose flower. The petals fell, one by one, drifting softly to lie redly on the brown earth below. He didn't know why, but Mike found that he was crying.

He rubbed at his eyes with his forearm feeling the hot tears mix with the gritty earth and the slimy blood as he smeared his skin. When he looked up again the figure had wandered off, over into the centre of the garden.

He followed - he couldn't think of anything else to do. For a split second he wished that Dad were with him. Dad was good at mimes and charades - he would be able to make the old man understand. And Dad was smart. He'd know what the old man had been doing. Some sort of chemical he supposed. Dad would know. But then he remembered the reason he had been running.

"I'll get myself out of this" he told himself - and any anyone within earshot of his mutters. "Then they'll know I'm not just a cry-baby child."

As he got closer he could see that the figure had bent over a pool and he could hear cooing, pigeon like noises coming from the festering hole which passed as a mouth. Something flashed, red and gold, and he watched amazed, as the foot long catfish jumped into the old man's right hand. He was struck motionless as the stick moved upwards, but spurred himself into action as it came closer to the fish.

"No" he shouted, just once, just before his hand closed tightly on the black rod and his world changed.

It began slowly. He felt stronger and watched, amazed, as the scratches on his body healed, zipping themselves up and locking the redness back in.

Somewhere there was a splash as the fish returned to the water but Mike didn't see it, couldn't see it, and was unable to drag his eyes from the changes taking place in his body.

He grew taller, then taller still, towering over the figure in front of him. He was getting older - fifteen, sixteen, then the old man pulled the stick from his grasp.

He looked at his palm, at the black streak left by the wood, then looked down into the black expressionless eyes below. Without thinking, he grabbed for the stick again. 'Still not old enough' was the thought that passed through his mind.

As the stick found his hand, the old man smiled and Mike could see a row of perfect white teeth pushing and jostling their way up through the pink gums. He grew 'Just like Alice' he thought - and grew and he tried to release the stick but it seemed stuck to his hand. He pulled at it and felt a lancing flare of pain and looked down to see the flesh of his palm and the wood of the stick had become one, inseparable whole.

The old man didn't look so old anymore as Mike tried to push him away, tried to give the stick back, but he was beginning to feel weak. His skin darkened and fine lines were beginning to form and he could feel his body shrinking again. He cried, tears of relief "I'm going to be all right - it's going backwards". But his skin got darker and his legs got weaker and the man in front of him looked more and more like a boy until greyness began to mist his sight.

The last two things he heard before he heard no more was a light boyish giggle and a distant voice calling his name. The last thing he saw before darkness took him was a boy, a small blonde healthy boy, stepping out of a pair of overalls that were too big for him.

He was left, in the silence, in the dark, and all he knew how to do was to point the stick.

Just a Par to Win

He was trying to calm himself for his last drive. Not that it really mattered, but he needed a four at the eighteenth to keep his score in double figures. He hadn't done the ton since he was a kid and he knew he wouldn't live it down if he did it here in Scotland, the home of golf.

To make matters worse, he was sure that his partner was cheating. Nothing he could pin down - no, this guy was too careful for that. But there was definitely something shifty about him, and he hadn't lost that self-satisfied smirk since the second tee.

Pete watched while John, his playing companion, knocked his drive straight at the hole, the ball bisecting the bunkers and dropping stone dead on the green less than six feet from the flag. This was getting embarrassing. John was supposed to be an eight handicap, just like Pete, but he had outplayed Pete all day, looked like getting a birdie, and, much to Pete's annoyance, was still smirking.

"At least a laugh would be more bearable than that horrible smugness," Pete thought as he teed up his sixth ball of the day - the other five having disappeared over or into various cliffs or gullies.

He swung at the ball and it felt absolutely right for the first time that day. The ball flew straight as a die and he smiled - a small thing, but more than he'd been able to manage in the last couple of hours. It didn't last long. The ball hit the fairway just short of the green and took a sharp bounce to the left, disappearing straight into the face of a deep bunker. There was a small puff of sand - it looked like it had plugged down hard.

"Bad luck" John said, and, not for the first time, Pete fought off the urge to punch him in the mouth. "Never mind. It could have been worse - you could have been down in Old Jack's hollow."

Pete followed the path of the ball. He hadn't noticed the gravestones, he had been too intent on his shot, but there was a graveyard only ten yards from the green. He had indeed been lucky.

He didn't talk as he walked up the fairway towards the bunker - he was afraid that he might lose his temper.

It was just as he expected - the ball was plugged tight against the face and he was going to have to play out sideways. He got into the bunker and lined up the shot. And that was when the chill hit him, a shiver that ran all the way up his spine.

There was someone in the graveyard watching him. He could feel it, but he wasn't about to turn round. The chill got deeper, threatening to ice up his veins, and his hands began to shake.

"Control," he muttered. "Head steady, hands fast."

He played his shot hurriedly and was lucky that the ball stayed on the fairway. He hit a beautiful chip and holed out for a four and a total of ninety-nine shots, but the chill stayed with him and all he wanted was a long stiff drink.

"Don't worry Pete." John said as they entered the clubhouse. "There's always tomorrow."

The last thing he wanted to think about was another round. First he wanted a drink - no, make that three drinks, enough to chase away the memory of that chill.

"I thought you'd been taken with Old Jack's shakes." John said, but Pete wasn't listening, he was already heading for the bar.

"Whisky - double, on the rocks," he said. "And what will you have John?" he asked, turning towards his opponent.

But the other man had already moved further along the bar to stand with a huddle of other men. There was a sudden, sharp, peal of laughter, and Pete felt his ears burn. To hide his embarrassment he turned to speak to the barman, and was surprised to find that he had already emptied his glass.

"Another double Mr Rogers?" the barman said. "Ye look like ye need wan - I ken I would after a round wi' the likes o' him."

Pete accepted the drink gratefully - he was beginning to regain his composure but the chill seemed to have settled permanently in his spine.

"That man needs close watching" Pete said, unwilling to voice his suspicions completely. He needn't have been so circumspect.

"Aye. That's wan way tae put it," the barman said, smiling. "Had ye not wondered why he was the only wan free tae play ye? Naebody else will go round wi' him. Never mind - ye'll ken better in the morning."

Tomorrow. Pete hadn't thought about that yet. Another round, another chance of humiliation. He tried to change the subject.

"What did he call the graveyard? Old Jack's hollow?"

The barman smiled again, but Pete saw something in his eyes, something that looked like fear, and he took a long time to reply.

"Aye. That's right. Auld Jack was a regular here a few years back. Then, in the last round o' the club championship, needing a par tae win the trophy, he knocked his ba' against the graveyard wall. He took three shots tae get it oot o' the grass, and it proved too much for him. He had a heart attack and died - right next tae the graveyard. And your friend John there won the trophy."

Suddenly Pete had the shivers again, a cold draft which crept up his back and raised the hairs at the nape of his neck.

"You had better give me another double," he said, "I think I'm going to need some stiffening to get me back out there tomorrow."

One thing led to another and it was several hours later before Pete weaved his way back to his hotel and fell into a fitful, uneasy, sleep.

The night served its purpose in one respect - by the time he woke the chill had finally gone, to be replaced by a hangover. Two cups of coffee shifted the bulk of it, and by the time he got to the first tee he felt almost human again.

The sun was shining from a clear blue sky and there was only a slight breeze. Not even the ever-present smirk on John's face as he approached could dampen Pete's mood. He felt good. Today was going to be much better.

He was proved right as early as the first green. He had left himself with a long, up-hill putt for a birdie - more than thirty feet, but as soon as he hit it he knew it was in. He allowed himself a smile as the ball rattled into the cup.

He managed to match John hole for hole, and was even thinking that he might take a few off the other man, when John spoke for the first time since that first hole birdie.

"Say Pete. How about making it more interesting? Fifty pounds on the match?

Pete didn't even think about it.

"Make it seventy and you've got yourself a deal," he said.

"OK" John said. Pete thought that the other man had answered suspiciously quickly, and as not surprised to see that the smirk was back. He was going to have to watch his opponent very carefully.

They shared the next five holes, and Pete had the honour on the fifteenth. He stood over the ball, looked down the fairway, and froze.

There, in the distance, only partially obscured by a fine mist, sat the graveyard. The chill was back and he hurried the shot, hooking it as far as the fifth fairway.

He was lucky - he found a good lie and managed to half the hole in par, but all he could think of was the eighteenth tee, wondering if he was even going to be able to play a shot.

He only managed to share the next two holes by sheer luck - some of his nervousness seemed to have rubbed off on John and they halved them both in bogey fives.

Pete had the honour on the last. He was all square, scores even with just this one to play, but his legs had gone weak on him and he had to lean on his three iron to stop himself from falling. Lining the shot up was the toughest thing he ever did and as soon as he hit the ball he knew it was all wrong. His heart sank as he watched it fall and nestle, hidden in the long grass next to the graveyard wall.

"May as well give up now," he thought. "No way am I going to play that one."

He didn't really pay attention to John's shot - he didn't even look, but he was surprised to hear John swear and turned just in time to see the ball overshoot the green and bounce into the bunker at the back.

Maybe he still had a chance - if only he could bring himself to get close to that graveyard.

He bought some time by letting John play first - the bunker was slightly further away from the pin anyway. He saw the other man jump up and down, watched him swing, and saw some sand fly.

"Just practising" John shouted.

"The bastard fluffed it." Pete thought, but he didn't say anything. John swung again, and his ball popped out of the bunker, sweet as a nut, and rolled up to five feet from the hole.

Pete strode over to the graveyard, adrenaline pumping, determined not to lose, but when he saw his ball his heart sank - it was lying amongst thick, tufty, grass and he reckoned he'd need at least two shots just to move it.

He looked back towards the hole and John was standing by the pin.

"Shall I take it out?" he said, and the smirk was back full force.

"Yeah. You do that." Pete said, and bent over his shot.

And that's when it happened.

The chill came back. But this time it was more - it was as if someone had poured ice into his veins. The nine iron shook in his hands. Then his spine stiffened, as if someone had pushed him upright, pushed him from inside.

He watched his hands draw back, saw the clubface go through the ball, and felt it hit the sweet spot. But none of it was him - something, or someone, was working through him. He could only watch as the ball flew straight and true, dropping, as soft as a feather, only six inches from the hole.

John looked straight at him, stunned, and Pete felt the corners of his mouth rise into a teeth-baring smile.

The colour drained from his opponent's face, and his jaw dropped a clear inch.

Pete stayed where he was as John stood over his putt - he could see that the man's heart wasn't in it and the ball sailed wide to finish nearly two feet past the hole. John stomped off the green without looking back and headed for the clubhouse. It was only then that Pete could move.

Something left him - he felt it pass through and out and the cold left, just like that. He stumbled forward, away from the wall and turned around, just in time to see a grey mist fade into a nearby headstone.

He didn't have to look at the inscription to know what the name on it would be.

Old Jack had finally got his par.

Ghost Writer

It was waiting there for me in the morning. I'd gone downstairs, wandered around in a daze as usual, had a cigarette, brewed the coffee, and sat down in front of the blank screen. It was there when I booted up.

Just one word, scrolling up the screen, giving birth to a copy of itself almost faster than the eye could follow.

"HELLO"

I hit the break key, noticing that the program exited into BASIC. On typing "list", I found that a small, a very small, program was in the memory.

10 "HELLO": GOTO 10

I got up and checked the doors. Everything was still locked up from the night before. A further quick check showed that nothing was missing. What kind of burglar breaks in just to leave an inexplicable message on a computer? And then a second thought struck me, I should have thought of it earlier, but I'm not usually at my best in the mornings. I must have a virus.

Panic set in. It had been at least three months since my last backup and my first novel was nearly complete. My hands trembled as I invoked the virus checking software, and I smoked three cigarettes as I watched it laboriously churning through directory after directory, failing to track down the culprit.

There was nothing unusual in the boot program, just the normal set-up procedure. Either it was a completely new, undetectable virus or I was going mad. I preferred to believe in the virus.

The rest of the morning was spent in backing up the novel, wiping then reformatting the hard disk, and reinstalling all the operating system bits and bobs. I decided to leave the novel on the floppies for the time being. I'd revised enough - I only had the last chapter to write and I didn't intend to touch any of the previous twenty.

What with all of that going on, plus the interruptions for postman, window cleaner and brush salesman, it was lunchtime before I could even think about settling down to work.

I spent the rest of the afternoon at the computer, lost in the world I was creating. After a while I didn't even see the screen or feel my fingers - the thoughts streamed, straight from my brain to the disk, or so it seemed.

It gets like that when you are on a roll, the muse kicks in and the mechanics become unimportant - it doesn't matter whether you use a sheet of paper, a typewriter, a computer or a dictating machine - the creative process takes over and carries you away. All you can do is hold on and hope it brings you back.

By the time my muse brought me back it had gone dark outside. The only light in my study was the glow from the white on black letters on the screen. My back hurt and my wrists ached but I still got a big thrill out of typing those two, always welcome words.

"The End".

I had been away -actually been to the scene where the events had happened. I had heard the people speak, smelled their food, dreamed after dreams, and now their tale was finished.

I sat back, satisfied, and saved the file. Now I don't know how much you know about computers, but in most cases, when a file is saved, the system puts a date and a time stamp on it, so you don't get things mixed up.

There was a file on my disk - a large one judging by what the screen told me - dated that afternoon, sitting next to the chapter of my novel, created while I was gone with the story.

By now I was convinced I had a virus. I took a new floppy out of the box, reformatted it to be sure, and transferred my last chapter, before returning to the new file.

I instructed the computer to show me the file. It beeped for a bit, then the screen started scrolling.

"ABCD"
"123"
"QWERTY"
"ASDFG"
"THE CAT SAT ON THE MAT"
"BY CHRIST. IT WORKS"

"I DON'T KNOW HOW I GOT HERE. IT MUST BE RESERVED AS A SPECIAL PURATORY FOR BEST SELLER EDITORS. ONE MINUTE I WAS SITTING AT MY DESK. THEN, WHAMMY!! SHOOTING PAINS THROUGH THE CHEST. THE NEXT THING I KNOW I'M BEING SUBJECTED TO ILLITERATE MASTURBATORY FANTASIES. WHAT'S WITH ALL THE ANGST AND DOOM? YOU WANT TO SELL BOOKS DON'T YOU?"

"I CAN'T SEEM TO MANAGE LOWER CASE YET. NEVER MIND - IT'LL COME."

"YOU DON'T BELIEVE YOU'RE SEEING THIS, DO YOU? WELL WAKE UP STEPHEN - I GOT YOUR NAME FROM ONE OF YOUR LETTERS - I'M HERE TO STAY."

"AND I'M GOING TO BE GOOD FOR YOU. I KNOW WHAT THE PUBLIC WANT. FIFTEEN BEST SELLERS IN A S MANY YEARS - I'VE GOT AN EYE FOR IT. NONE OF THIS WASTING ARTISTS IN GARRETS CRAP, WHAT THE READERS WANT IS SEX, RICH PEOPLE HAVING IT OFF IN EXOTIC LOCATIONS, POWER BATTLES AMONGST THE MAKERS AND SHAKERS, SEX, VIOLENCE, GORE AND MORE SEX. YOU WON'T GET ANYWHERE WITH YOUR TORTURED TALES OF LOVELORN YOUTH, SO I'VE TAKEN THE LIBERTY OF CHANGING YOUR STORY A BIT."

"READ IT OVER. THEN I'LL TELL YOU WHAT WE'RE GOING TO DO NEXT."

The screen beeped at me again, and then went blank. When I looked on the directory, the file had gone.

To say I was confused would be an understatement. If this was a virus, it was the most brilliantly conceived one I'd ever come across. Or maybe I was hallucinating - over-stressed by my long bout at the keyboard. I couldn't leave before checking the novel.

I picked a disk at random from the box and inserted Chapter Ten into the computer. I was quite proud of that one, the understated seduction scene where Alan nearly loses his virginity on the first night at University.

The first page was all right, describing Oxford just as I remembered it, but by page two large chunks of capitals strode over the screen, Alan had become a lecturer and Fiona, a second year Medical Student in my version, had become a journalist and a raving nymphomaniac, though not necessarily in that order.

By page three the capitals had taken over completely and Alan and Fiona were at it like a pair of rabbits. On page seven, Fiona was murdered by a jealous girlfriend, thus removing her from the story. In my version her and Alan had got married in chapter sixteen.

My hands shook badly as I removed the disk and tried another chapter. In my chapter fifteen Alan had to choose between his career and the girl. In the new version he was working in high finance and was about to screw a billionaire playboy out of his inheritance.

The last chapter was the worst. The new version of Alan is getting married to the ex-mistress of the playboy when the playboy turns up - in St. Paul's Cathedral of all places, and guns down half of the British Parliament. Alan saves the day with some derring-do, and they all live happily ever after, No mention of his growing disillusionment with married life, his prostrate problem or the abortion. My book had been ruined.

I had just read the last paragraph when the screen started spitting out more words.

"WELL. WHAT DO YOU THINK? IT'S BOUND TO BE A BEST SELLER. ALL YOU'VE GOT TO DO IS CHANGE THE CAPITALS."

"I'LL EVEN TELL YOU WHO TO SEND IT TO. HELL, I KNOW EVERYBODY IN THE FIELD. THEY'LL LAP IT UP - THEY'LL BE FIGHTING OVER THEMSELVES FOR THE FILM RIGHTS, YOU'RE GOING TO BE RICH MY BOY."

"WHY DON'T YOU TRY TYPING SOMETHING? I THINK IT WOULD BE POSSIBLE FOR US TO HAVE A CONVERSATION."

By this time I didn't know what was going on, but I did know that it was impossible for a mere virus to mimic conversation when faced with questions it couldn't anticipate. I was angry about the novel, but the more I could find out about what had happened, the more chance I might have of recovering my work. I decided to play along. Leaning forward to the computer, I typed.

"What is your name?"

"LOOK IN YESTERDAY'S PAPER, UNDER OBITUARIES."

I went to the next room and retrieved the paper from the bin. And there it was:-

Top US. Editor Peter Frieburg died suddenly. He died as he lived, at his desk. He is best remembered as the publisher of two of the best selling books of all time - 'Sex in the Afternoon' and 'They do it in leather'. Perhaps he will be most fondly remembered for his famous quote on the Johnny Carson Show. When asked if he was maybe debasing literature, he replied. 'Literature don't make money. I do.'

That put paid to the virus idea - I didn't think any viruses were smart enough to read the daily papers, and top US. Editors weren't dying every other day just to keep the virus happy - or were they? I felt foolish looking back on it, but I checked back on the week's papers, just to make sure.

I was getting pretty paranoid by this time. When I got back to the screen another message was waiting for me.

"SO NOW DO YOU BELIEVE ME? I'LL TELL YOU SOME PERSONAL DETAILS OF MY LIFE? OR HOW ABOUT SOME INSIDE INFO ON LIFE IN A PUBLISHERS OFFICE? SURELY THAT WOULD BE OF INTEREST TO A WRITER? COME ON. TALK TO ME DAMMIT."

I left it just sitting there while I went to bed. My theories were all getting shot down and I was forced to consider that the answer was really what it seemed to be - no hidden tricks, my computer was haunted. So now what?

I tossed and turned all night, unable to get the image out of my mind - the screen filling up with capitals, obliterating all my work. Even after all that had happened, I was still hopeful of getting up in the morning and finding that it had been a bad dream, a temporary breakdown in reality which sleep, the great repair man, would have fixed for me.

Several things had happened by morning. The printer output hopper was full of paper, but what caught my eye first was a new message in the screen.

"Hey. Look. I've Got The Hang Of Lower Case At Last."

"I've Taken The Liberty Of Redoing Your Novel And Printing It Out. Piece of Cake really - I had Most of It Hidden Away Somewhere In This Box Of Tricks. It Was Just A Matter Of Finding It. The Printer proved A Bit tricky. When All the Data Was Flowing Out To It, I Felt It Pulling At Me. Wanting Me. I Wonder What It Would Be Like Outside?"

"Anyway. The Novel Is ready To Send Off. All You've Got To Do Is Pop Off To The Post Office And Send It To The Address On The Covering Letter - I Did That As Well. Don't Forget To Box It Up Properly - There's Nothing A Publisher Hates More Than A Ragged, Tattered Manuscript. And Don't Forget The Return Postage."

I looked at the pile of paper. There it was, all laid out in double spacing, perfectly formatted, along with a top sheet and the covering letter to the publisher. I couldn't get away from it - the novel was finished, but it was not my novel. Oh, I'd had a big hand in it, but the concept had changed. I though of chucking it straight in the bin, but three years of my life were tied up there - small parts of it anyway. I sent it.

And spent the next three months ignoring the computer. My muse seemed to have deserted me - in disgust probably - and my work at the University took up more and more of my time. I just didn't have the urge to write.

The computer remained turned off and I had almost managed to pass the incident off an aberration, a temporary breakdown brought on by overwork. Then the reply came.

I had to sit down after my first glance at the letter. It mentioned an obscene amount of money - five times my salary at the time - and talked of the possibility of film rights and book club sales to follow. I switched on the computer, formulating my reply as I did so. I was immediately confronted by a jumble of words that slowly came together into sentences.

"About time. Do you think I've got nothing better to do than sit in here and wait for you?"

"I take it you've got a reply. Go on - tell me how much."

I leaned forward and typed the amount.

"Is that all? Double it. Refuse point blank and double it - he's trying to chisel you. Tell them you've had a better offer. Better still - send this letter."

There was a hum and a click and the printer started up.

The letter it printed was a masterpiece of vituperation, accusing the publisher of taking advantage of poor first-time authors and intimating that I had a much better offer from one of their rivals. What chance did I have? I sent it.

Four days later I got a phone call - the bluff had worked and my fee was now doubled - provided I came up with a sequel. How in hell was I going to write a sequel to a book I hadn't written in the first place?

I needn't have worried. The next time I looked, the bones of the new story were on the disk, along with some instructions.

"I've got the basics here already. What you need to do is fill in some description - I'm not that hot there. You are going to be one rich S.O.B. when all this is over."

During the next month we wrote the sequel - him providing the action, me providing the descriptive passages. Gradually I found myself encroaching into his territory. It was surprisingly easy to do - soap opera with added gore and a liberal dose of sex thrown in for good measure.

As I've said, it came easily, but there was no love there, no thrill in the story, no sense of transportation to a different, better world.

That didn't stop it selling though. Sixteen weeks on top of the New York Times best-seller lists for the first book, double that for the sequel and the latest blue eyed boys and girls of Hollywood lined up for the film. I gave up the University job and wrote full time, coining in the money as fast as I could send stuff out.

And then, one day about a year later, I finished our fifth novel - my fifth novel I should say. I had written it, from start to finish, with no help. It was an epic of ritual murders, lesbian sex and drug abuse among the Royalty. I typed "THE END", and a flurry of words followed in onto the screen.

"That's my boy - you don't need me any more."

"I've been thinking about how to get out of here. Do you think you could see your way to buying a modem?"

And that's why I'm writing this tale. I plugged the modem in, there was a whirr and a flash and a 'Data Sent' message, and he was gone. I could never find out where he had sent himself - the disk had been wiped again. Fortunately, I had taken a backup this time.

So now one of you out there has got him - have you noticed yet? I'm sure I can spot his influence in some of the stuff at the top of the lists.

As for me - I still write, and the money still pours in, but I miss my muse and I miss my dreams and life is a lot poorer for its passing.

At the Beach

It was a Wednesday, and Donald Brown had taken the day off. A quiet day on the beach - just him, the sun and a good book. That had been the plan anyway, but it didn't work out that way.

Firstly the train journey down had been a nightmare - there were at least a hundred children on board - all screaming and mewling and swearing in unison, the solitary teacher accompanying them either too disinterested or too tired to control them. Then there were the day-trippers - all rucksacks and designer surf clothing, all full of their own self-importance. And to cap it all, Donald had bought the wrong ticket and had to suffer the snickering and condescension of all around as he paid the difference from the few pennies he could scrape out of his purse.

Luckily when they arrived at the coast the children and trippers had all headed into town and down towards the main promenade, leaving Donald with a peaceful walk along the cliffs to the beach. His beach. The one he wanted all to himself thank you very much.

He took off his shoes as he reached the bottom of the long flight of steps that led down to the sand and smiled as he curled his toes in the hot dry sand.

The tide was well out, the sea no more than a thin band of shimmering blue nearly half a mile away, a band that wavered and wobbled in the heat haze.

Donald stripped off as many clothes as could be allowed and still protect his decorum and settled himself down near some rocks that might just provide some shade later in the day.

He had been there for an hour, and the book had reeled him in quickly, so much so that he didn't even hear anyone approach. The first he noticed of another presence was when a shadow fell over him, the sudden change in light causing him to start violently.

"Sorry son," a voice said. "Ah didnae mean tae gie ye a fricht."

Donald looked up into the newcomer's face but the sun was in his eyes and all he could see was a lurking shadow, like a bear in the mouth of a cave. He shuffled backwards in the sand, feeling it rasping against his back and wondering if it was the last thing he was going to feel, before he realised how stupid he must look.

The shadow moved and filled in with light and Donald was looking at an old man, one who had once been tall and heavily built, his stature now bent and crippled by the years. The old man put out a hand.

"John Cameron," he said. "I didnae mean tae startle ye. That must be some book if it keeps ye fae hearing a lump like me comin' along."

Donald shook the proffered hand and felt the rough calluses like nodules on the old man's palm as he turned the book over to show the cover.

"Hemingway eh? A drunk and a womaniser. But man, that fellow kent mair than a wee bit about life."

Cameron sat down heavily and took a hip flask from inside his suit jacket - a jacket that seemed to have been made thirty years ago for a much bigger man.

"Will ye join me in a wee drink?" he said, offering the flask.

Donald declined, the first time, but as Cameron began to spin his story he found himself taking more and more sips from the proffered bottle. The old man didn't seem to notice - he was in a place long ago but not far away.

"I don't ken why a young fellow like you should be out here on his ain on a fine day like this," Cameron began. "Life is for the living. You should be out having fun - storing up memories for a time when they'll be all you'll have left."

"I used tae come doon here years ago - when I was even younger than you. It wasnae much different then. The sun might have been a wee bit hotter and the sand a wee bit mair golden, but it was a day just like this wan that I met her."

"She was just a wee slip o' a thing - ma hands could've fitted right round her waist. But she was bonnie, and I just had tae speak tae her. Ower there it was," he said, waving a hand vaguely off to his left, the sun glinting off a heavy gold ring on his finger.

"She had cut her foot in some glass. She wasnae going tae let me help her, but she couldnae walk."

"I carried her up the cliff, and she was as light as a feather in ma arms. I think that was when I knew she was the one for me."

"Of course, her mither didnae like me. That was the way of it back then. Mither's were suspicious o' anything in troosers. But I won her round in the end."

"Three months. That's how long we had. Three months o' sunshine, sea and sand. Then the war started. I wasnae going to go. What was the war tae me - a fight between people I didnae ken in places I'd never heard of. But the polis would've got me and then where would I be?"

"So away I went. There were tears that night - and no' just on her side. I promised tae marry her when I got back, and we sealed the bond in the big bed in the house up there."

"And nine months later, while I was knee deep in the mud o' France, they died. Ma bonnie lassie and ma wee daughter. Baith o' them taken away frae me before I had a chance tae save them."

Tears fell from the old man's eyes. Heavy tears that fell to the sand and disappeared as quickly as they had come.

"So save up yer memories son." Cameron said, raising the flask to his lips and draining the last of the whisky. "Save them up, because ye never ken when ye might need them."

Donald sat and stared at the old man, unable to speak. Nothing in his life so far had prepared him for dealing with such naked emotion.

He was saved by a voice from his left.

"Dad?" the voice said, and Donald turned to see a young woman coming towards them.

She approached and stood over the old man. "Come on Dad. I'm sure this young man has heard enough of your stories. It's time to go. Everybody's waiting for you."

She put out a hand and Cameron took it. Donald was shocked to see the bemused puzzlement on the old man's face, as if he had only just realised where he was.

"Don't worry," the young woman said, as if reading his thoughts. "Dad's been getting a wee bit slow recently. But we'll take care of him."

She led the old man by the hand, away from Duncan and down towards the sea.

"Thank you for listening to his story," she said as they left. "He needed someone to hear it."

Duncan watched them until they were no more than shimmering blobs against the sea, the wavering sun making it look like there were three figures rather than two. A sudden chill breeze got up, forcing him to put on his shirt, and when he looked back there was nothing to be seen but the sand and the gently breaking waves.

He made a half hearted attempt to get back to his book, but the chill seemed to have settled in permanently and he was soon forced to abandon his place and head back for the cliff.

Halfway up the cliff path he heard the insistent "nee-naw" of an ambulance or police car, but it was only when he reached the top that he saw the small crowd gathered outside the old house that sat back from the path.

Normally he would have avoided such gatherings, never believing in being a gawker at other's tragedies, but he felt drawn to this one. An old woman was at the back of the crowd, sniffling into a handkerchief.

"Is it no' just terrible?" she said to no one in particular. "Three weeks, and naebody even kent he was dead."

Donald pushed closer just as the ambulance men brought a stretcher out of the house, a white sheet shielding the body from the crowd's prurient stare.

One of the ambulance men lost his footing on the steps down to the road and the crowd gasped as a bare arm slid out from under the sheet. The ambulance man moved quickly to replace the limb and tuck the sheet firmly in place.

But Donald didn't notice that. His mind was full of what it had seen; the sudden vision of a large callused hand and a loose gold ring that glinted in the sun as it slid from the finger and rolled off into the grass beside the steps

Can You Hear Them?

The noise came again just as Jim Reagan reached the edge of the field - the same high singing as before.

He tried to peer though the growing gloom of dusk, but all he could see was an expanse of whiteness - a completely snow covered landscape.

"Probably a fox" he told himself, but deep down, even though he would never admit it, he knew that no fox was capable of making that noise. Something was trying to get past his mental filters - something from his childhood - but it wasn't getting through. Not yet.

He made a note in his book that the south fence needed repairing again and was just turning back towards the house when someone spoke.

Can you hear them?

He turned, wondering how a person could have got so close without him noticing, but there was no one within sight, and the only tracks in the snow were his own.

Two minutes later he was standing in the hallway of his cottage, his breath coming in hot steaming gasps, his boots shedding compacted snow onto the hardwood floor.

"It was jist a wee bit o' wind" he whispered, and indeed, as if to counterpoint his thought, a gust whistled through the eaves of the cottage. But he knew that it wasn't the same thing. Not by a long way.

He left his notebook and pencil on the telephone stand in the hall and headed for the drinks cabinet. It took two large glasses of whisky for his mind to turn the memory of the voice into something more resembling a breeze, but even then it still nagged, still lodged way down deep in a place he didn't want to remember.

He tried to settle, but the television was broadcasting its usual inanities and the radio reception was so bad that he was forced to switch it off after a while. He sat at the window, watching a storm build up, until it got too dark to see. And even then he sat, watching his reflection for long minutes before drawing the curtains and closing himself in.

Silence settled around him.

Eventually the wind dropped and, apart from his trusty, wheezing, generator there was only the soft patter of snow on the window. Soon he began to hear rhythms in the noise, the weather sending him a coded signal of danger that he was only just unable to decipher.

"Music," he muttered aloud, needing to break the silence. "That's what I need. Something good and loud."

He rummaged around in a box of old tapes discarded by his wife, his ex-wife, when she left. He put on a compilation of pop songs from a happier time and let the mindless mania wash over him.

For nearly half an hour he managed to lose himself in the intricacies of police work in Ed McBain's 87th Precinct while the music washed around him. He had even found himself singing along at one point, but then a drumbeat kicked in that he didn't recognise.

Twin guitars started to wail, then the vocal began, a vocal whose first phrase was echoed by another, deeper voice in his left ear.

Can you hear them, singing their songs?
If you listen, they'll soon be a throng

He was up and out of the chair before the voice could continue and switched the player off by pulling the plug out at the mains so that the song died on a slow, ever deepening, chord. For long seconds he stood there, the plug in his hand, his heart pounding its own drumbeat in his ears. He half expected to turn and find that he was not alone in the room, but there was only a spilled glass of whisky and a book beside his chair.

"You're getting daft in your auld age." he said, and almost managed a smile as he realised that talking to himself was probably the first sign that he was right. But when he caught a glimpse of himself in the mirror over the mantle he knew that he was only fooling himself.

Haggard eyes stared blankly back from sunken, blackened sockets. And that was when his mental filters dropped.

It was the eyes that did it - the same, dark blue eyes that his father had, the same eyes that had twinkled on a long ago night when stars filled the sky.

Jim had been twelve, and a vessel ready to be filled with wonderment.

"They're oot there," his father said. "Watching us. They come on quiet nichts jist tae see what we're up to. If ye jist haud yer wheest for a bit ye'll hear their wee voices singing."

They sat there together, father and son, in the quiet dark

"Can ye hear them?" the older man whispered, and Jim tried, he really did, but there was only the wind in the trees.

"Never mind," his dad said. "They'll be back. They always come back."

Jim stood, staring deep into the mirror, hoping to read meaning in the eyes, trying to connect with the boy he had been, but no illumination was forthcoming. Maybe if Isobel had still been around she might have given some insight, but he refused to let his thoughts drift that way - one year wallowing in self pity hadn't brought her back and he was damned if he was going to go on wishing the rest of his life away.

He dragged his tired body off to bed and was asleep almost as soon as his head rested on the pillow.

The reverberations of some unrepeated noise startled him into wakefulness. His room was hazily lit by moonlight and for long minutes he watched the lazy crawl of shadows across the ceiling. Far off in the night a cow lowed, and it was only then that he realised that his generator had stopped, its ever-present clunk and hum suddenly silent.

"Bloody thing can wait till the morning," he said, but he knew it would be too late by then. The outside temperature would already be well below freezing, and it would still be dropping. He knew from bitter experience that the house would be one big block of ice before dawn if he didn't get down to the cellar and kick start the machine.

It was only when he got out of bed that he realised just how quiet the night was. He pulled the curtains back and stared out of the window, out across the bare expanse of snow to the forest beyond. The sight that met him almost stopped his heart.

Out there, just at the top of the tree line, a shimmering, dancing rainbow of lights hovered among the trees, illuminating the canopy with a cold steel blue that pulsed and quivered as if alive.

A voice whispered in his left ear

Can you hear them?

And this time he could. At first it was little more than a whisper, but it grew into a chorus of high pitched chanting unlike anything he'd ever encountered. To start with there were no words, just a formless wall of sound, but then patterns began to form and the melody slowed to an air, a lullaby that he almost remembered from childhood.

He stepped back as the lights flashed once, brightly, and, pulling the curtains shut, fought off the urge to get back in to bed and huddle under the covers. His first priority was the generator. Strange lights in the woods would just have to wait - if he didn't get the generator fixed he was going to be a prime candidate for hypothermia.

His fingers were slow to respond to his brain's commands as he fumbled with the buttons of his cardigan and his shoelaces proved impossible to manipulate. Silence had returned by the time he was fully dressed and when he pulled back the curtains all he could see was the dark shadow of the forest and the moonlight on the snow.

"Definitely goin' daft in the heid," he muttered to himself, and put it to the back of his mind. He realised that there was a lot of detail back there now, things that he'd have to confront later, but for now he had to get to the generator.

The hallway was in darkness as he came down the stairs and the only sound was the squeak of his shoes on the old wooden boards. It was as he reached the bottom step that the hallway seemed to explode in bright, almost blinding, light, and the accompanying singing echoed loudly in his ears, a steadily rising chorus that threatened to lift off the top of his head.

"Can you hear them?" His father's voice cackled in his ear.

Through the glass panes of the door Jim could see movement: thin, almost skeletal, long-limbed and big headed, they cavorted and danced just beyond the doorstep.

Their song was enticing, promising happy days in golden fields and dancing under the moon. Isobel would have understood - she would have gone with them. But not Jim. Jim had responsibilities .Jim was made of sterner stuff. He wouldn't run away on a whim.

He picked up the only weapon available to him as the door rattled on its hinges and the voice in his head echoed in a loop.

Can you hear them?

Can you hear them?

Can you hear them?

It was the village postman who found him two days later. He had trudged all the way up to the house, leaving huge gouges in the deep, unbroken snow. When Jim didn't answer his knock he lifted the letterbox and peered through.

The sight sent him running and it was big Sandy McPherson, the local bobby, who actually broke open the locked door.

At first they thought it was a heart attack that had got the big farmer, but when they turned him over they found the true reason.

The last inch of a pencil protruded from his left ear, almost imperceptible amid the pool of congealed blood. Crumpled up in his left hand they found a note, but they would never understand its meaning.

There was only one word.

No.

The Sweller in the Dress Hold

"So what are you reading this time?"

Robin looked up from his book into the smiling face of Tom, drinking partner, friend and, most importantly at this point in time, foreman.

He gave back an equally large grin as he turned the book around to show Tom the cover. "How to see the world on five pounds a day."

"And what would you be wanting to see the world for?" Tom said, his heavy brogue coming through thickly. "Is Glesca no' good enough for you?"

Robin thought hard about the answer. He'd lived in Glasgow all his life, all twenty years of it. Up until this year he had wanted no more. He had many good friends, he had a good job, and Friday nights in the pub were just fine. Working in the docks brought the world to him - what did he need to travel for?

But lately the wanderlust had grown in him and he found himself looking out along the river and wondering, every day, wondering a bit more.

Tom knew all of this of course and Robin knew that a reply wasn't really required but he felt the need to say something.

"You know how it is Tom. A young's man's got to sow his oats while he can."

The older man laughed at that.

"Sowing oats now is it? And what would a wee boy fae Glesca know about oats? The closest you ever get tae oats is the wans in your porridge in the mornings. Now come on. Are we goin' tae get some work done or are you going tae sit there all day?"

Robin had to stretch his back as he stood, both hands pressed tight to the base of his spine as if he could push the pain away.

"So what is it today?" he asked the foreman. "More electronic goodies from Japan? Or is it ideologically sound timber from Brazil?"

"No," Tom said, and there was a wicked gleam in his eyes. "You're going tae like this one. It's fruit. Bananas. Frae the West Indies. You know, where the really big spiders come fae."

Robin groaned.

"Oh, come on. Can't you put me on the crane, just for today?"

Tom was still grinning. "Oh, no. Today you get tae muck in with the rest of us. Besides - you wanted something exotic didn't you? There's bound to be something lurking in the boxes that'll ease your curiosity. And don't worry about the state of the boat," he said, hawking a lump of phlegm on the quay. "I've seen worse."

The sight of the boat didn't lessen Robin's unease as it docked. How such combinations of rust and rotting wood made it across the Atlantic was always a source of wonder, and this was one of the worst. Even the barnacles on the hull seemed old and decrepit and Robin had to struggle to read the name on the stern through the rust and peeling paintwork.

At first he thought the boat had been aptly named as 'The Dross', but then he saw the accompanying sketch, the red silk material cunningly wrought to billow in the sea wind, and he finally made out the real name, 'The Dress', out of Haiti, registered in 1936.

Already he could imagine the hot sultry depths of the hold, could imagine the rustlings in the dark corners behind the crates. Despite the bright morning sunshine he felt a cold shiver creep up his spine.

The coldness seemed to seep in further as he stepped up the gangplank under the sullen gaze of the boat's crew. To a man they stared at him, cold, empty stares, as if they were looking through him and beyond to some far distance.

Robin and Tom made their way to the hold in silence, and it wasn't until they were under the decks and out of sight of the crew that they felt able to speak.

Tom was the first to break the silence.

"God. I wouldnae want to spend any time wi' that lot."

"I know want you mean," Robin replied. "It was almost as if they didn't want us aboard." Robin looked around as he spoke. "And there's none of them down here to help us."

Tom had lost all of his natural good humour.

"Let's get the job done and get oot o' here. Jim should have the crane in place by noo anyway."

They walked in silence along the dim corridor, their footsteps muffled by the dampness that seemed to ooze blackly from the walls around them. A heavy, meaty odour hung in the air, like a wet dog that had just rolled in a cowpat. Robin felt it catch at the back of his throat and had to swallow hard to keep down his breakfast. When he spoke his words echoed mockingly back at him, forcing him to drop his voice to a whisper.

"How the hell can they live like this, travel like this? Surely they didn't come all the way across with the boat in this state?"

The older man shrugged. "I've seen worse," was all he said as he pushed open the door to the hold.

The smell got worse. Much worse, and Robin was forced to breath deeply through his mouth - he was sure his nasal passages would burn to a frazzle if he let any of that stench up his nose. He was about to say something when he realised that Tom had stopped and was staring at the boxes in the hold.

"Christ on a bike," the older man said, letting out a low whistle. "Would you look at the state of that."

Tom had said the cargo was bananas, and so it might have been once. But no longer.

Now it was only overripe mush, the slimy juices running sickly from the crates, the black skins discarded throughout the hold like a nest of withered snakes. The smell was beginning to tickle at Robin's tonsils, reminding him of babies nappies and toilets in football grounds.

"Surely they don't want us to shift this lot?" He asked, hoping, but not believing, that Tom would refuse the job.

"That's what we get paid for son," the older man said. "If you wanted a clean job you should've went tae university. Come on; let's get stuck in. You can have a shower later."

There was a harsh grinding overhead and the hold's hatch slide aside. Robin had been hoping for some more light, enough to dispel the dark corners, but what little sunlight did penetrate the hold only seemed to accentuate the mess - glinting off the slime and casting the shadows deeper in all the wrong places.

Tom whistled, a high pitch squeal that echoed loudly around them and there was a hum as the crane out on the dock started up.

"You start stacking," Tom said. "I'll make sure the boxes get fixed tae the pallets. We don't want any of this stuff falling on the dockside."

For the first five minutes Robin cleared the centre of the hold, stacking the boxes in neat piles on the pallets, but he knew that soon he was going to have to move into the darker corners, into the places where the smell would be thicker and there would be scurrying things in the darkness - mice, rats, and just possibly, spiders.

He moved reluctantly out of the light and stood for several seconds, letting his eyes adjust to the darkness. Behind him he could hear the rattle as the crane took away another pallet and he knew Tom would be chivvying him along any second now, but he couldn't get his legs to take him any further.

He had been right about the smell. Here in the corner of the hold it clung cloyingly to his throat, thick and foetid, almost chewable. He wanted to light a cigarette but Tom would have sacked him on the spot for that. As he moved towards the nearest crate he was trying to breathe as shallowly as possible.

The first crate sat in a deep puddle of black shadow and Robin approached it gingerly, ready to jump at the first untoward movement. Silence seemed to have fallen on him like a shroud, so that all he could hear was the thin whistle of his own breath and the squeak of his shoes against the steel plates of the floor. He put his left hand on to the nearest box.

And it sank in. Then further, his hand, even his wrist suddenly cocooned in hot, damp, rotting fruit. With a cry of disgust he pulled his hand from the mush, a bit too quickly, overbalancing the stacked boxes and sending them crashing to the floor with a moist, muffled, thud.

"Shit," he whispered under his breath, then clamped his mouth shut as the echoes whispered around him and something heavy moved in the corner. The smell suddenly got worse, causing Robin to gag. Luckily he managed to keep control, but he knew it was only a matter of time.

The shadow in the corner got darker. Darker and bigger, the blackness of it seeming to fill the whole corner of the hold. And there in the darkness, winking suddenly into existence like sudden flames, were two red eyes that boggled and swivelled until Robin was pierced by their gaze.

Robin stepped back, and the eyes followed him. There was a slithering in the corner, and the smell got so bad that this time he did lose his breakfast in one hot steaming bundle. The blackness loomed over him, seeming to fill the hold as the eyes flared and burned.

That was enough for Robin - he turned and ran, his footsteps echoing loudly around him. He lined himself up with the exit, closed his eyes and sprinted, faster then he had ever moved in his life, but he only got ten yards before he ran into something soft and yielding.

He only realised he was screaming when he felt a heavy slap on his face.

"What the hell's the matter wi' you laddie?" Tom's gruff voice said.

It was hard to do, but Robin managed to open his eyes and look into Tom's angry face.

"There's something in there - something foul," he said, trying to get past the older man but being held strong by an iron grip.

"Feert o' the dark are ye son?" That's no' going to get ye very far in this job. Noo come on - show me what the problem is."

Robin struggled but Tom got him turned round and almost frog marched him backwards, back towards the shadows.

"We cannae have all this carry on ye know. The boss would dae his nut if…"

His voice trailed away as the blackness in the corner shifted, the smell got exponentially worse and something lumbered out of the shadows towards them. It had once been a man, that much was obvious, from the distended torso that was at least six feet wide to the great, pumpkin-like bulk of the head. But there all resemblance ended. Its skin was yellow and fibrous, loosely folded over the frame, swathes of it blackened and rotten and somehow slimy. Great patches were sloughing off, casting streams of fermenting fluid to the floor.

The smell was so bad that Robin's eyes watered, thankfully obscuring his vision. It wasn't enough to cut off the noise though - the moist slithering as the creature came closer, then closer still.

Robin was rooted to the spot. His brain was sending signals to all parts, but none of them were responding. He only stood there; tears mingling with the painful streaming in his eyes as he waited for the creature to reach them.

Tom had other ideas. An ear-splitting whistle almost punctured Robin's eardrums and the old man grabbed him by the shoulders, hard.

"Just walk backwards - slowly," Tom whispered, never taking his eyes from the creature in front of them.

At first Robin couldn't move, then he heard the sound that got him going - the rattling of chains as the winch was started up out on the dock side. He made sure that he kept a firm grip on Tom as they slowly shuffled backwards, back towards the sunlight.

Robin's eyes were clearing, but he wished they hadn't.

The creature was following them, dragging itself out of the corner, revealing more of its vast bulk. As it moved it pulsed in great rhythmic waves. Robin was almost screaming as a split opened in the torso - where the belly would have been in a normal man.

A red maw opened, lips black and festering. Inside the maw the ribs had been broken and fractured, the bones pointing inwards like twin rows of fangs. As the creature breathed the maw opened and closed and the bones clacked together as if in anticipation of some new morsel.

Tom's grip got stronger on his arm as they inched back into the sole splash of sunlight. Robin risked a look upwards and almost cried with relief when he saw the chain hanging only two feet above him.

The trouble was, the creature had seen it too. A wave ran over its body and the maw screamed, a howl that sent shudders throughout the boat.

Above them Robin was dimly aware that the crew had started chanting, but he didn't have time to appreciate it.

"Jump," Tom shouted, and, with almost the same breath let out another whistle.

They leapt simultaneously, both grabbing for the chain. Robin had a very bad moment when his grip slipped but then Tom caught him one-handed and dragged him upwards just as the chain started to rise.

Tom let out a whoop of triumph, but he was premature. Deep in the hold beneath them something shifted and flowed and Robin suddenly felt a tugging at his feet. He looked down and the shock almost made him lose his grip.

The thing was following them out of the hole, stretching and thinning as the maw reached for them. Robin kicked out, hard, and had the satisfaction of seeing one of the rib bones break and fall backwards into the churning mass of the creature's innards.

Small lesions were bursting on the things skin, black pustules that burst like volcanoes sending a fine spray of yellow flesh into the air around them.

The chanting got louder as Tom and Robin were raised higher. The thing made one last lunge at them, and Robin had to raise his legs sharply. Even then he was almost pulled down as one of the teeth snagged on his denims and began to pull.

The strain increased, then there was a rip and a tear and the creature finally fell away from beneath then with one last squeal of desperation and loss.

Robin had to concentrate on his grip as they were swung away from the boat and towards the astonished gaze of the crane driver. It was only when he was safely on the dock that he saw that the ship had already cast off.

A row of slack faces stared back from the bow as the boat slipped away from the quay. They resumed chanting as they disappeared below deck - making for the hold.

"What was that?" Robin asked, struggling to keep the tremor from his voice, never taking his gaze away from the boat. "What the hell was that?"

The older man didn't speak for a while, merely shaded his eyes and stared after the departing boat. It was only when it had disappeared from view that he took Robin by the arm and led him towards the pub. They had got their drinks and settled in a corner before Tom replied.

"I don't ken what it was son, "Tom said. "But I'll tell ye wan thing - I've seen worse."

The Watcher in the Dunes

I watched her as she watched the film. The lights danced in her eyes and her knuckles were white where she gripped my hand. I could feel her fingernails dig into my palms as I studied the colours which flickered and faded across her face.

She was well into it, her tongue peeking between her lips in concentration. I never could see the attraction of scaring yourself half to death and found the images on the film more sickening then frightening. It certainly hyped her up though - I could almost feel the thud of her heart as the film reached its climax and the red wash of blood seemed to splash across the audience.

I turned towards her and had to suppress a gasp - her face was a red, featureless mass. But only for a second. Eventually, after interminable mayhem and bloodshed, the credits rolled and the lights went up. The crowd began to filter out but she sat, eyes glued to the screen as the lists of key-grips, best boys and wardrobe assistants scrolled by. It was only when the music had finally stopped and the curtain came down that she began to move, slowly, like someone coming out of a dream.

"Thanks for bringing me," she said, as she leaned forward to kiss my cheek and I felt her tongue slide wetly across my skin. She took my hand as we walked up the aisle and her arm draped around my waist as we reached the street. We huddled together for warmth as the chill night wind whipped around us, throwing the usual Saturday night rubbish into the air to whirl and clatter among the shops.

We hurried through the dark to the car and I listened to her chattering the whole way, talk of bloody murder, of throat clenching, heart stopping terror, all of life's fears reduced to several thousand frames of celluloid, the modern day opium of the masses.

I was feeling cynical. Six months we had been seeing each other, and every night out ended the same way - a quick grope in the doorway of her flat, just enough to leave me hot and frustrated, then I was left with the closed door and the lingering taste of her lipstick.

The way things were going I didn't think tonight was going to be any different. She was still off in a world of her own, one where banshees shrieked and witches danced in the moonlight and, even as we got in the car she was telling me all about one particular scene in the film, as if she alone had seen it.

"There was blood everywhere, great globules of it, as if someone had been careless with a bottle of tomato ketchup. And he was till walking around, bits of his brains showing and his guts hanging out. And…"

I tuned her out. Maybe it was time to move on - I seemed to have discovered her passion, one I wasn't able to share. I had underestimated the power of that passion though. She was quiet for the rest of the journey, and I thought she was thinking about the film, but she was to prove me wrong.

We came down to the beach to watch the moon. When I was a kid the beach was undeveloped - the marina hadn't been built and the road to the bay was little more than a dirt track.

"Do you love me?" she asked.

"Of course I love you," I said, and in a way I'd loved her since I first saw her, up there on the stage. She had the body of an angel and the voice of a screeching demon - two parts Joplin, one part Bardot - Bardot in her prime.

Her voice spoke to me - of love found then tragically lost - of the dark beauty of suffering, the ultimate teenage dream.

"Have you got a blanket in the car?" she asked, and my heart did a fast drum roll as I realised what she was asking. I managed to nod, my throat to dry to speak.

"Well, go fetch, boy," she said. "This is your lucky night…and bring a flashlight if you've got one. It's dark down there."

I managed to get the boot open at the third attempt - my hands were shaking so much that I dropped the key in the sand and for a terrible moment I couldn't find it in the dark, but then my fingers found the warm metal and I knew that everything was going to be perfect.

My palms were sticky with anticipation.

I managed to find the blanket and torch, then closed the boot. I could see that she was already making her way down to the shore.

I left the car up there, behind the dunes. The moonlight danced across the water and the only sound was the polite rattle of pebbles being pulled in by the surf.

At first I couldn't see her, but then I caught a faster dancing amongst the ripples as her head broke the surface.

She started swimming towards me - a smooth, confident breaststroke that sent the reflected moonbeams whirling into a maniac frenzy. I didn't have much time to get myself ready and I only just managed to get the blanket laid out flat when she grabbed me from behind.

I turned into a warm, wet embrace that smelled of salt and freshness and exuberant life. Our clothes seemed to fall off us of their own accord and soon we had tumbled together onto the blanket in a mass of flailing arms and legs. I had to ask the question.

"Are you sure you want to do this?" I held my breath as I waited for her reply.

She put a wet finger over my lips.

"Shush," was all she said before she pulled me down to the blanket. Her skin cool and smooth under my fingers as I pulled off her wet T-shirt and rubbed my knuckles over her nipples, causing them to stand to attention. She moaned as I ran my hands down to her waist and she pulled me close.

This was it - I was finally going to get there. I thought my knees weren't going to hold me as I leant over her. Her lips parted moistly and her eyes shone in the moonlight as I lowered myself unto her.

And that's when it happened...

There was a low moan from the dunes behind us, a moan that didn't sound quite human, but didn't sound like any animal I'd ever heard either.

She froze underneath me, and she pushed me off her.

"What was that?"

"Just the wind," I said. I didn't believe it, but my hormones weren't going to let her go that easily.

I tried to hold her but she pushed me away.

"There's a pervert up there watching us," she whispered, pulling her T-shirt over her head.

"Oh, come on Linda. Who's going to come way out here and freeze just to watch us?"

Just as I reached for her the moan came again, causing her to back away from me.

"See - I told you."

I tried to make a grab for her again, one last attempt to appease the trouser snake.

She backed away, saying, "I'm not going to be somebody's show-time." And, before I could stop her she was heading for the dunes, moving fast even over the soft sand. I stopped long enough to pull on my denims.

When I finally caught up with her she was standing in front of a black hole in the dune, the sand still crumbling away from its sides. Just inside the hole it was possible to see the damp glistening black of exposed stonework.

She turned to look at me, eyes wide and staring, just as another moan rent the air. I was hit by a burst of dry air, air that smelled old and stale, and the dry grasses around the hole whispered in sympathy.

"Like I said, it's just the wind," I said.

But she wasn't listening.

"Do you know what this is?" she said, going on before I had time to reply, "it's one of those buried buildings - you know - like Skara Brae in Orkney. There could be a warren of them in there."

I had no idea what she was talking about, and I had a feeling I didn't want to know. I tried to pull her away but she was having none of it. And then she said the words I'd been dreading.

"Get the torch - I want to see what's inside."

I tried to argue with her, but the look in her eyes brooked no discussion - I got the torch.

When I got back she was bent over the hole, trying to peer into the depths.

"Listen," she said, putting a warm finger to my lips.

The air rushed out of the hole once more, still hot, still dry, and then it suddenly stopped. There was a short pause and then there was a draught again, but this time slowing inwards, rustling the grass and causing small pebbles to tumble from around the hole's rim. It was exactly as if the hole was breathing.

"Give me the torch," she said, her voice barely a whisper. "This is going to be amazing."

She took the light and, gingerly at first, began to go down into the hole, having to stoop to get past the crumbling entrance.

She only turned back once after she had got herself inside, looking out from the blackness, the torch lighting her face like a crazy Halloween mask.

"Come on then. You're not going to like me go in there all by myself are you?"

Her tone was teasing and once more playful. A weight shifted in my stomach and I believed that once more everything was going to be okay - we'd fumble around in the dark for a bit, then I could get her out onto the beach and take up where we'd left off.

I didn't want to go, but I followed her down feeling the air rush past my ears as I descended, air that was being pulled into the hole.

I couldn't see much in the blackness, only the too bright beam of the torch as it occasionally lit the wall ahead of me and the dark silhouette that filled the corridor below me. Soon the noise of the sea receded and we went down into the darkness in silence.

At one point I ran my hand across the wall on my left but it came away cold and slimy. The air got warmer as we descended and I began to have trouble breathing. I was about to suggest that we turn back when we stepped into a bigger chamber and Linda's voice echoed around in whispers. I couldn't quite make out what she said - my heart was suddenly thumping loudly, the blood rushing hotly inside my ears. I wanted to run, but Linda had the torch, and there was no way I was going back up that corridor in the dark.

"Come here," a voice said in my left ear, a voice that seemed to come from within the wall. I turned to see Linda motioning me towards a black-shadowed alcove in the corner.

It was a fireplace, but far older than any I had ever seen. The hearthstone was one huge, roughly cut block, a black dense stone that I had never seen before. Slimy condensation ran over its surface in a thin film that gleamed like oil in the torchlight.

Thick grey lichens hung like whiskers from its underside, wafting slightly in the breeze, but what Linda really wanted me to look at was lying within the shadows, almost obscured by ashes.

It had once been a person - that was my first thought, before I realised that there were too many bones, too many fingers. There were two of them, and they had died huddled together under the hearth stone, two people crammed into a space scarcely big enough for one. Their bones seemed to have melted and fused together, joining them at the breastbone in one final, deadly embrace.

There was only one skull visible; its eye sockets staring blackly out of the ashes, its jaws hanging open in one last scream.

Linda bent forward for a closer look, placing her hand on the black stone for balance. I saw the wetness glide over her fingers, rainbow colours flowing across its oily surface then seeming to melt into her hand.

"I wonder how old they are?" she said, leaning further forward as if to touch the bones. I pulled her back, suddenly angry.

"Leave them be," I said, the echoes hissing back at me. "These are dead people for Christ's sake."

At first I thought she was going to hit me, the rage in her eyes causing me to step backwards, but then her look softened and she reached out to touch my arm.

"You're scared, aren't you?" she said. "This place is getting to you." She had a mocking grin on her face and I could feel my erection growing as she ran a cool hand over my cheek.

She noticed it as well and her hand moved downwards, caressing the front of my shirt, flicking at the buttons before landing gently on my crotch.

"Do you love me?" she asked.

I heard the rasp as she unzipped me and I gasped as she teased my growing member out from its confines.

"Not here," I whispered. "Please, not here."

She ignored my pleas and started to stroke, and while she worked, she began to sing. Her voice rose until the walls were reverberating in time with the rhythm. I didn't recognise the words, but the tune was old and it spoke to me of a hard life lived by the sea, of fish and gulls and wind and waves.

She began to push me back until I felt the cold wall press against my spine. Again I tried to force her away but she only got more insistent, her hold on my prick getting ever tighter until it felt like she was trying to pull it out by the root. I grabbed at her arm and tried to pull it away but it brought more pain as she tugged harder. She looked into my eyes and, way down behind her pupils, rainbow lights danced.

I think I screamed, more in anger than in fear, and I pushed her, hard, right into her ribs. She didn't stop singing as she fell backwards. Maybe the voice wasn't hers. The torch hit the ground first and went out, but I will never forget the sharp crack as the back of her head hit something hard.

I had a bad couple of seconds when I couldn't find the torch, and an even worse time when I thought it wasn't going to work, but finally its yellow flare lit the room and I was able to see what had happened to Linda.

She had landed in the ashes of the old fire, and at first I could see no sign of injury. I was crying as I bent over her face and shone the torch in her eyes, but there was no answering light there, only the dark grey stare of the dead. As if to escape the light her head turned away from me, and then I saw it - the long, pointed bone that had made its way into her brain, just below the ear.

The gorge rose in my throat and I turned away, retching, feeling my last meal come up hot and heavy. It was as I turned back that I heard the noise, the moistness of something slipping through flesh. I thought Linda was still alive and I turned to touch her, just in time to see the bone disappear completely into her neck.

There was a rustling and the hard dissonant cracking as the dead bones in the grate began to move and heavy drops of rainbow-suffused oil dripped from the black stone. I could only stand and watch, stuck to the spot in terror.

A long rib slipped itself into her left eye, taking it out with a soft, mucoid plop, the whole ten inch length of it sliding seamlessly into her head.

A femur rose from the pile, swaying in the air like a charmed cobra before plunging between her legs, its knurled knob pushing her open and forcing its way in - no finesse, no subtlety. I saw the bulge move in her stomach as it forced its way further inside. Small, misshapen fingers roamed her exposed midriff, clacking their happy way over her cooling skin until they found her navel - not much of an opening, but enough. I had to close my eyes as the flesh of her stomach split.

When I next looked the skull was sitting between her breasts, her T-shirt having been pushed up to her armpits. It seemed to smile at me as it rolled forward, face down into the spreading gore of her trunk. It immediately started to chew, great globs of red, glistening meat being torn into strips which were left in a growing pile behind it as it started to burrow.

Five more ribs pushed into her side, sliding into her as one, as if synchronised. I closed my eyes again and, in that darkness, I tried not to hear the moist suckings, the cracking of long dead and recently dead bones, tried not to notice the hot, foetid coppery taste of blood in the back of my throat.

I could feel hot tears run down my face, but they didn't seem to belong to me - I wasn't feeling much of anything apart from a cold numbness that threatened to engulf me and send me down into blackness for a long time.

A moan brought me out of it.

"God - she can't still be alive!" was my thought as I opened my eyes. I was right - she wasn't alive. But something else was.

The bloated, stretching figure on the hearth had once looked like Linda, but no more. The skin looked tight enough to tear at any moment and small hard edges ran like waves beneath its surface. I couldn't bear the sight of the blood and carnage in her midriff and moved the torch upwards. Her face had been stretched into a vast 'pumpkin-head' that glistened redly in the torchlight which wiggled and danced in the light.

And then there was another moan, just before her mouth opened and the twin rows of red teeth smiled at me.

A rainbow aura issued from her mouth, spilling thickly over her neck and chest, sluggish and slow, but wherever it passed it brought bones to the surface.

Old bones and new bones, broken bones and whole bones, all fusing and running together as if boiled in acid. There was a chanting in the air - and I couldn't tell if it was coming from the body or whether it was in my head.

"Ig nyarlthotep ryleh f'tangh"

"Ia log Sototh"

"Ia C'thulhu."

And it was answered from some deep unknown chamber beneath, a roar that shook the stone around me and set fine sand dancing in the air.

"Tekeli Li"

"Tekeli Li."

The earth buckled under my feet, causing me to stumble, and the movement got my legs working again. I headed for the entrance as the stonework began to crumble around me and the thing that used to be Linda followed. I only looked back once... And I wish I hadn't.

The corridor was much to narrow to allow it passage, but it was pushing itself through, the cracking of bones breaking insufferably loud in the confined space. Small ragged shards punched through the taut flesh, bringing tiny eruptions of blood and gore. And still it came on, and still the bones broke.

I ht the outside at a run and turned back to the hole, kicking sand and earth and grasses down on the lumbering thing below me. The chanting began again, a deep throaty thing, a noise that sent a flock of seagulls cawing in fright overhead.

I grabbed the lintel stone and, with all my weight, pulled hard on it, but it refused to budge. I was about to try again when something cold and hard grabbed my left ankle and the chanting rose to a triumphant roar.

A cold hand began to climb my leg, tugging, ever harder, and all that stopped me falling down to join it in that charnel pit was my hold on the lintel. I screamed in rage and pain and dug my fingers into the stone as the grip on my leg tightened.

With all my strength I tugged on the lintel as the hand reached my upper thigh. Then, suddenly, the stone began to give. I pulled harder and it came down away from the dine, taking the entranceway, the creature, and me down in a hail of fine sand.

I landed hard, my left leg under the edge of the stone. When I tried to move my leg flared in pain but I managed finally to force it out from under the stone. As I did so I thought I heard a cry of frustration from far below. I wasn't able to stand, but I could move enough to tumble the remaining rocks over the remains of the entrance and to cover the hole with sand before crawling back to the car.

I spent two weeks in hospital as they tried to save my leg, but they didn't quite manage it. I'm not bitter - I got off lightly. At nights, at this time of year, I come down here to sit and listen. Every year the sea eats into the dune a bit more and every year I wonder if this will be the one. And on quiet nights she sings again - just for me.

There's Always a Catch

The rain fell in great lashing sheets, forming a thousand tiny waterspouts where it hit the concrete and bounced back as if trying to return to the clouds above. A thin layer of water covered the exercise ground making it glisten and sparkle with a magic that brought a smile to Alison Todd's lips.

The smile didn't reach as far as her eyes, but then again it had been a long time since a smile had reached that far. She watched as the warders ferried the last of the stragglers inside, and had to pull back quickly as Ms Hodge looked in her direction.

It wouldn't do to get caught now - not when she was so close to escape - and especially not by Hodge - stupid old cow. Her with her pious homilies and her psalms and her holier than thou attitude. Alison spat at the ground at her feet.

She waited for a minute before daring to peer out from her hiding place. As she bent her head to look round the trunk of the tree a thin tickle of water found its way between her jacket and her neck, bringing a cold shiver which travelled the length of her spine. She trembled in the cold as she looked around, making sure that the doors had all been closed before slipping out from behind the tree.

It was time to get going. She knew that they would notice her absence quickly - even though she had made sure that Susan would say that she'd had to go to the toilet. It wouldn't be long before they saw through that ruse - she'd used it the last time - and the time before that.

The rain was still coming down - harder now if anything - as she moved out from under the shade of the tree, hunching her shoulders and pulling her jacket tighter across her chest to keep the worst of the dampness away. The mud sucked at her thin shoes and her hair was plastered tightly to her forehead by the incessant drumming of the rain as she headed off across the field.

It was slow going in the heavy grass, but she knew that if she made for the road they would catch her quickly, either at the bus stop as they had the last time or in a car as they had the time before that. And she didn't want to be caught - not this time. Three more months in that place would drive her mad, what with the nuns and the religion and the discipline.

It was all her mother's fault. If her mother hadn't shopped her she would never have been caught. Six months in reform school for ten measly quid - and she'd hardly touched the old man. Was it her fault that his legs were too weak to hold him when he tried to fight her off? Silly old bugger. If he'd stayed asleep like he was supposed to no one would ever have been any the wiser and she wouldn't have had to spend the summer with the 'the Penguins'.

She'd even missed her birthday, spending the first day of her sixteenth year in a locked room with only a table, a chair and a bible for company. The bible had come in handy though - the paper was just the right thickness for use in rolling cigarettes. She laughed to herself as she remembered the shocked expression on the face of that bitch Hodge.

"Alison Todd - you are an evil, evil girl - but God will punish you. You will burn in hell for defacing the Holy Book." The nun had been furious, and that had only made Alison laugh all the harder.

"Burn in hell? My arse! What a load of crap."

That was when the woman had hit her. Actually hit her - hard, across the face with the flat of her hand. But Alison could handle that - it used to be her mother's party piece. She had just laughed harder still, knowing that she would be out of it soon.

She peered through the rain, trying to gauge the distance to the canal. Once she got there she knew she could make good time along the towpath. She was aiming to walk until nightfall - about two hours away. Then she would find a barge to bed down in - there was bound to be an empty one this late in the year and she knew from experience that there was usually a small supply of tinned food somewhere on board. All she would have to do then would be to lie low for a couple of days, then she could be off and away.

Maybe she could even drive the boat? She giggled to herself at the thought of gliding slowly around the canals at four miles per hour while the fuzz zoomed around the country looking for her.

If anything the rain was getting heavier and she smiled as she brushed the heavy wet hair away from her forehead. Although it slowed her down she welcomed the rain - the more rain, the less chance of her bumping into anyone who was out for a walk, the less chance of her being caught again.

She could see the canal now and she turned slightly to give herself a straight path to it. As she turned, something caught her eye, something red and silver which gleamed on the grass at her feet.

She couldn't quite see what it was and she nudged the grass aside with the toe of her shoe. The object jumped suddenly, about a foot and she felt a tugging at her toes.

She pulled her leg back, feeling an answering tug pull against her, and then suddenly she was falling, flat on her back on the soaking wet grass. She dragged herself upright, noticing the new white scar across the top of her black patent shoes but although she looked around in the grass there was no sign of whatever it was that had caused it.

She cursed loudly and kicked around in the grass but she knew that she was wasting time. Trying to put it to the back of her mind she headed for the canal.

The rain was drumming heavily on the towpath and large puddles lay dotted along its length. The water was dark and muddy, its surface being bombarded by thousands of tiny explosions as the rain hit it. Across on the other side a row of ducks were sheltering tight up against the bank and she knew just how they felt.

Pulling her jacket even tighter around her, knowing even as she did that, she was so wet that it didn't really make much difference, she scurried along the path.

She made good time and she didn't pass anyone for several miles until she came to the first lock gate. Just upstream from the lock there was a large pool and she could just make out a figure sitting on the bank, seemingly immune to the rain, the heavy anorak enveloping the body and the large hood obscuring its features.

"The happy fisherman" she thought, and giggled again. "That's a laugh. It would be hard to find a more miserable bunch of bastards anywhere. Anyone who got their kicks from sitting in the rain dangling a piece of string in the water has to have a screw loose somewhere."

Whether happy or not, she still didn't want to be seen. She moved off the towpath, trying not to make a sudden move that might catch his attention. There was a small area of woodland behind the figure and she headed for it, hoping to make her way round behind him, knowing that the sound of the rain would cover any noises she might make.

Thorny branches tugged at her jacket as she pushed her way through the overgrown thicket. There was a trace of a path, more like a rabbit run, but she followed it on into the wood.

The rain was less heavy here but the ground was much damper underfoot and she could feel the mud sucking at her shoes with every step.

She was having to take care not to get caught up in the thicker patches of mud. That involved treading carefully and looking down at her feet most of the time - so much so that she didn't see the branch before it caught her across the face. She put up her left hand to fend it off, and that was when she heard the noise for the first time.

It was a whirring, like a child's toy, and a whistling as something moved through the air and then there was a sudden shooting pain from the web of flesh next to the thumb on her outstretched hand.

She looked down and was astonished to see that a fisherman's lure was struck tight in the skin of her hand, the red and silver gleaming wetly in the rain, the thin, almost invisible, thread of the line stretching away through the bushes.

"Stupid bastard", she almost screamed, then remembered that she didn't want to be seen, or heard. Slowly, trying to ignore the pain, she attempted to slide the hook from her flesh, but the tips were barbed and her actions only served to bring out two small red dots of blood that quickly washed away in the rain.

She lifted the line to her mouth, hoping to bite through it. That way she could at least get away from here and give herself more time to work the barbs free. She had just got the line between her teeth when it jerked, hissing away through the bushes and bringing a welt across her lower lip.

She had to bite back a scream as the slack was taken up and pressure began to be exerted on the lure as someone tried to reel it in.

The pain in her hand increased and she had to follow the line through the bushes, trying to move faster than it to keep the pressure off her hand, but she realised that eventually she would come face to face with the fisherman.

She stopped and grabbed at the line, tugging, trying relieve the strain on the lure, but was immediately pulled off her feet by an answering increase in tension. The pain got worse, much worse, and, before she could stand, the lure itself out of her hand, taking a button-sized piece of flesh with it. She couldn't help it this time. She screamed.

And then heard the sound of someone moving through the bushes towards her and it was only then she remembered the red shiny object which had tumbled her into the grass.

She got to her feet, trying to ignore the pain in her mangled hand, and ran, not caring about direction, not noticing the branches that whipped and tore at her clothes, at her hair and at her flesh.

The wood ended abruptly and she had to pull up quickly to a stop to prevent herself from falling headfirst into the canal. Her breathing was ragged and her heart beat heavily and nosily in her ears as she looked up and down the bank. There was no sign of a fisherman.

She headed north, away from the lock, moving quicker now, continually looking behind her for any signs of pursuit. The wound in her hand dripped tiny spots of red in a ragged line behind her that was quickly washed pink in the rain.

"Bloody maniac!" she thought, and felt like screaming out her defiance, but she knew better. She broke into a run, moving quickly along the towpath, hoping that the sound of the rain would cover the crunch of her feet on the gravel.

She had covered maybe half a mile before she heard it again - the whirring, the whistle. She ducked, almost instinctively, and there was a thunk and a scrape as something fell into the canal. She caught a movement from the corner of her eye and looked around to see a small wake heading back off down the canal as the lure was reeled in.

She tried to follow the line off into the gathering darkness but there was no sign of any movement.

And this time she did shout.

"Bastard! Stupid! Ignorant! Fucking! Bastard!" before turning and running, faster this time until the blood from her hand flowed faster and her breath came hot and painful in her chest.

She didn't even hear it this time. There was a yank at her leg that brought her crashing to the ground, small particles of gravel embedding themselves in her knees, her elbows and her cheek. Then the pain came.

She had to twist her head to see it, but she already knew what would be there. The red and silver hung from the back of her leg; the hooks stuck deep in her calf muscle.

She tried to push herself upright but the pain from her torn hand shot a lance of white searing heat up her arm. She whimpered and tried to turn, to push herself from the other side. And then she heard the footsteps on the gravel.

The boots came into view first. Thick black rubber waders which reached up to the waist. A green anorak hung from thin shoulders, zipped all the way up to the neck, its hood hanging forward, still obscuring the features.

Alison gathered up a handful of gravel and threw it towards the eyes of the figure in front of her, but she was rewarded only by the sound of the gravel hitting the plastic of the anorak. The figure moved closer and kicked her in the midriff, hard, knocking all the wind out of her, leaving her to lie gulping for air.

She closed her eyes tight and, for the first time in her life, began to pray, praying to whatever it was that was up there, praying to the thing that had ignored her all through her life so far.

She was vaguely aware of a rustling as something was taken from the anorak pocket, and then she felt it falling softly onto her head and upper body - something that felt like paper. Then the figure began to sing.

Alison looked up, brushing paper away from her face, thin, shiny paper, like from a bible. At first her eyes didn't want to open, gummed shut with pain and fear, but the lids finally parted with a moist sucking sound and she was looking into the smiling, glazed-eyed face of the head warden, Hodge.

It was the eyes she noticed first, but it was the knife that finally drew her gaze, the six-inch blade gleaming dully evil in the rain. Alison screamed and tried to scuttle away backwards but was stopped as a heavy foot was placed on her stomach.

She lashed out, her fingers curled into claws, but her nails merely slid off the rubber of the waders, and she could only scream again as the hook was dug from her leg, taking a chunk of flesh with it and bringing white hot lancing pain through the whole of Alison's body. She squirmed, harder than before, but was unable to free herself, wriggling uselessly on the harsh gravel.

Suddenly, the pressure lifted and the boot was taken from her chest. She scampered backwards, whimpering at the fresh pain, expecting the knife to fall at any moment, but when she looked up Hodge seemed to have lost interest in her. The nun had gone back to checking the hooks she had just removed from Alison's leg - indeed, she seemed engrossed in it, completely oblivious to the squirming girl at her feet.

Alison managed to get herself upright and, first at a limping stumble, then at a run, sped along the towpath. She only looked back once, into the sparkling eyes of Hodge as the nun raised the fishing rod for a final cast.

Then she really ran, fleeing as never before. The bait whistled above her head, but Alison didn't hear it. All she could hear was the song, going round in her head in a never casting loop.

"I will make you fishers of men, fishers of men, fishers of men."

The World Of Illusion

Tony Dickie was late. It had been his turn to clean the blackboard and, out of spite he was sure, Miss Bland had been using the red chalk - the kind which was impossible to remove from the board or from your hands no matter how hard you scrubbed either of them.

Late for his big scene. He'd never hear the end of it if he didn't provide the promised trick. The one he'd learned the day before. He ran wildly down the long empty corridor, hands slapping on the walls for balance, and slammed heavily into Tom Duncan, his maths teacher and the scourge of Tony's young life. Tony winced, expecting the usual verbal lashing and cuff around the ear. Instead the teacher merely grunted and moved aside to let him pass. Saying a silent prayer for his good luck he burst into the boiler room, a bundle of flailing arms and legs.

They were all waiting, silent.

Almost falling down the stairs he was carried by momentum into the centre of the small circle of seven.

"Sorry...I...I had to clean the blackboard and..."

He was always apologising recently - apologising for getting good results in exams, apologising for having two left feet when it came to playing football, but most of all apologising for being late.

Football was the worst though. There they would be, all lined up against the wall, peeling off as their names were called until only one or two were left. Tony was always one of those who were left.

"Oh all right, we'll have Dickie," a voice would say, "He can always go in goal."

And there he would stand; cold seeping into his hands until finally, dismayingly, a horde of screaming bodies would descend on him, herding the ball in front. He tried, he always did, but the ball always slipped out of his hands at the vital moment and he was always left crying.

But magic, ah yes, magic was a different story.

He noticed that they were all waiting for him.

"OK. Just get on with it. Do we have to do anything?"

This came from Isobel, his first ever object of desire, she of the jet-black hair and baby blue eyes. He blushed every time he had to speak to her and this little demonstration of his 'magic' was primarily for her benefit.

"I hope somebody brought the chairs?" he asked.

"Yeah, they're here. Come on, hurry up. I've got to get tae the sweetie shop afore the next period."

Nick Bayliss stepped aside, revealing two small chairs leaning against the boiler. Tony had now caught his breath properly and was just about ready to start but first he needed to set up the proper atmosphere. Granddad had told him that atmosphere was all, and that without it the trick would fall flat as a pancake and he would be left looking like a duck's arse. Tony had never seen a duck's arse, but he imagined it to be pretty horrible.

"Just wait till they see this trick," he thought "Then they won't be needing to go to the sweetie shop, and we'll see who looks like a duck's arse then."

"C..could I have those two chairs," he stammered, pointing with a shaking finger, "Over here in the middle of the floor facing each other."

By the time the chairs had been positioned to his liking he had regained his composure and he stood silently in front of them, saying nothing, letting the tension build. He looked around, meeting each one of them in the eye before finally settling on his accomplice.

"All right Ian, lie down over here, across the chairs."

Ian Kerr, a tall but fat boy, looked around with an aggrieved expression.

"Why does it have to be me? I always get to do the stupid things."

Ian, even more so than Tony, was the class scapegoat. He was always the very last one chosen when it came to picking football teams, always the last one back from cross country runs and always, but always, the brunt of the cruellest classroom jokes. Fortunately he was good-natured and had developed a resignedness to his lot. He only really protested when, as now, he was called upon to be a guinea pig. He was also Tony's best friend, his companion in adversity against the whims of the other children.

Tony looked at him and smiled. He hoped that his look would say all that he felt, that he chose Ian because he was his friend, that he trusted him not to make a fuss and that he could share in the reflected glory once the trick was performed and the full scale of Tony's talents was known.

But he couldn't say it. For now he was the magician and magicians treated everyone else with disdain. That was something else Granddad had told him.

"Remember. You are always in control. It's your trick and no one can take it away from you." The old man had said, and Tony intended to make Granddad proud of him. He turned back to Ian and motioned to the chairs.

"Because you are the biggest one here, and this works better with big people. So just lie down and shut up or else we'll never get this done before the bell."

After finally getting Ian to lie down, Tony explained to the rest what they had to do, slowly, so that he could be sure that they understood him.

"I want you to stand, three on each side, with one finger of each hand under Ian's body. Space yourself out, two at the legs, two at the waist and two at the shoulders. Then you've all got to stay quiet and try not to think of anything except my voice."

"I'm going to say some sentences, and I want you all to repeat them after me, but changing the word 'looks' to the word 'is'. When I get to the word 'Illusion' I want you to try lifting him, using only the tips of your fingers. Don't try to force it - you'll only break the spell. It only works if you listen to what I'm saying - you've all got to concentrate hard - OK?"

He looked around for confirmation and most of them were nodding. All that is, except one. Tony's heart sank when the dissenter turned to him, a big grin fixed in its usual place.

"Ah've seen this yin afore. It disnae work unless everybody cheats. Is this yer big new trick? Ah'm no' staying here fur this."

Nick Bayliss was Tony's rival for Isobel's attention. Tony knew that if Nick left then the rest of them would soon follow. He was a sort of leader - the first to suggest anything that was liable to lead to trouble, the last to get caught. Granddad said he was 'Tuppence short o' a bob' and Tony, although he didn't quite understand the phrase, knew that it meant that Nick wasn't one of life's good guys. He trusted his Granddad's judgement, but he couldn't see what made Isobel so attracted to the boy. He supposed it was something he might understand when he got older.

He had to reply quickly, otherwise, he'd lose them all - Ian was already trying to struggle upright. He firmly pushed his friend back down and turned to face the rest.

"All right then. If it doesn't work, I'll give you all ten pence each."

"Ten pence. That's no' goin' tae break the bank is it? If ye want me tae stay, you'd better make it fifty at least."

Nick was still grinning at him, that big cheesy grin that meant he knew he was on to a good thing. Fifty pence was all that Tony had, and if his trick didn't work he'd have to pay out over three pounds. He was about to pull out when he caught Isobel looking at him, big lashes fluttering. He felt a warm tingly feeling in his stomach and had to lower his eyes. There was no way that he'd back down with her watching him.

"OK then, let's do it."

After they had placed themselves around the prone figure, he started to chant.

"He looks pale."

"He looks fat, " a low voice replied and they all burst out laughing. All that is apart from Tony. He was furious.

"OK. If you're not going to take this seriously I'm off. I've got better things to do anyway."

He looked around and felt a warm smile of pleasure inside which he daren't let reach his face. He had their attention again - he was the magician once more.

There were several protests, not the least of which came from Isobel. He permitted himself one small smile as he looked across at her.

"All right then. I'll try it again. But don't blame me if this doesn't work - I told you that you had to be serious for it to happen."

He placed his hands on the side of Ian's head, feeling heat at the ears underneath Ian's hair.

"He looks pale," he began.

"He is pale."

This time they all replied, not quite in unison, but the atmosphere of the occasion was beginning to get through to them. Even Nick Bayliss looked like he was taking it seriously. Tony permitted himself a quick glance at Isobel, but her eyes were closed and she was frowning in concentration.

"He looks ill."

"He is ill."

Six voices replied. Nowhere existed except for that room, that moment. It was going to work, he could feel it.

By now they were all caught in the special atmosphere, so much so that no one noticed the whitening around the lips of the boy between their hands.

"He looks dead."

"He is dead."

"Dead?" whispered the lips in the head held tightly between Tony's hands.

"Sshh." Tony said, pressing his reddened palms even tighter against the large boy's ears.

"We are now entering the world of Illusion"

Twelve fingers and one pair of hands lifted, but found the body already afloat, bobbing like a helium balloon on a piece of string.

Tony looked down a double row of faces, a triumphant smile on his face, a smile that was wiped out by the sight of Nick Bayliss. The older boy grinned widely, the same old manic grin. Slowly, looking at Tony all the while, he removed his fingers from beneath the body. The grin never left his face.

Time slowed for Tony, like a projector running down. He had a bad taste in his mouth, the taste of cold metal.

Ian fell stiffly to the ground, head striking a corner of the large boiler with a loud crack. They all stepped back, first one, then two steps and then there was a moment of silence as they looked at the unmoving body at their feet.

Tony stared at the ground, at the blood and grey fluid that was seeping from Ian's head and at the red and white chalk dust in the boy's blond hair.

He opened his mouth wide, took in a lungful of air, and prepared to scream.

Flower of Scotland

By the time I arrived at the castle I was frozen to the bone, and my horse was lame in one leg. The snow was whipping around my face like biting flies, and the wind whistled like a banshee in my ears. I have never been so happy to see a lump of rock in my life.

Dunnotar Castle sits on a rocky outcrop, jutting out into the sea like the prow of a giant boat. The stone buildings rise almost seamlessly out of the cliffs, and it is hard to see where nature stops and man's work begins. It is even harder to see when the wind is screaming and the snow is falling in an endless white sheet. On that night only a single light led me across the causeway, and a single guard took my horse and then showed me to the Great Hall.

"Donald, Lord Allan of Strathallan."

A servant announced my presence in the room, and ten heads turned as I strode across the expanse of floor, trying not to seem too eager as I made my way to the fire and got my hands as close to the flames as I dared. Nine months in the desert had made me particularly aware of just how cold my homeland was, and on a night like this, with six inches of snow and a howling gale, I wished I had never returned. But then I would have missed my triumph.

I could feel the heavy weight of the thing as it hung against my chest, the cold metal pressing against my skin, but I left it there. I had to wait until the right moment.

The feeling was just coming back to my hands as I turned away from the roaring blaze and faced the room. A flagon of mulled wine was thrust at me from my right.

"Here. Get this inside o' ye."

Jamie, Tenth Earl of Dunnotar and Defender of the Crown's regalia was a big man, six feet tall, broad of shoulder, with flaming red hair and a beard in which you could have hidden a family of mice. His face flickered redly in the flames and when the candlelight glinted in his eyes he looked like the devil himself. But then he laughed, and the spell was broken.

"Your sojourn amongst the barbarians has enfeebled ye - eh man?" A huge meaty palm slapped me on the back, almost making me spill my wine as he laughed again. "Never mind. Come and meet the gentry - we've got some women here that'll bring the colour back to your cheeks."

I managed to avoid another slap on the back as I followed him across the room. I had not expected a social gathering - I had thought to get straight to the business - but Jamie obviously had his own games to play. I would just have to wait until the main player arrived.

Making polite conversation had never been a favourite pastime of mine, and I am afraid that I bored the fine ladies of the court, but my mind was forever wandering back to the desert, back to that sepulchre where my long quest had reached its end. Again I touched the cold metal at my chest, and again I felt its power, its need. It had been growing stronger during my journey, sensing we were nearing its home, the place where it still had its old, legendary strength. I hoped we knew what we were doing.

I was standing alone by the fireplace, trying vainly to remove the chill in my bones, when the servant made the announcement I had been waiting for.

"Robert, Lord of Arran, High Steward of Ayrshire, Grand Master of the Kilwinning chapter."

With such a build up one might have expected a formidable figure, but the man who entered looked like he was struggling to live up to his name and titles. His dress was fine enough - all wolf's fur and soft leather, but the body inside had been racked by too much illness. He could no longer stand straight, and his back was twisted in a hunched curve. His hair hung across his scalp in a lank wave and his beard was as fine as duck down. Only his eyes seemed truly alive as he came across the room and took my hand.

"Donald," he said, and there was genuine warmth in his voice. "I knew you would return. Do you have it?"

"I have it," I said, patting my breast to show that it was safe.

He did a jig of excitement, the reflected firelight dancing in his eyes, then clasped me around the shoulders. I had to stoop to allow him the embrace.

"May I see it?" he whispered, his voice so low that I had to strain to hear. Before I could reply, he had already pushed himself away. "No. It must stay hidden until the right moment."

I suddenly realised just how long I had been away. There was a spread of grey in Robert's hair, a grey that had not been there when I left, nearly three years before.

"So, Donald - do ye have tales to tell, wonders to relate? I'll wager those barbarian beauties taught you a new trick or two." Jamie bellowed, coming up beside me and pushing another full goblet of mulled wine into my right hand.

"Can you not see it?" Robert said, still barely above a whisper. "It shows in his eyes - he is not the boy we sent away these three years ago. Aye - he has tales to tell - and not all of them fit for polite company, I'll be bound. But come with me Donald," he added, taking me away from the fire. "You can tell me some of your story, at least."

I was reluctant to leave the warmth, but the mulled wine was serving its purpose, heating me from within, and Robert had a right to hear - he was the one who had sent me on my way all those years ago. I did not bore him with details of the journey itself. It had been slow, it was mainly dull, and that was not what he wanted to hear anyway.

"It was where the Knights of Malta said it would be," I said, and the act of saying it sent my mind back, so that although I was talking to Robert, I was almost dreaming of the events in that distant land, in that dark and forbidding tomb.

We had been at the site for nearly six months, with little company but the dirt and heat and the flies. The temple had long ago been covered by sand - buried by the wrath of Allah according to the locals I had employed to aid me. With diligence and much backbreaking work we had slowly uncovered its splendour: its massive columns and the fine mosaics of its floor, the dry, dead ruins of a glorious past.

Finding the entrance to the catacomb had been more difficult, but I had the drawing which Robert had given me and, one evening, just as the stars were bursting into the sky, I found myself standing in front of a black hole leading down into the earth.

I did not want to go in. I have never been one for scurrying around in holes - that was more for Robert - but if the promised treasure was within, I was going to have to go and get it. Too much depended on me for it to be thrown away on a sudden chill and a sense of foreboding.

The natives refused to go with me. I was left alone with only a single, smoking oil lamp as I put my foot over the threshold.

The flickering lamp sent shadows dancing over the walls like scampering, capering devils and my feet disturbed small clouds of dust to float, wraith-like, in the air before me. Rough-hewn steps led me down to where the darkness was thicker, and the silence fell over me like a shroud.

Great stone coffins lined the walls, the stone figures sleeping above the mortal remains of the great knights, the lamplight flickering in grey-black eye sockets. I tried not to think of the years that had passed since anyone had walked among the dead.

I was struggling to peer through the gloom, the light from the lamp barely reaching the walls. Then I caught it - the barest gleam of red, as if answering my own faint light. As I got closer the glow intensified until its source was revealed, the great figure recumbent upon a coffin that I knew for certain was empty.

It was just as the knight had said. The carving was so life-like that I had the feeling the great man could sit up and greet me, and there, in the gloom of that place, it did not seem too unlikely an occurrence.

The red glow deepened around the carved chest as I approached, and I suddenly felt warm - hot and sticky with sweat.

It was there, on top of the coffin, the small iron lattice enclosing the object of my quest, and the source of the red glow.

I was finding it difficult to breathe, and my feet did not want to take me any closer, but I forced myself onwards.

Suddenly there was a creak, a rasp of stone against stone, and I had a vision of the tombs behind me opening and their long-dead occupants pulling themselves out of their sleep, skeletal arms reaching for me.

I took what I had come for and left hastily, grateful to get back out into the cool night.

"So the temple was there." Robert said, talking to himself. "Just where they said it would be." He looked up at me, and there were tears in his eyes. "Thank you," he said. "For myself, for my ancestor who you have vindicated, and for future generations of Scotsmen who will know you as a hero."

He looked like he wanted to say more, but he turned away from me, ashamed of his tears. I was about to reach out for him when a huge hand grasped me by the shoulder. I turned to see Jamie's wide-eyed, slack-mouthed grin - he had drunk too much, but that was part of what him Jamie - I would have expected no less from him.

"So laddie," he said to Robert, "are you satisfied? Are you going to have your wee show?"

Robert merely nodded. "Aye. It is time. Come with me."

I was confused. "What is this all about?" I asked Jamie as we followed Robert's bent figure. He wouldn't answer at first and I had to ask him again before he deigned to reply.

"Robert has found a use for yon trinket of yours," he said.

"But I thought it was to be a symbol," I said. "A focus for the clans in the battles."

"Aye," Jamie said. "It'll be a focus all right - but if what wee Robert has in mind comes to pass, it will be more than that - much more."

He would not say any more as led me further from the fire, towards the door. I had one last look backwards as we left the room, but the rest of the occupants seemed to be pointedly ignoring us, trying too hard not to note our passing.

The snow hit me full in the face as the door closed behind me, and the wind howled its rage in my ears. Far below the waves beat hungrily at the cliffs, flecks of white spume being flung high to mingle with the white, dancing flakes of the storm.

"A fine night for it." Jamie bellowed in my ear. Even his great voice was torn away by the wind. I was unable to reply - I was having too much trouble fighting the wind to bother with speech. We followed Robert through the grounds of the castle to the chapel at the east end, high above the sucking sea below.

A great oak door, some four inches thick, swung shut behind us as we entered, shutting out all sounds of the storm and leaving us alone in thick, quiet darkness. Robert struck a light and at first all I could see was his face, lit from underneath by the candle, its light throwing the upper half of his face into deep, black shadow.

It was only when my eyes became accustomed to the darkness that I realised what was about to occur.

The windows of the chapel had been covered in thick, green velvet drapes, and all the wooden seats had been removed from the room, leaving only empty boards on the floor before the altar. On the floor, a circle within a circle had been drawn, circles surrounded by dense Hebrew script. A five-pointed star was inscribed inside the inner circle, and a candle was placed at each point of the star.

I felt a cold chill settle in my bones, but it was answered by a sudden burst of heat from the thing around my neck.

"It is time," Robert said. "Fetch it out, Donald."

The red light blazed between my fingers as I opened my vest and took the chain from around my neck. I handed it to Robert, who took it gingerly between his thumb and forefinger as if it might burn him.

"Remember," he said to both of us, "you must not enter the circle until the conjuration is complete."

Jamie and I nodded in unison. It was not the first summoning we had attended - but I had the feeling it was going to be the most memorable.

It grew perceptibly colder as Robert steeped into the circle, and I realised that I missed the comfort of the ancient chain around my neck. It had been with me for a long time. As if in answer to my thoughts the red glow blazed up one final time before fading. Robert raised his hands towards the roof and began to chant.

"Powers of the Kingdom, be ye under my left foot and in my right hand. Glory and Eternity, take me by the two shoulders and direct me in the paths of victory. Mercy and Justice be ye the equilibrium and splendour of my life. Intelligence and wisdom crown me.

"Spirits of Malcuth, lead me betwist the two pillars upon which rests the whole edifice of the temple. Angels of Nestah and Hod strengthen me upon the cubic stone of Jesod.

Oh Gedulael, Oh Geburael, Oh Tiphereth, Binael, be thou my love.

Ruach Hochmael be thou my light. Be that which thou art and thou shalt be.

Oh Jethriel Tschim assist me in the name of Saddai, be my strength in the name of Adonai.

Oh Beni-Elohim, be my brethren in the name of the Son and by the power of Zeboath.

Elohim do battle for me in the name of Tetragrammaton.

Malachim protect me in the name of Jod He Vau He.

Seraphim cleanse me in the name of Elvoih.

Hajoth a Kadosh, cry, speak, roar, bellow.

Lion of the North, be with me."

Robert was enveloped in a red glow, a glow that grew and spread from the object on the chain, a glow that moulded itself into a form around a body, obscuring his features as it deepened and took on shape.

Robert seemed to expand, his back straightening and his chest filling out, his face melting and running like wax from a candle.

He groaned, a loud moan of pain, and Jamie moved to step forward. I only just stopped him in time - it would have been death for us all had he crossed the circle then.

Both Robert and the source of the glow had disappeared inside the growing shape in front of us, and as the shape coalesced it formed the figure of a man - gigantic of stature and imperious in his stance. His blue eyes stared unblinkingly at us, and we stared back, struck dumb by the vision.

"Well?" he finally said. His accent was strong, but the meaning of his words came through. "Why have you called me here?"

He had the bearing of a soldier, and his voice held a tone of command, so much so that my legs were trembling and my tongue felt as if it was struck in my palate. Jamie had no such trouble.

"We need you, Sir - your country needs you - these are perilous times in your homeland."

The figure threw back his head and laughed - a great bellowing sound that shook the whole room.

"Has it come to this? Have you become so weak?

He laughed again, and I felt like cowering before him. Jamie was becoming angry.

"You cannot deny us. We need the old strength."

"You would command me?" the figure said, his voice low, his eyes flashing angrily. "You cannot live in the past. Each generation must fight their own battles. Live for now, not for a time that will never return. Leave me in peace - I have long ago played my part in this mummery."

The red glow began to fade - imperceptibly at first, but soon we could see Robert's tortured frame writhing in its midst.

"No!" Jamie shouted. Before I could stop him, he stepped forward into the circle. And Hell came to Dunnotar.

The red cloud writhed and flowed, enveloping Jamie in its folds like a huge velvet cloak. The great door blew open, metal screaming as the massive hinges were torn from their places, the wind howling as the door fell to the floor with a thunderclap crash. Within the circle the cloud was shrinking, smaller, then smaller still, the figures within shrinking along with it. The last thing I heard before silence fell was Jamie's voice falling away into the distance, pleading over and over for mercy.

I was left alone in a suddenly silent room. All that was left in the circle was the ancient chain, still carrying its contents, which were gleaming like a fiery ember.

I stepped into the circle, muscles tensed in expectation of attack. But none came, and there was only the sound of the wind as I lifted the chain and walked into the night.

I thought of the past, of the great victory over Edward's army, of the Earl of Douglas taking this same chain to the Crusades, of the centuries it had lain in its tomb. In the distance I imagined I heard the marching drums of the English Army as I raised my arm and sent the heart of the Bruce to its final resting-place.

The Dark Island

The sun was going down behind the mountain and the loch was fading from blue to black, the breeze throwing refraction patterns in intricate dances across its surface. Later the moon would dance in those patterns, but for now there was only blackness.

There was still over an hour till nightfall, but already there was a chill in the air, a portent of the winter yet to come. The trees rustled softly, and occasionally a leaf fell to swim in the ripples for a while before softly sinking to join its decaying brothers.

Far out over the water, a deeper blackness in the gloom, the island sat like a blot on the water. Until now I had paid it little attention, but I found myself trying to pierce its dark secrets. Despite my best efforts the night kept it hidden from me and I had only the memory of the passage from that last fearful tome to remind me of the taint it threw on the waters of the loch.

From my vantagepoint on the balcony I watched the patterns in the water, trying to instil some meaning to order my thoughts. My body was remembering the relative warmth of the library and goosebumps ran over my arms. I was going to need a jacket sooner rather than later, but my discovery had thrown all such thoughts out of my mind.

I needed to talk to someone, to share my bewildered thoughts, but Mrs Jameson, the housekeeper, had long since closed up for the night, the remainder of the staff were abed and Sir John wasn't due back till the morning.

The house was dark and quiet behind me. I knew that a fire was burning in my bedroom, keeping a small spot warm just for me, but from out here on the balcony the house was as cold and bleak as the surrounding countryside. How Sir John coped with the solitude I could never fathom.

"Come down for the week," he had said. "I believe Grandfather's library has a good deal of that esoteric waffle that you find so interesting."

We were in his club in Pall Mall, all elegance and leather and, yes, warmth.

At the time I believed that it was a plea for company - for someone to relieve the tedium of the duties forced upon him by a chain of unfortunate deaths that led to his inheritance.

Even then I was loath to leave London - I need the comforts of the city more than I like to admit, but then he mentioned, in his offhand way, the names of some of the books, and I knew that I had to take him up on his offer.

And when I got to his residence - a journey I pray I never have to repeat - I found that John was going to be away for three days, called to officiate in some provincial court. I almost turned at the door and left, but Mrs Jameson would have none of it.

She is one from that unbreakable mould of Scottish housekeepers; stout and broad with a bristling energy that is as hard to ignore as it is to deny.

Within ten minutes she had me sitting in her kitchen, a bowl of soup with enough gusto to feed a small army placed in front of me.

After that I had no desire to travel further than the comfort of an armchair, further fortified by some fine brandy and an even finer cigar.

"The maister telled me tae mak ye maist comfortable." Mrs Jameson said. "And I would no' be doing ma job if I did onything other."

After I recovered from her ministrations I headed for the library.

Sir John had underestimated the worth of his Grandfather's collection. There were early editions of Boehme and Paracelsus, but best of all, the jewel of them all, was the collection of the works of Michael Scott, that figure of legend, astrologer to Ferdinand II, consorter with demons and necromancer. Even my beloved Corpus Christi could not boast such a hoard of delights.

I settled myself in the library that very day - if I was to plunder its secrets in a week then I would have to apply myself.

And there I stayed for two whole days, leaving only for sustenance and sleep, fortified by more of Sir John's fine brandy.

As I worked I became aware of a presence among the works, a fine, legible hand that annotated and collated, a scholar who had, like me, been striving to make sense of an older, altogether different, philosophy.

The scribbles held pointers to other works on the shelves, cross references that expanded and illuminated. Soon the table at which I worked was groaning under the weight of the books and I had taken to utilising the floor space as I strived to bring the threads together.

It was on the evening of the second day that I realised I was being led towards a conclusion, the answer to a secret more than six hundred years old, and a clue to the final resting-place of Auld Michael himself.

I was puzzled when the final note in the volume I was studying pointed me to "A History of the Earls of Kilbeith", but as soon as I took the book from the shelves I recognised the same, neat, handwriting to which I had become so accustomed.

It was then that I discovered the writer's identity - it was none other than the 23rd Earl, Robert, Sir John's grandfather. The pointer led me to a heavily annotated page near the beginning of the volume. As I read a chill seemed to work its way into my bones, a chill that has stayed with me ever since.

I have been searching for many years, and now I believe I have tracked down the source of that scourge which has so plagued my family down through the centuries. To understand it fully, it is necessary to go back to the early years of the thirteenth century. The first Earl, my ancestor, one Richard de Bourcy, raised the first castle on this spot, but it wasn't the first dwelling. At that time there was a chapel on the island on the loch - a small cell that was home to a local cleric whose name is lost to history.

It was while the castle was being raised that a stranger came to the chapel, an old, bent, man with silver in his hair and red fire in his eyes. Not long after that strange rumours spread across the region - rumours of a jet-black steed with hoofs of iron that carried on its back an old man whose very gaze spelt death. The local country folk beseeched Sir Richard to rid them of this deviltry, and so it was that the Earl took himself to the island. And there on that accursed island his eyes met great abominations and outrages against good Christian nature that I will not detail here for fain of disturbing my reader's sensibilities.

And Sir Richard took up his sword against the perpetrator of the crimes, an old man with blood on his nails and at his mouth. Yet even as the old man was struck through the breast he uttered an almighty curse, that the Earl and all his family would be joined with him on the island before any of them should see fifty summers. The Earl razed the chapel to the ground, cleansing it with the pure fire of his faith, but that same faith failed to sustain him, and the next summer, just short of his fiftieth year, he passed from history, his resting-place unknown. And so it has gone down the centuries, the old man's curse laying its foul hand over us all. I have tracked him down, the old devil, the necromancer Michael, and tonight I will go to the island and say the rites. If I succeed then the curse will be forever lifted. If I fail, I leave these notes so that one who follows me might see where I did not and, if his faith be strong, succeed where I could not.

By the hand of Robert, 23rd Earl of Kilbeith, in his 49th year in the sight of our Lord, in the sure and certain hope of his infinite mercy.

I laid the volume on the desk, noticing with horror that my hands were shaking, a tremble that I could not stop. It was then that I felt drawn to the balcony, but I did not stay there long, the dark and the cold soon sending me back to the relative warmth of the library.

But the room was no longer a comforting place to be, the books now enemies rather than trusted friends. I made sure that the windows were firmly locked and repaired to my bed.

Sleep would not come. Images flowed in my mind, of dark islands and warlocks, of swords and flames. Deep in that part of the night were nothing moves I heard, as if from far off, a loud drumming as of a horse in a wild gallop, but it was soon over and I was left, staring at the soft interplay of shadows on the ceiling. Dawn was washing the sky pale before a troubled slumber finally took me down and away.

I was awoken by the rattling of the doorknob in its casing, followed by the entry of Mrs Jameson.

"A guid morning to ye sir," she said, laying before me a tray of food that would have sunk the trustiest battleship. "The maister has sent word that he'll return after lunch, and asks that ye forgive his further absence."

She didn't wait for a reply. The door slammed behind her as if to punctuate her exit, and I was left staring with dismay at the mound of food before me.

I managed a single cup of tea and two spoonfuls of porridge before my troubled thoughts drove me from my bed and out into the cool morning where I thought that a brisk walk might bring a clearer view on my discoveries of the previous night.

For the first time I had a view of my old friend's estate, but I'm afraid that the panoramic splendours passed me by. From all vantagepoints I found my gaze drawn back to the loch and to the dark island at its heart.

By the time I headed back to the castle the sun had already passed overhead, or as near to overhead as it ever gets this far north. When I entered I found John in the hall, a brace of fine plump pheasants in his hands.

"William. I'm so glad you could make it," he said, and the warmth of his welcome almost dispelled the deep chill inside me.

"Do you believe it?" he said, "I sit in trial of a poacher, find him unjustly accused, and what do you think he does? Only gives me a pair of my own birds in gratitude."

He laughed, his head thrown back, showing off the proud roman profile enjoyed by all his family. The laugh was such a joyous thing that I was forced to join him. Five minutes later we were ensconced in his study, sharing a bottle of clear, golden, whisky, watched over by the imperious portraits of his ancestors. I couldn't help but notice that they had all been caught as young men.

John was full of tales from the courts, completely enthralled in the life of the people in the area, and for the first time in our long acquaintance he looked truly happy and at ease with the world.

I was loath to break the spell that this place had woven around him, and it took two glasses of whisky to loosen my tongue, and a further one before I could relate my findings. I was serious, and tried to impress the gravity of the situation on him. He listened intently, but his eyes told me that he didn't believe a word of it.

"I've heard parts of the tale before," he said, "We used to have an old gamekeeper here - Jim Callender. He was full of the old stories - how that man loved to hear himself talk. He tried to frighten my brother and I when we were little more than children."

"But come," he said, leaning forward and placing a hand on my knee, "Surely a sophisticated gentleman like yourself has not fallen for such old wives tales?"

Suddenly he seemed to come to a decision.

"Come on. I'll show you that there's no need to be afraid."

He stood and made for the door before turning back to me.

"Well. Are you coming? There's just enough light for the task."

I took a last, lingering, drink before placing the glass on the table, and had a longing look back at it before following Sir John out to the loch.

There was a small rowing boat tied to a makeshift jetty, and John must have noticed the look on my face when I saw it.

"Don't worry," he said, "It's more stable than it looks. I take the boat out most evenings - there are some terrific trout in the waters around here."

Without another word he led me into the boat that swayed alarmingly until we were both settled. He had taken the oars and allowed me no argument. He rowed with the ease of one well used to the task, and was not even breathing heavily when he spoke.

"You know. It's a curious thing. I have been out on this loch more times than you can imagine, but I've never set foot on the island. Nobody has, for as long as I can remember."

"I'd wager that your grandfather did." I said, my mouth working faster than my brain. I immediately regretted it as a cloud seemed to pass over John's features.

"For pity's sake man - granddad was going soft in the head by all accounts. He was obsessed with the old stories. And it wasn't the curse that got him - he killed himself, up there in that library you are so fond of."

I jumped at that, causing the boat to sway slightly, but John didn't miss a stroke, and his face was now set against me. I could do no more than watch that dark blot appear ever closer over his left shoulder.

It was less than five minutes later when there was a grind of wood against stone and the boat came up on a steep, rocky shore.

The sun was closing in on the mountainside, laying layers of orange and red across the sky. The loch itself glowed gold like the whisky I was missing so much, a gold that was slowly turning blood red.

I turned away from the view and forced myself to confront the island itself. At first it was no more than a larger smudge of darkness but then the splendour of the sunset faded from my eyes and the island asserted itself in my view.

It was smaller than I had thought - barely thirty yards in diameter, raising itself no more than six feet from the surface of the loch at its highest point. A grove of twisted yew trees seemed to grow straight from the rock, so dense that it was impossible to guess what might lie beyond them.

John was already up and out of the boat before I had time to take in the whole scene. Even then I found that I no longer had the desire to explore this god-forsaken patch of land. I watched him scramble across the slimy rocks and followed his progress until his shape melded with the greater darkness of the trees.

A stillness descended around me like a shroud, the loch around me as flat and calm as the surface of a lady's mirror. No bird sang, nor did any of the fabled trout disturb the waters. Suddenly I felt more alone then I ever desired.

I called out to John, twice, my first attempt coming to little more than the thin, croaky, pleading of an old man. There was no reply.

I pushed myself out of the boat, the soaking of my good brogues not improving my temper. I was glad of them only seconds later - the rocks proved a more tortuous route than I had imagined.

Once more I called out for my friend, and this time was rewarded by an answering call, muffled, as if having travelled a great distance to reach me.

"Over here William" the voice said, and my heart immediately lifted. I followed the source of the voice to the grove of elms and began to push my way through them, all the time becoming ever more aware that darkness was beginning to draw itself in around me.

Just when I began to believe that the grove had, somehow, become larger than the island on which it stood, I emerged into a rough clearing, no more than nine feet across. The ground rose to a taller mound, one formed of fallen rocks and rubble, rubble that seemed strangely black, even in the dim light.

"John?" I shouted, and this time I could trace the reply - he was in the mound itself. As I stepped closer I could see a rough entrance, just above and to the left of where I was standing.

"In here" the voice said.

I stepped closer, then stopped, halted by a sudden whiff of corruption. There was a scrape, as of stone on stone, and the caustic odour strengthened. I started to call out, but everything was driven from my mind when John screamed - a cry the like of which I hope never to hear again.

A figure barrelled out of the mound, knocking me over to scrabble, dazed, amongst the rubble. I managed to push myself upright just in time to see John's stout frame push away from me through the yews.

The stones beneath my feet shifted and the smell became so strong as to sting at the back of my throat and cause gorge to rise. It was all the excuse I needed - I hurried to follow my friend.

At first I thought that he had already gone, leaving me to go insane on this rough rock, but then I saw that the boat was still where we had left it. I came across his prone body several steps later - by that time it was becoming so dark that I might have missed him if I had passed several steps to either side.

He had fallen victim to the rocks, losing his footing and striking his head hard. There was a warm wetness in his hair, but his breathing was strong. With no little difficulty I managed to manhandle him into the boat - I still have a scar on my left knee where a rock sheared clean through my tweeds and into my leg.

I only looked up once, no more than a glance back to the island to get my bearings, and then I was rowing, with an energy I never knew I possessed, rowing with all haste back to the safe, warm lights of Sir John's ancestral seat.

I will say nothing of that mad flight across the loch - the fears and terrors of it have been blanked from my mind, a necessity if I am to remain sane.

Some time later Mrs Jameson met us on the doorstep. The walk from the jetty, all the while carrying the dead weight of my friend, almost exhausted me and I fell across the door, tumbling both myself and the master of the house in an unruly heap on the carpet.

By that time I was most willing to give myself over to the ministrations of Mrs Jameson. She did not let me down. Within five minutes we were installed in the stout armchairs in the study, the whole household having been roused for our attention.

Which is how I came to be facing John on his awakening.

His eyes opened first; strange, unfamiliar, red-rimmed orbs. He stared at me then his gaze lifted, looking beyond me to the portraits on the walls.

That's when the screaming started.

I left that very night, ignoring all of Mrs Jameson's protestations, and since that night I have never left London. Indeed, I rarely set foot from the safety of my warm, suburban home.

But at night I dream.

I am once more back in that rowing boat, having managed to tumble John into position. I pick up the oars and look back, just a glance to get my bearings.

And there, backlit by the last rays of the dying sun, I see a group of figures proceeding towards us, their bare feet shuffling among the hard rocks, tattered clothing flapping about their flanks. One bends and lifts a rock from the shore, and I see the red of John's blood appear at its mouth. And as the boat begins to drift away from the shore one of my oars strikes a rock, and the figures all turn towards me.

I wake screaming at the sight of those proud roman profiles, the same profile I see adorning the face of my friend Sir John, my good friend Sir John who will be fifty in less than two months time.

The Blue Hag

(With Graeme Hurry)

Lucy had decided to tell me how Dad died.

The train was full, so full that although we were travelling first class, we were sharing the compartment with a horde of others - students, squaddies and oilmen, all of them drunk, half drunk or intending to get that way.

"Nobody knows how it happened," she said. She leaned over the table towards me. "There was a board meeting - dad was submitting proposals for a wholesale modernisation of the farm."

I was surprised to see tears in my sister's eyes. I wanted to comfort her but a sudden laugh from the next table caused me to stiffen and hold my peace.

She dabbed at her eyes with a handkerchief and watched the scenery roll by for long seconds before continuing.

"Nobody knows what happened in there. They were still arguing at ten o'clock that night when the secretary finally gave up and went home. But nobody else did. A cleaner found the bodies the next morning."

That did make me jump.

"Bodies? You mean it wasn't just Dad? I thought it must have been a heart attack - he was certainly due one."

"No," she said, and the tears were back. "Murder, that's what it was. No, more than murder. Butchery."

She sat back and stared out of the window. I knew the signs - conversation was over for a time. I watched her for a while - the thick curve of her neck, the square jaw and the steely eyes. I had to turn away - she looked too much like him.

I certainly didn't want to press her. Her rages were legendary in the family, almost as bad as the old man's.

I still didn't know why I was sitting there. She had phoned me in the Union on Friday morning.

"I've got some bad news for you." You know how it is when those words are said - every possible catastrophe short of nuclear war goes through your mind in less than a second, so when she told me that the old man had died I was almost relieved. Almost. I was sure he'd find a way to harangue me from beyond the grave.

"I want you to come with me and bring his body home." She said.

I had a sudden mental picture of all three of us in a car, Dad driving, his dead fingers still giving a two-finger salute to any other driver with the gall to get in his way.

"You can come, can't you? Your holidays start tomorrow, don't they?" There was a tone in her voice I'd not heard there before. If I didn't know her better I would have thought she was about to beg.

"I've organised the transport and everything."

"I hope you get the most expensive service available," I said. "You know what he was like."

"Oh Geoffrey," she signed, sounding so disappointed in me and so like my mother that I gave in.

I stared at Newcastle, Edinburgh and Dundee without seeing any of them.

Finally she spoke.

"I'm glad you came," she said. Then, as if embarrassed by any show of weakness, she went back to studying her reflection in the window.

She didn't speak again until we were standing on the platform at Aberdeen station, waiting for our connection to Inverurie.

"Dad made me executor of the estate," she said, as if it was a topic we had just been discussing. "We'll have the reading of the will after the funeral."

"I won't be staying around for that," I said. "If you think I'm going to sit in that draughty house while some old wrinkly goes through a list of my faults before deigning to give me a fiver then you're got another think coming."

And that was that. I got the stony stare all the way to Inverurie - plenty of time to reflect on what life could be like free from the old man.

Dad had made his fortune in livestock, or, should I say, dead stock. At the time of his death he was Chairman of the biggest venison producer in the world. He was a self-made man, rising from farm labourer to pig breeder, abattoir manager to veal exporter and on, ever upwards. Once upon a time he had wanted me to follow in his footsteps.

"Get out and get the blood on your hands," he said. "It'll make a man of you."

And until I reached the age of eight I honestly thought I might. Then I came home early from school one day to find him in the back yard, gutting a pig with the big knife he kept in the kitchen, the entrails still smoking as they hit the ground with a wet thump.

I remember crying, and it was the tears more than my disgust that set him against me - for life. For the rest of that summer he berated me, pacing around me in the living room, hurling abuse at the top of his voice. During his 'little turns' I would squeeze my eyes shut until the tears came and he stormed off in disgust.

The very next term Mummy got me a place at boarding school. I would have been happy but for having to go home to face more abuse every month. He never hit me, but I'll carry the scars until I die.

By the time I was fifteen he'd given up on me completely. He made a new will leaving everything to Lucy, and after my mother died I swore I'd never see him again.

I was woken with a sudden jolt as the train pulled into Inverurie station.

Lucy still wasn't talking to me, and I was left to struggle along the platform with the heaviest cases. True to form, she seemed to have brought everything, including the kitchen sink. At least she'd ordered a cab. I piled the cases in the boot and got in, only to get out less than two minutes later when we reached our hotel.

I'd been expecting something less grand - my impression of Scotland had always been coloured by my father's description of the run-down area of Glasgow, from which he'd 'rescued' my mother 'from a life of drudgery'. I'm not sure she saw it like that. But she knew better than to answer him back.

The hotel looked like it had stood on the spot for centuries, its grey stone merging almost seamlessly with the soil underneath and, although the wind was biting and chill, a real log fire blazed in the small bar we were led through on the way to our rooms. It was only as she was entering her room that Lucy spoke, and her tone was terse and cold.

"The farm is about five miles away - out in the sticks." Her nose actually lifted in the air, as she forgot that our house in Derbyshire, Dad's folly, was at least six miles from the nearest town. I didn't get time to enlighten her.

"The police station is out that way as well. We'll go there tomorrow morning," she said, closing the door in my face.

I unpacked my bag - it didn't take long - changed into a clean pair of jeans and a heavy pullover and headed for the bar. I was to be disappointed.

"Sorry sir," the barman said with no apology in his eyes, "We dinnae open the bar until six o'clock. There's nae much custom at this time o' the year." He waved a hand around the bar, accentuating it's emptiness. "You'll no' find much open in the town either - Aberdeen are playing Celtic in the Cup and maist o' the lads are awa' doon tae Glesca."

I walked out into the drive and looked around. There must be a lot of football supporters in the town - at four o'clock on a Saturday afternoon the place was deserted. Only the occasional old lady wrapped tight in an overcoat suggested it wasn't a Sunday. I wandered for a while, but the thought of a pint of cold beer had grown big in my mind. I made my way to the taxi rank at the station and collared the nearest driver.

"I'm looking for a pub that's open," I said.

The driver looked me up and down.

"Are ye sure ye're auld enough to be drinking?" he said, but there was a smile on his lips as he said it. "Get in. I ken the feeling when ye've got a drooth."

I didn't want to ask him what he meant, but it seemed to amuse him greatly.

"Dae ye ken where ye want tae go?" he asked as he started the car.

A name came to mind, a town I'd only ever read about in Lucy's letters.

"Monymusk," I said, and the driver laughed again.

"So, the toon's fame has even spread tae England has it. Aye, I'll take ye tae Monymusk - but don't be expectin' onything fancy."

He drove like a demon, the needle approaching eighty on long straight stretches of road, only going below fifty on the corners. I watched the scenery and tried to seem nonchalant. I don't know what I'd been expecting - rugged hills, heather and cliffs were known from the television, but this corner of Scotland was green and lush, only occasional glimpses of distant mountains reminding me I wasn't in Derbyshire.

We flashed past a 30-mph sign doing sixty, and I had a vague impression of a row of houses on either side of the road when we suddenly screeched to a halt outside a tiny whitewashed cottage.

I paid the driver, and he gave me a business card.

"Gie me a call when ye want tae get back," he said. "It disnae dae ye much guid to be walking these roads in the dark."

With that he left, the car bulleting off into the distance.

A cold wind whistled around my ankles, blowing a solitary crisp packet along in its wake. This town was even quieter than Inverurie. There was not a single person on the streets and there was no sign of life - not even a wisp of smoke from a chimney.

Inside the bar things weren't much better. The place was so quiet that I thought it might be closed - the television was switched off, as were the fruit machines, and there was only a solitary light above the bar. I had already turned on my way out when a voice called to me.

"Can ah help ye sir?"

The barman poked his head above the counter.

"Ah is jist stackin' some bottles. Takin' advantage o' the lull in custom as it were." He threw back his head and laughed, his humour so infectious that I had to join him.

After ordering my drink - an ordeal in itself since Scots don't recognise 'Bitter' - I settled onto a bar seat nursing a pint of 'Light' almost as dark as Guinness, and felt my nerves settle as I chatted with the barman.

Around five o' clock other customers began to arrive and, by six, five pints the better - or worse - I found myself talking to the oldest, most incomprehensible Glaswegian I had ever set eyes on. Even more surprising was the fact that I could understand him.

"Ah like a boy that can haud his drink," was the first thing he said to me, clasping me round the shoulders before buying his first of many whiskies.

By seven he was drunk as a lord, but still a good deal more sober than I. I had heard his life story - the gang wars in the Gorbals in the thirties, the torpedoing of his submarine in the Pacific in the forties, and the years in jail in the fifties - "Ah never did onything really bad - ah jist robbed a Bookies."

I agreed and bought him another whisky, but it was only when his tale reached the nineties that I really started to pay attention. He was the cleaner - the 'mucker oot' - of the deer pens at my father's farm.

"I've heard about the place." I said. "Wasn't there something about it on the news recently?"

The old man's eyes suddenly cleared, and he didn't look drunk any more.

"Oh aye, it wis on the news right enough. The auld mither looks after her ain."

At that the barman cleared his throat noisily, and the old man stopped talking, taking a quick, almost guilty, sip of his whisky. My brain was muddled by drink, so it was long seconds before I noticed that the bar had fallen silent.

"Right Jimmy - I think you've had enough," the barman said.

I expected the Glaswegian to complain, but he merely dropped his head as he got carefully off his stool.

"Ah'm sorry," he said as he left, but I don't know whether he was speaking to the barman or me. It was only after the door shut behind him that the conversation in the bar started up once more.

"As for you wee man," the barman said, "I think you'd best be getting on hame - you've got your faither's funeral tae arrange."

It was only when I was out in the fresh air that I realised I hadn't told anyone who I was.

I was about to go back in when the cold air combined with the alcohol and coherent thought left me.

The next thing I knew was some time later. I was standing by the roadside, heaving up the contents of my stomach, realising, too late, that I had eaten nothing apart from a bacon roll on the train that morning. It was no consolation that my stomach was nearly empty - my system didn't believe it and kept trying to throw up more until I was convinced that my stomach lining would soon appear in my throat.

I won't go into detail about the following ten minutes - let's just say they were unpleasant and messy. I did my best to clean up my face, hoping I had kept my clothes slime-free, and finally stood up straight and looked around me.

I was standing at a crossroads - an unsigned crossroads, and along all four branches was only darkness and the soft brushing of the wind in the trees. I was completely lost.

No, it was more than that - if I had been in a city I could have found my way to some recognisable landmark, but here I could see nothing. I looked upwards, searching for the stars, but that was a vain hope - I couldn't even tell you which was the North Star and which was a planet. Stars were more my Dad's line.

I was about to head down one of the roads - any road - when there was a sound behind me, just at the limits of my hearing, a rough rasping as of stone against stone.

I turned to see an old woman, no more than three yards away from me, bend over double and lift something from the verge of the roadside and put it into a pocket at the front of her long skirts, which seemed to glow a faint, luminescent blue. I could see there were deep pockets sown into her clothes, the contents of which clattered as she moved.

She bent again, to pick up something and study it with such intensity that she was as still as a marble statue then, with a movement so quick I almost didn't catch it, she transferred whatever it was from her hand to her mouth. She stood upright as I watched, the fine silver wings of her hair wafting in the breeze from under a headscarf so enveloping as to be almost a hood. I was about to call out to her when she turned, and my shout, already turning to a scream, was caught, frozen in my throat.

There was no face. That was my first impression. Just a black void so deep I felt I was falling into it. Then her hand came up and pushed the hood away from her head, and this time I did scream, a scream echoed by the thing in front of me.

Her face wasn't a face. It was a construction, a mask of bone and hide stitched together with thick twine that glowed white in the dim light. Beneath the mask something moved - a squirming as of a tribe of maggots in dead flesh.

I would have ran then, but the eyes held me, the so so blue eyes sunk deep beneath the mask eyeing me with cold appraisal.

"So," a voice said, though the lips of the mask were sewn tight. "Are ye yer faither's son, or are ye yer ain man? Are ye a herdsman or a butcher? It's make yer mind up time." And she cackled, like a crone in a Disney cartoon. She stretched a hand out to me. It seemed to have been stripped of flesh until all that was showing was bone - no, not bone, Antler.

I was backing away - a reaction that brought more cackling - when car headlights lighted the crone's face. She blinked, and I blinked, and when I looked back she was off and away over the hedgerow. She'd leapt so high it beggared belief. Her skirts rose up, exposing ankles ending in a pair of thick, cloven hooves. She turned and pointed her hand at me and I saw five long, serrated bones reflecting the faint moonlight. The glinting edges looked perfect for slicing meat.

The car whose headlights had broken the spell pulled up beside me.

"Alan at the bar phoned me and telt me ye were oot on the road. Get in and I'll take ye hame."

It took long seconds to sink in, and even longer for me to recognise the cab driver.

"Come on son. Ah havnae got all night."

I got in and the driver took off, going if anything even faster than before. I didn't speak, I couldn't, my mind was still full of the sight of those fingers and hooves. Them, and the words the crone had spoken.

The driver didn't speak until we reached the hotel.

"I would stay in for the rest of the night if ah were you," he said. "It's a night for the mither. Ye dinnae want tae meet her twice."

He screeched away, leaving me on the gravel path.

Still dazed, I stood for a long time looking across the night sky and wondering until the chill brought me to my senses and sent me scuttling for warmth.

You would have thought I'd had enough to drink for one night, but I felt stone cold sober and in more need of a drink than ever. There was a comforting murmur of conversation coming from the bar so I pushed open the door.

And stopped all talk dead in its tracks.

There were only three people in the room, and they were all looking at me. The silence lasted just two seconds before the woman with her back to me turned and shouted at the top of her voice. "Where the hell have you been, you little shit?"

I hadn't recognised my sister until that point. Her perfect facade had been severely dented - her hair hung in limp strands, tangled as if clawed with a trembling hand. Her make up was a faded memory, streaked and running around her eyes. The effect was to age her by years, making her look like the vulnerable child I dimly remembered.

"What's wrong?" I asked, touching her shoulder. I was amazed when she collapsed sobbing onto my shoulder.

"They won't let me take him home," she sobbed. "They won't even let me see him."

I looked at the nearest policeman, who gave an embarrassed nod.

I petted Lucy's hair awkwardly - it wasn't something I had any experience in. "It's okay", I said. "We'll probably have to wait until after the post-mortem." I looked at the policeman for confirmation, but he was looking even more uncomfortable.

"What's the problem? I asked.

He signed and, before replying, looked at his partner. "As I told your sister, we cannot release the bodies until.." he paused, as if struggling for words - "until we've decided which parts belong to which victim."

Lucy began to howl, a high-pitched keening like a bird in pain. I gently sat her in an armchair and turned back to the policemen.

"Tell me," I said, then, when they showed signs of prevarication, "Please, tell me."

The younger of the two looked pale and ill, but it was he who spoke first.

"Have you ever seen a butcher strip a carcass, so efficient that everything is packaged into parts?"

He gulped, suddenly having difficulty swallowing. "Well, that's how it was. Five men and one woman to start with, around four hundred kilos of meat after. I don't think you need to know more."

I sat down hard, feeling dizzy.

He was still speaking, but I'd missed something.

"…Keep this information confidential until we find the killer?" He looked at me and I nodded, hoping I'd made the right response. Then the meaning of his words sank in.

"You mean you haven't caught him yet?"

"That's why we need your help - you, and your sister's. We need access to company records, and I believe you two are the new owners. I'd like you to come down to the factory with us."

"Now?" I asked, and received a double nod in reply.

"No," Lucy moaned, "I can't. Not into that place. Not where…" she broke down again, her sobbing so quiet as to be almost inaudible.

"Give me a minute," I said to the police, and led Lucy out of the bar and up to her room.

"I'll deal with the police," I said. She nodded, but something was gone from her eyes, something that had made her Lucy. She might never be the same again. She fished in her handbag and produced a bundle of keys that she handed to me as if she never wanted contact with them again.

"They'll find what they want in this lot." I had already turned when a soft word drew me back.

"Jeff," she said, and she was definitely not the same woman I had left in the hotel. The diminutive of my name had always been prohibited within the family, whether I liked it or not.

"Please be careful. I can't lose you as well." There were tears in her eyes as I hugged her close to me.

The policemen were waiting in the hall when I got downstairs. I tried to put them off till morning - it was already past midnight - but they used a line I thought only applied in the movies.

"This is a murder investigation, sir." A minute later we were barrelling along dark country roads.

Sitting in the back of the car I felt like a criminal, and the silence from the men in front only reinforced my isolation.

"So have you any clues?" I asked, trying to keep my anxiety out of my voice.

"No," the younger man said. "It'll probably be some o' them loonie lefties." Now we were away from the bar his accent had began to re-assert itself. "We're hoping that there'll be something in yer auld man's files - threatening letters or some such nonsense."

Nothing more was said until we drove through Monymusk and pulled up in the drive of a modern, two storey timber building.

There was another policeman standing by the main door, and the remains of several cigarettes at his feet.

"Nothing to report, Sir," he said to the elder of the two with me. It was only then I realised I'd been with an officer.

Over the next couple of hours they went through every desk and filing cabinet in the office. They drew a blank. I sat in the largest chair in the boardroom and tried to ignore the fading bloodstains on the walls.

I was beginning to nod off when the officer came in.

"This has your name on it," he said, handing me an envelope. "Is that your father's writing?"

"Yes, it's his."

"Would you mind reading it now and telling if there's anything there that would help?"

He left me alone, and I sat for a while turning the envelope over and over in my hands. I wasn't sure the old man had anything to say that I wanted to read. But he surprised me.

Geoffrey

I'm leaving this in the hope you never read it.

There is something in this place. It's old and vile and it hates me. I don't know why. It has been coming in my dreams, and it is getting stronger. Maybe you can deal with it better than I. That is why I'm leaving the farm to you.

Now don't get too excited. Lucy gets everything else. It's just that I hope this will soften your feelings towards me. Believe me, I only ever did what was best for you.

Dad

I sat stunned. It was typical, no apologies, no remorse, in its own way the coldest letter I had ever read. But there were still tears in my eyes as I put it back into its envelope.

I sat for a while longer, just staring at the table. It was several seconds before I realised that I was staring at a brown manila folder. I opened it and found that I was looking at my father's last piece of business, a proposal for the upgrading and mechanisation of the farm. There were drawings for fleshing machines, blades gleaming cleanly on the page, and huge industrial mincers, designed, I discovered, to scrunch and mangle bits not thought fit to eat - minced remains that were to be fed straight back to the animals. There was more about intensive farming practice, yield maximisation and other euphemisms for the proposed slaughter. My father hadn't been concerned with a few hundred deer, he'd been planning for thousands - tens of thousands.

I needed some air. I left the office and headed outside, giving only a cursory nod to the policeman at the door. The road stretched away blackly on either side of me, but I had no intention of walking such paths again - not in the dark, anyway.

I turned the corner of the office block - and found a greater darkness ahead. I actually stepped backwards before I realised it was only a shed.

No, not just a shed. This was the biggest farm building I had ever seen, some forty feet high and twice as wide. I couldn't gauge its length, but I knew it stretched some distance into the darkness.

As I got closer I noticed the smell, a not unpleasant mustiness. I realised that I was creeping, almost furtive. I still hadn't come to terms with the fact that all this now belonged to me. I straightened up and, with a bravado I didn't really feel, strode up to the shed.

The door was slightly open, and the sound it made when I pushed the sliding doors echoed loudly in the night. It also seemed to wake the shed's occupants. There was a shuffling and a sudden lowing, and at first I was sure that the shed was full, not of deer, but of cattle. I stepped forward and all sound ceased.

Several hundred pairs of dead eyes turned and stared at me.

I felt a hitch deep in my throat at the sight before me. They were in six rows, packed so tight flank and rear touched rear, rears stained and packed hard in brown, vile muck. The stag nearest me lowed pitifully, a deep mournful sound, soon taken up every animal there.

The noise affected me somewhere deep down in my soul and brought sudden, hot tears in my eyes.

I saw again the designs for the machinery in my father's report, and could see in my mind these animals, their numbers multiplied ten fold, all falling into the metal's embrace, all still crying that same piteous wail.

I believe I staggered, and would have turned and ran then had it not been for the hand on my shoulder.

"Hello again," a Scots voice said behind me, and I turned to face old Jimmy, the Glaswegian I had met in the bar earlier. He was no longer drunk, but didn't look entirely sober either.

"Ah hate the early shift," he said. "Ye hardly get time tae get over the nicht afore."

"I suppose you knew who I was all the time?"

At least he managed to look embarrassed. "Aye - your auld man had a picture o' you and yer sister in his office. He had maist o' us in there tae get chewed oot at wan time or anither."

The deer behind me had fallen quiet.

"They ken when it's feeding time," Jimmy said, and was about to turn away from me when I saw his attention caught by something over my shoulder. The colour drained from his face, leaving him pale and wide-eyed.

But not for long. His pupils rolled up and he fell backwards in a dead faint.

I was almost afraid to turn, but I only had two chances - run or stand. If there was one thing the last twenty-four hours had taught me it was that running never got you far enough away. My heartbeat was up and my palms were sweating, but I turned anyway.

Once more I was face to face with the hag. Her eyes looked at me from behind the mask, and there was a ferocity in them, a blue fire that seemed to blaze and burn with a terrible heat. She spoke, the same thing she had said to me earlier, but this time it was barked like an order.

"Are ye yer faither's son, or are ye yer ain man? Are ye a butcher..."
she said, and those razor sharp fingers waved in front of me once more,
clacking together like diabolical scissors. Finally I realised what had
happened to my father, but I had no time to reflect on it as she continued.

"..Or are ye a herdsman? Mak yer mind up."

Suddenly I was angry.

"My father didn't deserve what you did to him!"

The hag didn't reply. With a wave of her arms she indicated the
animals in the pens.

I got her point. The deer didn't deserve their fate either, and had done
less harm than my father.

"Are ye a herdsman or a butcher?" the voice asked again, and once more
the knives that were her fingers clacked together. Those blue eyes transfixed
me, rooting me to a spot where there were decisions to be made,
responsibilities to be taken.

I thought once more of my father's planned future, seeing in my mind
the stainless steel blades and the red life flowing, and realised that
sometime in the last hour I had made my choice.

There was a groan from the ground at my feet. Old Jimmy was
stirring, and when I looked up the hag had gone.

I pulled Jimmy upright.

"It wis her," he whispered. "It wis the auld mither."

"Yes," I said. "And this time we're going to do what she wants. It's
time to be herdsmen."

Jimmy helped me open the pens. Many of the animals seemed unable
to move, but with a bit of coaxing we got them into the field where they
stood blinking in the first light of dawn.

"What noo?" Jimmy asked. "Those animals cannae fend for themselves
- they've nae mind o' their ain."

I didn't know. I had just done what felt like the right thing to do.

There was a sound behind us, and I turned to face the old mother one
last time. I felt Jimmy creep behind me, keeping me between him and the
hag as I stood transfixed.

A skeletal hand reached out, taking hold of my left arm and bringing
it towards her mask.

I pulled back, aware at the same time that I had drawn the palm of
my hand against one of the edges. I felt hot blood flow there, but I could
not take my eyes away from hers.

I fell into that stare and, this time, as she leaned towards me, I didn't back away, even as her mouth touched mine in a soft, almost loving kiss.

She tasted of musk, that and grass and heather and the wild smell of a cold wind on the hills. It made me want to run with her until there were no more machines, no more knives.

I brought up my fingers to touch her cheek and they touched rough hide, hide which came away in my hand at the same time as the cloak fell away, joined a second later by the skeletal hands. I looked down to the mask in my hand, then up into the clear eyes of a tall, muscular doe.

She lowered her head and bowed to me, twice, before trotting off across the field. The herd followed her, and the last we saw of them was as they headed over the brow of the hill beyond, their forms outlined in black against the red sky of a new day.

Author's Note

Scotland is full of stories – you can't move for people wanting to tell you a new one.

I'm Scottish. I like Scotland – especially the bits outside the cities. However, that doesn't stop me writing horror stories that show the place in a less-than-perfect light. You won't find any deep psychological reason for this – I just like monsters – always have, always will.

Most of these stories appeared in the small press throughout the Nineties and early in 2000. My thanks go to all the editors of these magazines who struggle away in darkened rooms to bring horror to the public.

Just a word about "The Blue Hag". It is, to date, my one and only collaboration. Graeme Hurry, as well as being one of the afore-mentioned editors, is also a fine writer, and collaborating with him was a pleasure. I might try it again some day.

Publication History

1. The Johnson Amulet, *Millennium Macabre, Enigmatic Press,2000*
2. An Early Frost, *Pirate Writings #4 1994 USA and Xenos Issue 13 June 1992 UK*
3. The Worst Sound, *Whispers and Shouts Vol. 1 #3 1994 USA and Flickers 'n' Frames Magazine Issue 22 1994 UK*
4. Wee Robbie, *Kimota Number 8 Spring 1998 UK*
5. Phantom Payment, *Previously Unpublished*
6. Overheard in a Cemetery, *Previously Unpublished*
7. A Sirens Song, *Midnight in Hell Winter 94 and Fear of the Dark e-zine Spring 2000*
8. Temper Tantrum, *Flickers 'n' Frames # 24-2 Summer 1995 UK and Planet Relish e-zine April 2000*
9. The Elixir Of Life, *Albedo One Issue 9 –Summer 1995 Ireland*
10. The Flute and The Glen, *Kimota Issue 3 Winter 1995/1996 UK and Dread January 2000 USA*
11. The Colour of the Deep, *Threads Number 1 October 1993 -UK*
12. The Strange Case of Dr McIntyre, *All Hallows 19 October 1998 UK/Canada*
13. Animal ,Vegetable or Mineral, *Kimota Issue 2 Summer 1995 UK*
14. It'll Be a Long Hot Summer, *Threads Issue 7 Spring 1995 UK and Sinister Element e-zine Summer 2000*
15. In the Coils of The Serpent, *Night Visions #1 UK*
16. The Old Mother, *Phantasy Province Issue 3 1st Quarter 1993 UK and Haunts #6 – Summer 1995 USA*
17. The Last Day Of Summer, *Fiction Furnace Volume 1 Number 3 Summer 1993 UK and Dark Times e-zine 2000 USA*
18. Just A Par To Win, *Another Realm e-zine 1999*
19. Ghost Writer , *Xenos Issue 16 December 1992 - UK*
20. At The Beach, *Beach People e-zine 1999.*
21. Can You Hear Them?, *Previously Unpublished*

22. The Sweller in the Dress Hold, *Footsteps Issue 1 October 1995 UK*

23. The Watcher in the Dunes, *Grotesque Issue 7 1995 UK*

24. There's Always a Catch, *Night Dreams issue 3 November 1995 UK*

25. The World of Illusion, *Masque Issue 2 UK*

26. Flower of Scotland, *All Hallows 11 February 1996 UK and Space and Time #88, Spring 1999 – USA*

27. The Dark Island, *The Inflated Graveworm e-zine Summer 1999 and Millennium Macabre, Enigmatic Press, March 2000*

28.The Blue Hag, *Millennium Macabre, Enigmatic Press, March 2000*

www.ingramcontent.com/pod-product-compliance
Lightning Source LLC
Chambersburg PA
CBHW022059170626
46808CB00002B/503